PRAISE FOR

HOW WE BECAME WICKED

★ "The vividly imagined and haunting landscape is not unlike the post-apocalypse world of *The Walking Dead*. . . . A creative and philosophical take on a zombie-esque apocalypse with a perfectly executed final act twist."

—*Booklist*, starred review

"A first-class sci-fi/horror story."

—*School Library Journal*

"Contains all the plot twists, rebelliousness of youth, and bits of romance that will make it a popular read."

—*School Library Connection*

Also by Alexander Yates

The Winter Place

HOW WE BECAME
WICKED

Alexander Yates

A Caitlyn Dlouhy Book

atheneum

New York London Toronto Sydney New Delhi

atheneum

An imprint of Simon & Schuster Children's Publishing Division
1230 Avenue of the Americas, New York, New York 10020
For information about special discounts for bulk purchases, please contact Simon & Schuster Special Sales at 1-866-506-1949 or business@simonandschuster.com.
The Simon & Schuster Speakers Bureau can bring authors to your live event. For more information or to book an event, contact the Simon & Schuster Speakers Bureau at 1-866-248-3049 or visit our website at www.simonspeakers.com.
Also available in an Atheneum hardcover edition
Book design by Debra Sfetsios-Conover
The text for this book was set in Stempel Garamond.
Manufactured in the United States of America
First Atheneum paperback edition August 2020
2 4 6 8 10 9 7 5 3 1
The Library of Congress has cataloged the hardcover edition as follows:
Names: Yates, Alex, 1982- author.
Title: How we became wicked / Alexander Yates.
Description: First edition. | New York : Atheneum, [2019] | "A Caitlyn Dlouhy book." | Summary: "A viral disease called 'the wickedness' plagues the world, and sixteen-year-olds Astrid and Natalie are two of the only people immune. The girls live in separate, isolated communities, but recent encounters with wicked people link their stories in unexpected ways"— Provided by publisher.
Identifiers: LCCN 2018003651
ISBN 9781481419840 (hardcover) | ISBN 9781481419857 (paperback) | ISBN 9781481419864 (eBook)
Subjects: | CYAC: Science fiction. | Virus diseases—Fiction. | Immunity— Fiction. | Survival—Fiction.
Classification: LCC PZ7.1.Y38 Ho 2019 | DDC [Fic]—dc23
LC record available at https://lccn.loc.gov/2018003651

For Eric,
my brother

PART I

GOLDSPORT

CHAPTER 1

The Lighthouse

ASTRID AWOKE TO FIND THAT HER BEDROOM WAS FILLED WITH a strange, warm light. It faded in an instant, leaving her blinking in the darkness.

What had just happened?

The clock said that it was four thirty in the morning. The whole sanctuary was on an electricity curfew, so the light couldn't have come from any of her neighbors. And it certainly wasn't a dream—Astrid didn't have those.

Then it came again.

Her whole bedroom pulsed, brimming with white light. It was dull on her wallpaper and bright on the glass of her picture frames. Then once more it faded, plunging her back into darkness. Silently, Astrid counted the seconds as they ticked by. Exactly a minute later, there was another flash.

A minute of darkness—a second of light. It could mean only one thing.

"Oh, hell yes," Astrid whispered to the walls of her bedroom.

She jumped out of bed and went over to the window. It was a clear night, and in the starlight Astrid could just make out the glittering crescent of Goldsport—the seaside sanctuary where she'd spent her entire life. The harbor was socked in with a low-lying fog that stretched out into the bay, all the way to Puffin Island. There was a lighthouse on that island. It had been dead for years. And just now, for whatever reason, it had come back to life. The beam arced out over the water and across the sleeping village. Each time it passed across Astrid's bedroom there was a flash, like a very slow *knock-knock*.

Anybody home?

Astrid turned to the window on the far side of her room, the one that looked out onto the Bushkirk house. She pulled up the glass. Cool air surged through the fine metal screen. "Hank," she hissed as loud as she dared. "Wake up."

Hank's bedroom window sat exactly opposite her own. The Bushkirks had lived next door to Astrid's family since forever, and Hank Bushkirk had been her best friend for as long as either of them could remember. As it so happened, Hank was also Astrid's ex-boyfriend. But that was a much newer development.

"Hank," she called again.

Still no answer. Astrid considered leaving Hank to his sleep. But no—the light on Puffin Island was too important to let him miss. It might not have been a ship on the horizon, or a plane blinking across the stars, but it was the closest thing to a sign of life out there that either of them had seen in years. And besides, it was also a good excuse to talk to him. They'd barely spoken since breaking up.

We didn't break up. You dumped me. That was, in point of fact, the last thing Hank had said to her, nearly a month ago now.

Astrid pressed her ear to the window screen, listening for the high-pitched hum of flying singers. When she heard nothing, she carefully worked her fingernails into the frame and pulled the screen back. It creaked, shedding little skins of rust. Astrid braced the screen open and plucked an old coin from the collection on her nightstand. The coin had a picture of a bearded man on one side and a picture of a house with columns on the other. It was called a penny. It used to be worth very little, and today it was worth even less. She had loads of them.

Astrid took aim and flicked the penny against the screen of Hank's bedroom window, where it made a loud, brassy *ping*. Astrid waited. She thought she could hear Hank rustling in there, kicking at his sheets. She flicked a second penny, and this one struck the wooden frame of Hank's window, making a loud *clack*. Finally, Hank's groggy voice rang out from his bedroom.

"Leave me alone, please," he called.

"Hank, get up," Astrid said.

"You're going to wake Henry and Klara," he said. He meant his father and stepmom, snoring away in their grand master bedroom. "Just because you can't sleep, that doesn't mean you have to bother us."

"Just get out of bed for a second," Astrid said. "Take a look outside."

A moment later she heard the sucking sound of his window sliding open. Hank appeared behind the metal screen, knuckling his eyes in the darkness. Then his gaze focused on Astrid, and he blinked. It dawned on both of them at the exact same moment that she was wearing only an oversize shirt and that Hank wasn't wearing a shirt at all. He quickly averted his eyes, and Astrid scooted back from the window and into the shadows of her bedroom.

It was going to take some practice, this whole just-friends thing.

"What is it?" Hank said, making his voice gruffer and deeper than normal.

"The lighthouse," Astrid said. "It's on."

"Oh . . ." Hank turned so that he could look out into the bay. The lighthouse beam swung dizzily toward them, racing across their windows. The sight of it seemed, for an instant, to bring him a smile. But he blew it away with a big, bored yawn.

"Yeah," he said, taking his eyes off of Puffin Island. "I could ask: Who cares? But the answer to that is obvious. You do. You're the only one."

"Come on," Astrid said. "You can't tell me you're not the slightest bit curious." She paused, giving Hank a chance to argue the point. He didn't.

"I was thinking I'd go up to the wall," she went on. "Want to come?"

"Why?"

"To get a better look."

Hank only shrugged. "It'll look the same from up at the wall as it does from down here," he finally said.

"Maybe . . ." Astrid was trying her best, but she wasn't about to beg. It wasn't a pride thing—she was scared that begging would give Hank the wrong idea. "I'm going to go anyway," she said. "You can come if you want."

With that she closed the screen, carefully fitting it back into place.

"I wish you'd be more careful with that," Hank said.

"There aren't any singers out. I checked."

"Just because you can't hear any doesn't mean they aren't there," Hank persisted. "Besides, if you keep bending that screen all over the place, you're going to break it. All it takes is one crack."

All it takes is one crack. Where Astrid and Hank were from, this was the informal town motto. Actually, it was more than that. In Goldsport, it was something akin to a single-sentence religion.

All it takes is one crack.

"If the singers get into your house," Hank continued, "they'll get into mine. They'll get into the greenway and the plaza and everywhere."

"You're right," Astrid said. "Sorry. Next time I'll just message you."

"Ha ha," Hank said.

Astrid slid the glass back down and drew the curtain. She was disappointed, both with Hank for being such a slug and with herself for being unable to pull him out of it. But there was no use dwelling—she'd tried. And she and Hank had the rest of their lives to figure out how to once again act like normal humans around each other. Astrid dressed, then grabbed her binoculars. The Bushkirk house was silent. Hank must have gone back to bed. But then, just as she was about to slip downstairs, he called out to her.

"Just wait for me at the junction, all right? I've gotta get my suit on."

In the darkness of her bedroom, Astrid smiled wide.

Astrid snuck past her father's room, down the plush staircase, and out the front door. But she didn't go outside. In the sanctuary of Goldsport, there was no such thing as outside. Her front door opened directly onto the greenway, a vaulted glass tunnel that crisscrossed the entire village, stitching it together. The tunnel connected directly to her front door, where the glass was sealed tight around the frame with molded rubber. It looked like something between a greenhouse and a hallway. Hence the name—greenway.

Every house in Goldsport was like Astrid's. Everyone had screens on their windows and glass around their doors. It was the only way they knew to keep the singers out. Astrid's own grandfather had thought it up. He was the famous Ronnie Gold—hotel owner, real-estate developer, and founding investor of the sanctuary that now bore his name. Grandpa Gold had been dead for twenty years, but the greenway had outlived him. It was a commonly accepted fact that without it there could be no Goldsport.

Astrid's footsteps echoed down the greenway as she made for the junction. Above her head the glass sparkled in time with the spinning of the lighthouse. Hank arrived just moments after her, the elastic cuffs of his puffy white pants pulled tight over the tops of his rubber boots. The upper half of his bee suit was unzipped, hanging loose around his hips. Under that he'd put on a shirt that read: WORLD'S 2ND BEST DAD. It had a picture of a rather shabby silver cup on it.

"I just want to point out," Hank said, "that going up to the wall is a bigger pain in the ass for me than it is for you."

"Noted," Astrid said. This was, after all, undeniably true.

Together they continued down the greenway, bypassing junctions that led to their neighbors' homes. They cut through the dairy garden, where the milk goats were all dozing in their stalls, and stepped out into the plaza—an open expanse of sandy ground under a glass dome. It was the largest safe space in the sanctuary, and if you closed your eyes and squeezed your toes through the sand, you could almost imagine that you were outdoors. Which was exactly the point.

"You want to go out the western hatch or the harbor hatch?" Astrid asked.

Hank paused to think this over. "I saw my father working

on the roster yesterday," he said. "I think Mr. Collins is posted to the western hatch."

Astrid snorted. If old Mr. Collins had pulled overnight guard duty, there was about a 5 percent chance that he would still be awake to hassle them about leaving the greenway in the near dead of night. "The western hatch it is," she said.

Sure enough, a few minutes later they came upon Mr. Collins in the last junction at the edge of town, at his post but dead to the world. The old man had dragged a beach lounger down the greenway and was curled up on it in a deep sleep. His little gold-framed eyeglasses had slipped off, snagged in the thick coils of his beard. Beneath the lounger lay his village-issued rifle, a paperback spy novel, and a mostly empty bottle of wine. It was the only stuff Mr. Collins ever drank, and rumor had it that it used to be one of the most expensive wines in the world. Mr. Collins had a whole cellar full of it. Apparently, he was once something called a "venture capitalist," though no one had ever successfully explained to Astrid exactly what that was.

"My father needs to take him off the roster," Hank whispered, looking down at Mr. Collins's peaceful, sleeping face. He gingerly removed the glasses from Mr. Collins's beard and tucked them into his shirt pocket so they wouldn't break. "He's just too old for this."

"Other than the two of us, who isn't?" Astrid asked.

Mr. Collins was a hair over seventy, but that still made him one of the younger investors in Goldsport. Meanwhile, Astrid and Hank represented 100 percent of the under-eighteen set, and the next youngest people they knew were their own parents. She'd never gone through the trouble of calculating it, but Astrid guessed the average age in town was somewhere around eighty.

"What do you mean 'us'?" Hank asked. "I've got two months on you. If anyone should be getting extra chores, it's a baby like you."

Astrid looked at him. "Was that a joke?"

"Could be," Hank said. He ran a hand through his hair, which was sticking out every which way. "Pretty amazing, huh? That I can crack a joke? After you smashed my heart and all?"

Astrid grinned. That, right there, was progress.

They stepped around Mr. Collins and continued down to the western hatch. Here a series of heavy woolen sheets, cut into slits and doused with insecticide, hung before an exit chamber. The insecticide was called "quiet," so everybody in town called this exit chamber—and the others like it—the "quiet room." It looked like a glass box affixed to the side of the greenway.

Hank could go no farther without putting on the rest of his bee suit. He pulled the top half over his shoulders, arms tunneling through the oversize sleeves, fingers sliding neatly into leather gloves pinned at the cuffs. His bonnet looked something like a birdcage, with a wire frame supporting a fine mesh veil. Hank fit it over his head, zipped up the front of the suit, and buttoned the fastener.

"Can you check my straps?" He held his arms up and

rotated in a slow circle. There were no gaps, but Astrid tightened a buckle here and there.

"All good," she said.

"Thanks." Hank completed his turn, and the two were suddenly very close, face-to-face. He fell silent. Astrid knew that in this darkness he must be able to see the purple in her eyes—jagged flecks of color that glowed like fox fire. If Hank looked really close, he'd be able to see those little shards of light wriggle and pulse. Even when the two of them had been more than friends, the sight of her glittering irises had freaked Hank out. There was a reason why he used to always close his eyes when they kissed, and it had nothing to do with romance.

Hank dropped his gaze from Astrid's face. Then he turned and pushed his way through the layered wool and into the quiet room. Astrid followed. There was no need for her to go through all that sweaty business of strapping into a bee suit. All she'd had to do before leaving home was pull on a faded pair of jeans and a hoodie. That was because Astrid was immune to the singers and the terrible disease that they carried. Her purple eyes, her dreamless sleep— these were just side effects of her condition. Astrid was the only person in Goldsport who could dare go outside with even an inch of skin exposed. The only person in the whole world, as far as she knew.

Not that that was saying much.

The world was a pretty empty place.

CHAPTER 2

The Wall

OUTSIDE IT WAS STILL DARK, BUT THE WOODS WERE WAKING up. Songbirds called from atop the pines. A barred owl hooted. And there, tucked into the spaces between these sounds, Astrid could detect the faintest purr.

It got louder as they approached the forest. There were different pitches—looping and dipping, knotting and untangling. A rich harmony of hums. This was the sound of singers, thick in their summer swarms. This was the song that had ruined the world. Still, no one could tell Astrid it wasn't beautiful.

Hank missed a step when he heard it. He was perfectly safe from those horrid bugs in his bee suit, but their song still sent a shiver through him. Astrid couldn't blame him. Just one bite would have been enough to undo the person that Hank was. Just one bite would have cast him down forever among the wicked.

That's what they called the disease—the wickedness.

It was a virus. Forty years ago it spread across the world, carried on the buzzing wings of the singers. The virus traveled through their beastly, sucking mouths and into the veins of the people they bit. There it wormed its way into your brain and unmade you. The virus silenced your imagination, and empathy, and kindness. It robbed you of your inhibitions, your instinct for self-preservation, and your ingrained sense that hitting people in the head with rocks is wrong. The virus could turn even the gentlest grandfather into a grinning, homicidal maniac. Infected sisters drowned their brothers in stopped-up sinks. Infected fathers set fire to the cribs of their children. So there was no word more fit for the sick than that: the wicked. They had torn the world, and everyone in it, to tatters. As far as anyone knew, only Goldsport had survived.

As for the singers, they were still a mystery. Astrid had read everything she could find about them in the sanctuary archives, but none of it amounted to very much. The singers resembled mosquitoes, so some scientists thought that they were a new species. Others guessed that they were just normal mosquitoes, and that the virus had changed them, as well. Whatever the explanation, the little purple monsters were tough as nails. The old-fashioned pesticides that worked on normal mosquitoes might as well have been bubble bath to the singers. They could survive being poisoned, crushed, gassed, and frozen. If they'd had more time, perhaps the scientists would have discovered where the singers came from. But then the world fell wicked, and there were no more scientists. Nobody left to answer questions. Hardly anybody left to even ask them.

"All right," Hank mumbled, half to himself. "Let's get this over with."

He set up the road quickly, keeping his eyes locked on the crumbling asphalt. Astrid followed, rushing to catch up. The wall stood atop a crescent of hills that ran the length of the Goldsport sanctuary. To get there they'd have to climb, passing through the singer-infested forest.

It wasn't long before Astrid and Hank could see them.

The singers drifted among the trees, dizzy and luminous as fireflies. Their wings glowed a dim but constant purple—the exact same hue that flickered in Astrid's eyes—which made them easy to spot as they twirled through the branches. Soon they sensed Hank's passing and descended. The singers' wings bled like watercolors as they moved, leaving fading violet contrails in the air behind them. One of them landed on the shoulder of Hank's bee suit, mouthing for holes. Others bounced repeatedly into the mesh of his bonnet. A few singers brushed against Astrid on their way to the feast, but they didn't pay her any mind. They didn't even seem to realize that she was there.

A short time later Astrid and Hank arrived at the wall. It towered over them, twenty feet high and topped with an opulent crown of razor wire. As with the greenway, Astrid's grandfather had built this wall. And as with the greenway, it was beloved by the old folks in Goldsport. It represented for them not just a promise of safety, but more important, a promise that had been kept. The wall loomed at the edge of their sanctuary like a silent, loving father outside his child's bedroom door. But to Astrid, the wall just looked like an ugly heap of concrete and twisted metal.

The wall had only one opening—a massive chain-link gate that cut across the road. The gate was locked, of course. But they could see through it. The road continued down the leeward side of the hills and into a sucking yellow bog in the valley beyond. Where it went after that, Astrid couldn't say. In her whole life, she'd never been farther from home than this.

To one side of the gate stood a watchtower, which rose up into the canopy. To the other was a rusting tank. It was a relic from years ago, long before Astrid was born, back when the singers first flooded into the woods and the wicked first began to grin and jabber and stab. The tank had its gun aimed directly at the gate. There was a word spray-painted onto its dusky metal flank—a name.

MOTHER.

"Come on," Astrid said, making for the watchtower. Hank followed, bringing along with him the little swarm of hungry singers. They climbed a rickety set of stairs and stepped out onto a windswept wooden platform up above the treetops. Layer by layer, the wind stripped away Hank's cloud of singers, and they swirled off into the night like sparks from a dying campfire.

"Man . . . ," Hank said as he gazed out over the harbor.

"Totally worth getting out of bed at four in the morning for this."

Astrid ignored him. She went to the railing and pressed her binoculars to her face. She could see the rocky shoreline of Puffin Island. The lighthouse was an ivory needle against the black ocean. The lamp up top blazed and spun.

Per the official story, Puffin Island was uninhabited. The lighthouse had come on a few times before, but whenever it did people would ignore it. Astrid's dad said that it was automated. According to him, the flickering light was due to nothing more mysterious than the aging, malfunctioning equipment. Failing engines and rat-gnawed wires. The slow death of everything that belonged to the world before the wickedness.

Astrid didn't buy it.

She couldn't say exactly why she didn't buy it. She simply didn't. She had no hard evidence—just a loose collection of odd coincidences that seemed to add up to something more. There was the way people in town would fall silent and drop their eyes to their shoes whenever Astrid asked them about Puffin Island. There was the fact that whenever they went out fishing, people would steer their boats clear of the lighthouse. And, of course, there was that one evening when Klara, Hank's stepmom, wondered aloud if they shouldn't bring some of their leftovers to "those poor people out there on the island." Though that last piece of evidence wasn't as good as it sounded—half the time Klara didn't know who Hank was, and the other half she got him and her own husband mixed up.

Flimsy evidence, all in all. But it was enough for Astrid. She was convinced that the whole town was lying about Puffin Island. Convinced that there were people out there, on that little rock in the bay. And for some reason that Astrid couldn't fathom, nobody in Goldsport wanted to admit it.

"You know," Hank said, joining Astrid at the railing, "it really looks different from up here."

Astrid pulled the binoculars from her face and caught him gazing down at Goldsport. They had a view of the entire sanctuary, from the beautiful Gold-family beach house to the empty ruins that littered the north shore. The greenway twinkled. With the domed glass plaza sitting at its heart, the whole town looked like a crystal octopus.

"I guess I always forget how small it really is," Hank said.

"Me too," Astrid said.

A lie. Really, she never, ever forgot.

Hank rested his elbows on the railing, shifting to get comfortable in his bulky suit. His eyes went from their town out to the little shard of light on the horizon.

"You know," he said, "even if there is a family living out there . . . I mean, what makes you think they're true?"

That was what they called people who hadn't been infected by the wickedness. It divided the world neatly into categories—wicked and true. Astrid was the only person in Goldsport who didn't fit into either of them.

"Well, for one thing," she said, happy to play along, "if the people on Puffin Island are wicked, wouldn't they have come for us by now?"

Hank shifted in his suit, looking askance at Astrid. "Maybe they don't have a boat?"

"I don't think the wicked work that way," Astrid said. "I think if they saw the lights in town and wanted to hurt us, they'd swim."

This was just a guess—Astrid had no personal experience with the wicked. In fact, their sanctuary hadn't had contact with any outsiders, wicked or true, in decades. The thinking was that everybody out there had either fallen to the illness or been killed by the ill. Which was exactly why Astrid found the prospect of strangers on Puffin Island, living out there on Goldsport's doorstep, so irresistible.

"Fine," Hank said, holding his gloved hands up in a gesture of surrender. Finally, he seemed to be loosening up. "I guess I can accept that. But then explain something to me: Let's say you're right and there are people on Puffin Island, and what's more, they're true people. . . ." He paused. "Same question. Why are they staying away from us? Why are we staying away from them?"

Astrid didn't answer. She'd asked herself the exact same question more times than she could count.

"I know, right?" Hank said. "That right there is a complication."

She turned once more to face the lighthouse. "If I'd known you'd be such a bummer," she said, "I wouldn't have asked you to come."

"Everybody needs a reality check from time to time," Hank said.

"Yeah?" Astrid gripped the railing and leaned back, letting her weight dangle and swing. She felt like a flag, taut in the breeze. As free as a person can feel when they're tied to one spot. "Is that what you are to me?" she went on, head tipping back and eyes to the sky. Above them the stars were blinking out as the sun rose. "My reality check?"

To her right Astrid heard the snap of buttons. Hank was unfastening the bonnet of his bee suit. The wind rushed across his cheeks and through his hair and into his big, smiling mouth. Astrid figured out what was happening only a second before it actually did—before she could do or say anything to alert Hank to the fact that it was a truly terrible idea. Suddenly his hands were on her back and his lips were mashing into hers. They were chapped from the breeze, and soft and familiar. Astrid straightened herself up, pressed both hands against the coarse fabric of Hank's bee suit, and pushed him away. For a second he blinked at her, confused. Then, realizing how badly he had miscalculated, Hank said, "Shit."

He popped his bonnet back on and fastened the snaps around the collar and veil. He retreated to the far side of the platform, turning to face the darkness beyond the wall.

"Shit," he said again. "I thought that you were . . ."

"I was absolutely not," Astrid said. Hank had tried the whole mixed-signals routine with her before, and she was not about to have that conversation again. The signals were only mixed because Hank ignored the ones he didn't like.

"I said 'friends.' I meant friends. Come on. . . ." Astrid

was at a loss for words. She had no desire to yell at him, but she also didn't know how to be any clearer than she'd already been. "When I'm being nice to you, that's me being nice to a friend. Because that's what you are. Or at least, that's what I want you to be."

Other than a mumbled "sorry," Hank had no response.

Astrid didn't know what else to say either.

Talking to each other used to be so easy. Ever since Astrid and Hank could speak, they'd spoken mostly to each other. As children they'd been inseparable, and the greenway took turns being their fort, their space station, and their enchanted castle made of ice. When they'd gotten older, their parents had allowed them to go out to the north shore by themselves, with Hank buckled tight into a child-size bee suit. Together they'd plucked starfish and hermit crabs out of the tide pools and watched seals basking on the rocks beyond the harbor. And then one day, shortly after Astrid turned thirteen, they climbed into Mother—the rusted tank guarding the gates to Goldsport—and shut the creaking hatch behind them. Hank pulled off his mesh bonnet, and they kissed. It was better than a first kiss between inexperienced friends had any right be—which is to say, it wasn't a disaster. But they got better at kissing over time. In fact, as the years passed, Astrid and Hank did a lot more than kiss in the safe confines of that tank. Not that anything like that would ever be happening again.

Whenever Astrid tried to retrace their steps, to see

where things had gone wrong between her and Hank, her mind always went back to the hours they'd spent making not-great decisions inside of Mother's metal belly. But that wasn't the whole story. Really, things began to sour between them once the community in Goldsport realized that Astrid and Hank were courting. That was the actual word they used: "courting."

It wasn't courting.

It was touching and pressing and not knowing where to look as whatever was happening was happening. It was two friends, stumbling ass-backward together into the great sweaty beyond. It felt good and confusing and brave and stupid. Often, when they left the tank, Astrid would see the smitten look on Hank's face and feel suddenly queasy. But never mind the details—the old folks of Goldsport were just tickled to have a pair of "young lovers" in their midst.

At first Astrid had enjoyed the attention. Or, rather, she'd enjoyed getting that kind of attention. People in Goldsport had always noticed her. They'd long been suspicious of her condition and were unsettled by her glowing eyes. Some even refused to touch Astrid, afraid she might carry the disease upon her skin. But once she and Hank were seen as a unit, all that changed. Astrid finally got the Goldsport seal of approval. Before long the investors began to treat her and Hank like some kind of arranged, intended couple. The old Abbitt twins asked her, in that casually morbid way of theirs, if she and Hank ever thought of moving into their big house at the edge of the plaza after the twins both died.

Then Mrs. Wrigley began making not-so-subtle hints that her old wedding dress would look just divine on Astrid. She'd even caught Mr. Collins saying, "When you two have kids of your own," like it was no big deal at all. Like the question of choice was totally out of their hands!

It made Astrid wonder—had she and Hank been friends only because they'd had no other options? And now that they were the only citizens of Goldsport between the ages of zero and fifty, did that mean they should be engaged by default? Did it mean that, somehow, love would just automatically follow?

Hell no, it didn't.

From the other end of the platform Astrid heard a soft sound. She was worried for a second it might be Hank crying, but then she realized that he was only chuckling. It was a quiet, sad, sorry-for-himself chuckle. But a laugh is a laugh.

"Okay," she said. "What's funny?"

"This," Hank said, flinging both arms out to his sides. "I mean, here I am. The last guy on earth—or, at least, the last guy your age. And still, you don't want me." Again Hank laughed. He must have figured that he'd reached the point of no return, embarrassment-wise.

Astrid crossed over to his side of the platform and looked out into the empty world beyond the wall. The sun was climbing at their backs, casting a glow across the treetops. "If you were the last guy on earth," Astrid finally said, "I'd start picking out furniture with you. But, Hank, I promise that you're not. I promise. Just like I'm not the last girl on earth. I just . . . I just know it. Which is good, right?" Astrid elbowed him in the ribs through his bee suit, hard enough that there'd be no room for misinterpretation. "Isn't it nice to think that someday you'll have choices other than me?"

Hank sighed. "I don't want other choices," he said. "I want you."

Oh well. Two steps forward, one step back.

CHAPTER 3

The Plaza

ASTRID AND HANK RETURNED HOME WITHOUT SPEAKING.

The singers followed close, filling the silence with a swarming serenade. Dawn had come and gone, scattering sunlight across the greenway. Up ahead Astrid could see the boxy quiet room and beyond that the glass-blurred figures of townsfolk moving down to the plaza. She'd been so focused on Puffin Island that she had nearly forgotten that today was Sunday—picnic day.

Radio day.

"You don't have to wait for me," Hank said. It always took some time for him to get that nasty bee suit off. "No reason for you to miss the show."

Astrid waved him off. "I'm the one who dragged you out of bed," she said. "What kind of friend would I be if I ditched you now?"

Even to her own ears, it sounded a bit ham-fisted the way she lingered on that word: "friend." But whatever. Astrid had tried subtle, and subtle hadn't worked. "Besides," she went on, "it's not like we haven't heard the show before."

"Suit yourself," Hank said.

He stepped through the heavy outer curtains, into the quiet room. Astrid followed, closing her eyes and pinching her nose. The curtains were doused with quiet every week. The smell made Astrid's eyes water. Inside the chamber there was a large barrel of foaming blue quiet, with a dipper bobbing on the bubbly surface. Hank filled the dipper and poured it over himself. The liquid streaked down his bonnet and then his back and legs. The popping bubbles hissed.

"Arms up," Astrid said.

Hank lifted his arms and turned in a slow circle while Astrid checked him to see if any singers had managed to avoid the poison. But he was clean. She opened the internal glass hatch, and together they stepped through another set of curtains and back onto the greenway. As soon as they were inside, they could hear a low murmur reverberating through the halls. Everybody must have been at the plaza by now, waiting eagerly to hear *The First Voice*.

It happened the same way every week. The old Goldsport investors put on their Sunday best and marched on down the glass tunnels like a colony of cheerful, geriatric ants. They gathered together in the plaza, spreading beach towels over the sand and unpacking picnic baskets. They passed around fresh loaves of bread, jars of strawberries, and tubs of soft goat cheese. People took turns manning the omelet station. Sometimes Mrs. Wrigley would even whip up a batch of her famous mimosas—a treat reserved for special occasions, due to a dwindling supply of powdered orange drink. Though Mrs. Wrigley liked to joke that at least they had enough genuine champagne to see Goldsport right on through Revelation.

The murmur of conversation grew louder as Astrid and Hank approached the plaza. By the time they arrived, it had reached a dull roar. Astrid scanned the crowd for her dad and saw that he'd already taken his place up on the stage with the board. Amblin Gold was shuffling papers and shaking hands. Astrid headed up to the stage as quickly as she could, weaving between the beach towels. Hank followed, his crumpled bee suit still dripping under his arm.

And . . . was it just Astrid's imagination, or did something weird happen as she and Hank crossed the plaza? Each little huddle of picnickers seemed to fall silent as they passed, and Astrid caught a few of them staring. She wondered: Could it be that everybody in town had already noticed the lighthouse? Had they all taken a moment before the picnic started to get their stories straight?

"There you are!" Amblin Gold called, lighting up as he spotted his daughter. "And Hank, too!" Astrid's dad lowered his notes and straightened up to his full height of five feet and zero inches. To go with that unimposing stature, Amblin had large blue eyes, a gentle face, and skin the color of raked sand. Two fringes of blond hair sprouted out at his temples, which against all of Astrid's advice he'd allowed to grow bushy to make up for the bald spot up top.

"A little late this morning?" her dad said, tapping on the bridge of his nose with one finger and giving them both a knowing look. Just about the mildest scold in the history of parental discipline.

"Sorry we broke curfew," Astrid said.

"Sorry?" her dad asked with a dramatic show of skepticism. "Tell me, Hank, do you think for a second that she's actually sorry?"

"Nope," Hank said, returning Amblin's smile. Astrid's dad and Hank had always gotten along like this—corny and friendly. When she and Hank had broken up, Amblin had taken it just as hard as Hank.

"Skipping right ahead," Astrid said, nodding down at the notes still gripped in her dad's hand. "Are you going to say anything about Puffin Island?"

"Puffin Island . . . ? I hadn't planned on it," her dad said. "Why would I?"

"The lighthouse. It turned back on this morning," Astrid said.

"Did it, now?" Amblin turned out toward the bay and squinted through the greenway glass. "I suppose so," he said, sort of bemused. "Who'd have guessed those batteries still had juice?"

If Astrid's dad was pretending, he was at least doing a good job of it.

"It's been two years since the last time it turned on," Astrid added.

"That long?" Her father's attention was already back on his notes.

"So . . . ," Astrid said, pausing. "Maybe we should go and take a look?"

Her dad dismissed the suggestion with a little snort. "No sense in motoring all the way out there just to visit a pile of rocks," he said. "Waste of fuel. And the boats don't need the stress."

Bullshit. They had plenty of fuel—brimming underground tanks hoarded from the world before the wickedness. And if their boats couldn't handle a simple trip across the bay, well, then what was the point of even having boats in the first place?

"All right," Astrid said. "But suppose, just hypothetically, that the lighthouse didn't turn on by itself?"

At this her dad's gaze surfaced from his notes. He looked from Astrid to Hank. "Don't tell me she's still . . ."

"Totally," Hank said with a shrug. "That's what we were doing this morning. Astrid wanted to get a better view from the watchtower."

"So what?" Astrid said, frustration taking hold. "Is it impossible that there could be people out there?"

"Listen, honey," Amblin said. "The island was empty the last time I went. And the island was empty the time before that. I'm not going to waste gasoline just so you can see that emptiness for yourself." Her father sighed. "I mean . . . what exactly do you think we're keeping from you, Astrid?"

"Who's keeping what from who now?"

Henry Bushkirk, Hank's father, had just lumbered up behind them. He was a large, unpleasant, and fashionably dressed man. That morning he wore a collared shirt tucked into a pair of pin-striped slacks. Astrid could see the jagged corner of an ancient price tag sticking out of one of his shirtsleeves.

"It's nothing, Henry," Amblin said. "Just the kids going on about Puffin Island. Rather," he was quick to correct himself, "just my kid."

"That so?" Mr. Bushkirk asked, rocking back on his wing tips. "Junior . . . ?"

"Sir." Hank's voice suddenly rose an octave, and his eyes dropped down to the sand. It was a tic he'd developed over sixteen years living under his father's roof—one that Mr. Bushkirk only pretended to dislike.

"I'm not down there between your toes, Junior," Mr. Bushkirk said. He snapped his fingers in the air and pointed at his own face. "Eyes up, please."

Hank's gaze made it only to about the center of his father's chest.

"I guess that's why we didn't find you in your room this morning," Mr. Bushkirk said. He glanced at the crumpled bee suit, still shining with blue quiet, slung over his son's arm. "Klara went in to wake you for the picnic. She got worked up to no end when you weren't there. You know how confused she gets."

"No harm done," Amblin said. "They only went outside

to get a look at the lighthouse. It turned back on—did you notice?"

"I asked him to come with me," Astrid said.

"Is that so?" Mr. Bushkirk said, chewing the words. His eyes went from Hank to Astrid and back to Hank. "Just the two of you?"

"Yes, sir," Hank said.

"Well, now, that has me puzzled. . . ." Mr. Bushkirk gave a little half grin and hooked his thumbs under his suspenders. "Help me out, Amblin," he said. "Does that mean our two kids are an item again?" Only Mr. Bushkirk could take a word like "item" and make it sound so sweaty and gross.

"No, sir," Hank answered before Astrid could.

Mr. Bushkirk licked his lips, and they shined a bright pink. "I wouldn't sound so defeated if I were you, Junior. What girl likes a quitter?" He threw Astrid a little shrug, as though to apologize for his son's lameness. Then he juked his head in the direction of the gathered picnickers, many of whom were stealing glances at Hank and Astrid.

"It certainly is a pity," Mr. Bushkirk said. "I suppose the audience will just have to get used to disappointment."

It took Astrid a moment to understand his meaning. But, of course—that's why people had fallen silent when she and Hank entered the plaza. News traveled fast in Goldsport, and everybody must have known that they'd skipped curfew together. Dammit. Astrid should have realized what kind of signal this would send.

"*C'est la vie*," Mr. Bushkirk said, climbing up onto the

little stage and carefully lowering himself into an open seat beside Amblin. Once he was settled, his attention returned to Hank. "But, Junior. Come on. Work with me here. What you and Astrid do or don't get up to isn't any of my business. I'm a reasonable guy—I can accept that. But when you disappear, like you did this morning, it really stresses your stepmom out. And when Klara gets stressed out, I get stressed out. So the next time you leave my house, Junior, you don't just tell me where you're going. You ask me if you can. Understood?"

"Understood," Hank said.

Mr. Bushkirk eyeballed his son for a moment longer before giving a little grunt. "Good boy," he said. Meanwhile, down at the other end of the stage, Mrs. Lee flicked the live microphone and caused an electric *thump* to echo through the plaza, rebounding off the yawning glass dome.

It was time for the show.

CHAPTER 4

The First Voice

THEY DECIDED IT WAS BEST IF THEY DIDN'T SIT TOGETHER—NO point getting people's hopes up any further. Hank made his way over to his stepmom, while Astrid headed for a row of empty chairs that sat against the rear wall of the plaza. Here the greenway glass overlooked the docks, where a few lobster boats rocked on the outgoing tide, pulling gently on their lines. Beyond the docks, Astrid could see the distant form of Puffin Island.

"Don't let them get you down, honey," said a familiar but unexpected voice.

Startled, Astrid turned to face her mother, who had slipped into the seat next to hers. Astrid hadn't noticed her mom in the crowd, but that was only because she hadn't bothered looking.

"Sorry." Her mom brushed a strand of hair from her own face. Her name was Ria, and she had the thickest, blackest hair Astrid had ever seen. "Did I sneak up on you?"

"A little," Astrid said, looking her over. Her mother's eyes were bloodshot, and her flannel shirt was spotted with stains and fish scales. Three of the buttons had been replaced with safety pins. Her trousers were rolled up to the calf, rigid with dried seawater. Ria clenched her brown toes in the sand.

"What are you doing here?" Astrid asked.

"I had to chat with your dad about something," Ria said a little absently. "And then . . . I figured if I was already on the greenway, I might as well stay for the picnic. It's been a long time since I've heard a show."

That it had been. Ria Gold wasn't exactly what you'd call sociable, and by Astrid's reckoning, this was the first Sunday picnic she'd attended all year. In fact, Astrid could hardly remember the last time her mom had put in an appearance at any of the Goldsport community events—she usually even skipped the annual commemoration. Which made her attendance this morning all the more odd.

"About what?" Astrid asked.

"I'm sorry?"

"What did you have to talk with Dad about?"

This, too, was fishy—Astrid's parents had been separated for years, and the only reason they hardly ever fought these days was because they hardly ever saw each other. In fact, her mom and dad had become near geniuses at avoiding contact. To help accomplish this task, Astrid's mother had moved out to an old house on the north shore. This was a part of their sanctuary that had been destroyed by the wicked many years ago—the one blemish in Goldsport's happy history. Astrid's own grandfather had been killed defending it, forever memorializing him as a saint to the other investors. The greenway up there was shattered beyond repair, and most of the houses had been burnt to ruins. Only Ria's was still habitable, though it sat untethered from the rest of town. That made Astrid's mom the only person in Goldsport who lived beyond the glass. She had her own screens and her own little homemade quiet room. Anywhere she went, she had to put on a bee suit. It seemed an awful lot of trouble, just to get away from your ex-husband. Sometimes it struck Astrid that Ria hadn't only divorced her dad, but also the entire sanctuary of Goldsport.

"Oh, nothing urgent . . ." Her mom took a breath. "I need a work crew for my roof. There's been a leak ever since the thaw, and I don't want it to rot through."

Astrid studied her mother. She'd stayed over with Ria just last week and hadn't noticed any leak.

"So it wasn't about the lighthouse, then?"

"What?" Ria didn't blink.

"That's not what you wanted to talk to Dad about?" Astrid paused. "The lighthouse came on again. Last night. It's still on now," she said.

"Oh? I didn't notice. . . ." Ria twisted in her seat to gaze through the greenway glass. Out on the horizon the lighthouse sparked, a flare in the sunlight. "Well, would you look at that."

Astrid would have pushed further, but at that point her

father took his place at the center of the stage. An instant later his voice rang out over the gathered crowd, delivering the weekly announcements. Goldsport investor Chipper Gregory had reported a humming sound coming from somewhere in his game room. Out of an abundance of caution, the board of investors had decided to put a weeklong quarantine on the Gregory house and to shut down greenway junction D-17. During this time, Missy Van Allen had kindly agreed to take Mr. and Mrs. Gregory in. In the meantime, investor Henry Bushkirk would search the house for singers. The board was looking for volunteers to join him.

"And on the small chance that there are no volunteers"— Amblin Gold smiled at this little joke; there were never any volunteers—"then the board will hold a lottery."

The crowd let out a collective groan.

"Listen," Ria said, leaning in. "What I was trying to tell you before is that I saw how weird everybody got when you and Hank walked in together. It's not my business if anything is going on between you two, but—"

Astrid cut her off. "Nothing is going on between us."

"Still not my business," Ria said. She ran her lean, chapped fingers through Astrid's hair. It felt good, but Astrid resisted it. She wasn't a little kid anymore.

"And it isn't their business either," Ria continued. "You and Hank don't owe them a thing. You just have to do what feels right."

"Yeah. Well . . ." Astrid huffed. "Being broken up only feels right to one of us."

"Honey." Ria smiled at her. "Believe me, I know the feeling."

At the other end of the plaza, Astrid's dad had finished up his remarks — he'd made no mention of the lighthouse — and together with the rest of the board, he began to clear the stage. Henry Bushkirk yanked the starter rope on the generator, powering up a ring of speakers rigged along the walls. Mr. Collins fiddled with the radio receiver. The crowd tittered, eagerly anticipating the radio show. It began as it always did, with the faint and rising call of trumpets, the opening fanfare for *The First Voice*. At the sound of the music, everybody in the plaza clapped and cheered.

"Mom, are you sure there's nothing else you want to tell me?" Astrid asked, speaking up to be heard over the ruckus. The coincidence was just too big for her to ignore. Ria and Amblin having words for the first time in who knows how long? The lighthouse coming back to life after years of darkness? How could these two things not be related? "Nothing about Puffin Island?" Astrid tried.

"Sweetheart," her mother said. "Hush. I want to listen."

A familiar voice sprang from the speakers. "Hello out there, dear true listeners," the lady presenter said, enunciating each word. "This is *The First Voice*, broadcasting to you live from the Quiet Lands, west of the majestic Rocky Mountains. Today is the first of October, in the twenty-fourth year of the wickedness, and it is a beautiful day indeed."

Other than the beautiful day bit — which was only a

coincidence—everything else the woman had said was wrong. First, it was actually July, and by the Goldsport calendar they were in the fortieth year of the wickedness. Second, the show wasn't live. And third, there was nothing to the west of the Rocky Mountains—at least not anymore. Though ... whether or not the mountains were still majestic was anybody's guess.

It hadn't always been this way. *The First Voice* used to broadcast a new episode every Sunday. It was an absurdly optimistic show. "Not the last voice of the old world," went their tagline, "but the first voice of the new one!" But whoever those people were, optimism wasn't enough to protect them. New episodes stopped broadcasting the same year Astrid was born. Ever since then, the final nine months of shows had simply repeated on a loop. Their sanctuary must have been overrun, and the people inside had either been killed or fallen wicked. Just like everyone else in the world. All that remained were echoes of their happy voices. Dying batteries and rusting wires.

"Twenty-four years." The announcer sighed. "It's an age, isn't it? But it's also a blink. A heartbeat. It goes by so fast. Those of you out there who are parents, you know what I'm talking about." She paused, commiserating with her unseen listeners. Nobody in Goldsport knew her name— she'd never said, and now she never would.

"So, as I promised you all last Sunday, today I'll be playing the second half of *Gone with the Wind*. And just like last week, I have my friend here with me to narrate the bits in between so that you can all picture what our lovers are getting up to. But before we pop the movie back in, I've got one very gentle reminder to deliver."

At this point, there was a general stirring in the crowd. Somebody stood up from their chair and hollered, "Mute, please."

It took a moment for Astrid to remember why.

"You might recall," the announcer continued, "that some weeks ago we brought you a special news segment on a promising new development in our ongoing struggle against the wickedness. Doctors in California are calling it the vex."

At the sound of this word, Astrid's stomach turned.

"Today I'd like to remind you all—"

"Turn it down, please," someone else hollered from the crowd. It was Mrs. Wrigley, her sun hat askew and a champagne flute tight in her gloved fist. "This part lasts for three and a half minutes," she said. "I wrote it down last time."

Mr. Collins hurried back up to the receiver, frantically putting his little gold-framed glasses back on. He began fiddling with the buttons and knobs. Still, the woman on the radio persisted.

"I think it's important," she said, "in light of some distressing news we've heard, to restate a few key elements of that story. As we said some weeks ago, at this point the vex cannot be recommended for any babies of more than six months of age. Do not—I repeat—do not—"

"Come on, Tommy!" This was Mr. Gregory, now standing as well.

"I'm sorry," Mr. Collins said, getting flustered. "I'm try—"

"Unplug it," Mrs. Wrigley yelled. "If you can't figure out the volume, unplug it." Her champagne flute was shaking in her hand.

Meanwhile, the radio announcer continued. She could never have known how unpopular this particular segment was with her loyal audience in Goldsport. "And even for babies within the recommended range," she said, "you still need to use discretion in how you apply the vex. What we've heard out of California is that the most consistent results might actually come if exposure is given in the first seventy-two hours after birth. Furthermore, they recommend exposure to at least—that's at least—five singers. I know that's frightening, but we're talking multiple bites, friends. That's what you need to get the required . . . What are they calling it? The required viral load."

"Get it together, Tommy!" Mr. Gregory was approaching the stage now, his gait jagged and unsteady.

"Now, it goes without saying that the potential rewards of the vex are just . . . They're just . . . I mean, 'wow' is all I can say." The announcer sighed longingly as her entire Goldsport audience grew more and more agitated. And for the second time that morning, people in the crowd turned, glancing nervously in Astrid's direction.

"But I need to stress that the doctors say there is no guarantee of immunity. And there are some risks involved. There's a chance that exposure to the virus could overwhelm a young immune system. The complications are potentially fatal. Now, the doctors consider the likelihood to be minor, but not—"

"Liar!"

Mrs. Wrigley hurled her champagne flute up at the stage, where it shattered against the edge of the banquet table, drawing a glittering orange bolt across the tablecloth. Mr. Collins was so panicked that he fell backward off the riser and into the sand. A moment later Henry Bushkirk arrived and killed the generator.

"You're a liar!" Mrs. Wrigley screamed again. She slumped back down onto the sand, sinking into the folds of her dress. The Abbitt twins, who had been sitting on the adjacent quilt, took Mrs. Wrigley into their arms.

"I'm so sorry about that," Mr. Collins said, nervously pushing his glasses back up the bridge of his nose. "I don't know how I forgot. . . . It was right here in my notes. Eight thirty-two—volume off."

Nobody spoke for the next few minutes as they waited for the rest of the segment to play out. Many stared at Astrid. She wished, as she always did when the vex came up, that she could disappear. After all, it might as well have been her that everybody was so upset about. Astrid was vexed.

She was the only one.

"Honey . . ." Her mother reached for Astrid's hand. "Try not to pay any attention," she whispered. "It's not about you."

"Mom," Astrid whispered back, "it's exactly about me."

She pulled out of her mother's grip and stood, heading for the rear hatch, which opened onto the Goldsport harbor. Even after she was through the quiet room and outside, marching down the dock and sending the gulls leaping off their perches, she still felt watched from beyond the glass. Astrid wished she could go invisible. She wished she could jump off the end of the dock, into the cool and clear water, and just swim away.

Years ago, when they first heard about the vex, everybody in Goldsport had been overjoyed. It wasn't a vaccine, but it was close—a way to shield the next generation from the wickedness. Just as *The First Voice* recommended, they'd carried their children and infants outside, naked under purple garlands of singers. By some fluke of the young immune system, exposure to the live virus at that early age was supposed to make the children forever resistant.

In Astrid's case, it had worked. When she was two days old her parents carried her off the greenway and let the singers taste her blood. As payment, she enjoyed a life free of bee suits and quiet. Most important, Astrid knew that she would never catch the disease—never fall wicked. But she was the only one.

Story of her life—Astrid was the only one.

The vex was supposed to free Goldsport's next generation, but instead it simply erased them from existence. Every other child died within months of being bitten. That included Hank's older brother and his twin sister. He had survived only because he'd been a sickly baby, the runt of the Bushkirk litter, and his parents had decided not to risk exposing him to the vex. To this day, his father had never forgiven Hank for being the one who'd survived. And as for the rest of Goldsport, they were all so traumatized that they were done having children. There would be no new playmates for Astrid or Hank. No new names to give or to remember.

"You okay?"

Astrid turned to see that Hank had put his bee suit back on and had joined her at the end of the dock.

"Yup," Astrid said.

"Liar."

"Yup," she said again.

Funny. Just an hour ago, up at the watchtower, Astrid had been puzzling over how her relationship with Hank had fallen apart. But this right here was why it had started in the first place. The vex had screwed up his life just as much as anyone else's. Yet here Hank was, side by side with Astrid, the living symbol of everything he and Goldsport had lost. It had been like this since they were little. Hank had accepted Astrid from the get-go. He didn't flinch. This feeling, this closeness, was all she'd ever wanted. As they grew older it changed and went places it shouldn't have. Astrid hoped, with all her heart, that they could find their way back to that friendship. It was one of the most important things in her life.

"So . . . just checking," Hank said. "Now would also be a bad time for a kiss, yes?"

Astrid laughed, and so did he.

"Yes," she said. Then: "Thank you."

They stood together in silence after that, gazing out into the bay. The gulls flapped around them, returning to their perches. They could hear the radio show once again, reverberating through the glass behind them. A minute passed, and then another. They both seemed to realize, at the same time, that the lighthouse out on Puffin Island had turned off.

CHAPTER 5

What Klara Remembers

TRY AS SHE MIGHT, ASTRID COULDN'T GET THAT LIGHTHOUSE out of her head. Over the following days she did her best to investigate. She popped over to her neighbors' houses uninvited, armed with questions. She lurked outside the council room, eavesdropping on the board of investors. She even signed up for shifts in the dairy gardens, just so she could interrogate the people on duty.

"Hey, did you happen to notice that the lighthouse turned on?"

"That's right! On Sunday morning. That's weird, isn't it?"

"How long has it been, actually? Two years? More than that?"

"Do you really think batteries can last that long? Seems odd to me!"

"When was the last time anybody even went to Puffin Island, anyway?"

"Wouldn't you agree that someone should go and check it out?"

"Aren't you the least bit curious?"

Astrid was so persistent that her neighbors stopped opening their doors when they spied her through the peephole. Investors began to turn and head in the opposite direction when they saw her coming down the greenway. Astrid was used to this—people had been weirded out by her for as long as she could remember—but not even Amblin or Ria would let anything slip! There was simply no cracking through their lie. And so, after a few days of getting nowhere, Astrid finally decided to try her luck with Klara Bushkirk.

Honestly, she felt a little guilty about it.

Klara was Hank's stepmom, and she was the oldest person left in the sanctuary. She'd been among the first investors and had stood right beside Ronnie Gold at the founding ceremony. Hank said his dad had married Klara only so that he could weasel his way into her big house and win himself a seat on the board of investors. Given what Astrid knew about the man, it checked out.

But none of that was why Astrid felt conflicted. The truth was that Klara tended to forget things. Sometimes it was small stuff, like a name or a date. Sometimes it was big stuff, like what singers were. She had even been known, from time to time, to forget literally everything about this new and wicked world in which they lived. Last year Astrid's father had caught Klara trying to go outside without her bee suit on. Her ear was pressed up against a dead cell phone, and she was complaining loudly about how poor the service was. It came in waves. She had good days, and she had bad ones. All of which was why Astrid felt so guilty. Interrogating Klara felt a little like taking advantage.

Mr. Bushkirk would never stand for questions about Puffin Island, so Astrid waited until Klara left the house. She followed her along the greenway, down the airlock, and into the underground grocery. It was a large bunker, dug directly beneath the Goldsport plaza, stuffed to the brim with treats and treasures from the world before, all specially preserved. The board had done everything they could to make it look like an old grocery store. The food was arranged in neat aisles. Cardboard signs advertised special deals. There was even a checkout counter and a cash register, filled with worthless paper money.

Klara Bushkirk retrieved a shopping cart and made her way into the baking section. Astrid did a quick survey of the aisles, and as soon as she saw that they were alone, she grabbed a basket for herself and wandered casually up beside Klara.

"Oh, Mrs. Bushkirk!" she said, hiding her shame under a big fake grin. "I didn't see you come in. . . ."

"Well, good morning." Hank's stepmom turned to face Astrid. She was dressed in a nice silk blouse, with all of the buttons done up right. She had her earrings in, and her makeup was immaculate. Good signs. "How have you been, sweetheart?"

"Fine," Astrid said, trying her best to seem interested in the items on the shelves. She pulled down a vacuum-packed bag of sugar and set it lamely inside her basket. "How about you?"

"Well, you know. I could complain, if I had a mind to." Mrs. Bushkirk smiled at Astrid. "Do you know that Missy wants us all to bake three cakes apiece for commemoration this year?"

Commemoration—far and away the biggest holiday in their sanctuary. It was held every July, on the anniversary of Goldsport's founding.

"Ha ha," Astrid said. "Three cakes does seem like a lot." She paused, trying to find a smooth way to bring up the subject of the lighthouse. But before Astrid could say anything more, Klara Bushkirk beat her to it.

"From what I understand, you've been pretty busy yourself." She arched one of her perfectly plucked silver eyebrows. "Carrying on about that island. To hear people tell it, you've been making yourself into something of a pest."

"Oh . . . ," Astrid said. "I didn't mean to bother any—"

"Sweetheart," Klara cut in gently. "I'm teasing you. A little."

She continued down the aisle without another word, dropping items into her cart. Astrid followed along, shopping for things she didn't need. Flour and powdered milk. Granola and freeze-dried ice cream. There was so much of everything. Astrid hadn't done the math, but she guessed

48

that everybody in Goldsport could have eaten nothing but chocolate-vanilla-strawberry for the next five years if they wanted to.

"So you don't think . . . ? You aren't curious about the light?"

"Not in the least." Klara stopped to lift a bag up, reading ancient calorie information. "It's a lighthouse," she said. "It's got a light. It's in the name."

"But why did it turn on again?" Astrid asked.

At this Klara only blinked. It seemed, for a moment, like she might be losing the thread of their conversation. But then she recovered herself. "Honey, you really need to give this up," she said. "You're upsetting people."

"I'm sorry," Astrid said. "I don't mean to."

"I know you don't," Klara said, softening. "We all know that."

Together they were quiet for a time. The sound of their footsteps filled the empty grocery. Astrid wanted to let it go. She really did.

She couldn't.

"But if you and the other investors aren't hiding anything, then why is everybody getting upset when I ask about the lighthouse? How come no one is even willing to talk about it?"

Klara shook her head, keeping her eyes on the shelves. "You'll forgive me for saying so, sweetheart, but that's a young person's question. When you go around asking about that lighthouse, what you're doing is bringing up the past.

And that's a painful subject around here. The past is a painful subject to anybody who's got one." With this she threw Astrid a withering look. "Honestly, Ria, I'd expect you to know that already."

Astrid almost crashed into a pyramid of canned shortening. Klara Bushkirk continued walking, turning a corner into the aisle of dried fruit. "I don't know why you can't be more like that nice Amblin boy," she continued. "He's got his head screwed on right. That young man is looking forward, not back."

It was painfully clear what had just happened. Klara Bushkirk had confused Astrid for a younger version of her mother. It was an easy enough mistake to make—other than the purple eyes, they looked all but identical. Astrid suddenly realized that for this entire conversation, Klara had been in the past. She'd been talking to a girl who had long since grown up.

Astrid decided to say nothing more. She helped Mrs. Bushkirk finish her shopping and then carried her bags back home for her. At some point, the old woman seemed to shift partway into the present. She thanked Astrid by name, slipping a hundred-dollar bill into her palm as a tip.

"You just spend that on whatever you want," Klara Bushkirk said, smiling.

Thoroughly discouraged, Astrid left the greenway. She headed up the road and into the singing forest. She wanted to be alone, but when she arrived at the wall, she saw that

Hank was already there. He was buckled tight into his bee suit, slumped atop the turret of Mother, the tank. He looked just about as glum as she felt. Their eyes met, and they nodded to each other. Astrid joined him on the tank, her legs dangling on either side of the cannon. Together they gazed out into the wilderness beyond the wall. For a long time they said nothing.

"Ice cream?" Astrid finally asked. "Or granola?"

"What?" Hank cocked his head.

"You want ice cream or granola?"

"Um, is that really a question?" A faint smile cracked beneath the wire mesh of his veil.

Astrid pulled one of the freeze-dried ice cream bars from her pocket and tossed it up in the air for him to catch. The foil wrapper flashed in the sunlight, and Hank snatched it out of the air. He stared down at the gleaming little rectangle, small in his gloved hand.

"So . . . just to follow up on the whole kiss thing."

"Still not a good time," Astrid said, forcing a friendly chuckle. She was happy to laugh at that joke as many times as Hank cared to make it. It was a heck of a lot better than the alternative.

"When did you go to the grocery?" he asked.

"Today. With Klara."

"Ah."

"I was asking her about the lighthouse."

"Of course you were."

Hank carefully opened one of the snaps on his cuff and

slipped the foil packet inside. Then he pulled his arms into the center of his bee suit, leaving his sleeves hanging limp and empty at his sides. His naked fingers appeared inside his bonnet, clutching the ice cream. He fumbled over the wrapper for a moment before peeling it open and jabbing the chocolate end into his mouth. Watching him, Astrid was struck once more by her good fortune. She was so lucky to be able to sit out in the open like this, totally uncovered. The breeze on her legs, the sun on her face. Nothing between her and the world. Nothing other than this big-ass wall, at least.

"Thanks," Hank said.

"Thank the investors," Astrid said as she tore open a foil packet for herself. This was another one of their town mantras: Thank the investors! A phrase Astrid and Hank were likely to hear far too often over the next week as the annual commemoration approached.

"So," Hank asked. "You get anything out of her?"

"Not really," she said. "She didn't remember who I was."

"The problem isn't so much that she doesn't remember," Hank said, shaking his head slowly. "Actually, I think Klara remembers everything. It's just that she remembers it all at once. She only forgets the order things go in." He paused to gnaw on his ice cream. The breeze picked up, causing his empty sleeves to flap at his sides. "It's hard to put a story together when you don't know what goes where," he continued. "When you don't know what the present is, or the past."

Astrid looked at him and raised an eyebrow.

"What?" he said. "I've matured a lot since our breakup."

Just the word brought back memories of the day itself. Hank weeping in Astrid's bedroom, inconsolable. Astrid standing awkwardly in the middle of the carpet, torn between a desire to comfort her friend and the surety that it would be a big mistake. You can't exactly reach out and touch someone after saying the words "I'm not in love with you" loudly and clearly, as she had. Of course she'd said other things too. She'd told Hank how much he meant to her, told him that he might be the most important person in her life. And it was all true. But the whole "not in love with you" bit had drowned out every other sentence.

They enjoyed their ice creams in silence atop the tank. From there they could see the bog, which filled the valley beyond the wall like stew in a pot. If Astrid looked closely she could make out the swarms of breeding singers—flecks of iridescent purple dotting the tufts of scraggly grass and pitcher plants, all belting out their strange and beautiful hymns. She leaned back, her hand coming to rest on the cool metal of the gunner's hatch.

Astrid could remember the creaking sound the hatch used to make when she and Hank would pry it open. She could almost smell the tinge of rust mingled with sweat, hear the sound of their whispers reverberating in the dark. Past and present indeed. For a moment Astrid felt the way Klara might. Like all of it was happening at once. She was still in her bedroom, watching Hank sob and forcing herself not to hug him. And she was also down there in the tank with her mouth on his, fumbling and mumbling and getting things right and wrong all at once. Only recently had it dawned on Astrid how profoundly creepy it was that they'd done all of their hooking up in an old army tank named Mother.

"Why can't you just stop thinking about it?" Hank asked, a smear of rehydrated chocolate on his lips.

Astrid glanced at him.

"The lighthouse," Hank said.

"Oh," she said. "I'm not sure why. But you're right. I can't."

Hank finished his ice cream, letting the wrapper drop into the baggy tent of his bee suit. Then his arms tunneled out into his sleeves again, fingers finding their place in his gloves.

"My father mentioned it," he said at last, nodding slowly. "How you were asking around about Puffin Island." He didn't say anything more for a while. When he spoke again, his voice sounded breezy and light. Artificial. "He said you maybe shouldn't."

"Maybe shouldn't?" She snorted. "Are those the words he used?"

"Not exactly," Hank said.

"Yeah." She glanced back once more at Puffin Island. She could see a thin trace of white where the waves hit the breakers, but they were much too far away for her to hear them crash. "Did your dad happen to mention why I shouldn't?" she asked.

"He said all you're doing is stressing the old folks out."

"I see," Astrid said. "No offense, but do you think your dad actually cares if I stress the old folks out?"

"No, I don't," Hank said. "And no offense taken. Nobody knows my dad's an asshole better than I do." He allowed the words to hang between them for a long moment before changing the subject. "We should probably get back to the greenway. Otherwise everybody is going to assume we ran off together or something."

Astrid and Hank scooted to the edge of the turret, but before either of them could dismount, they caught sight of something moving on the other side of the gate. It was a rabbit, cautiously crossing the road. Astrid and Hank stayed still as the animal approached. It arrived at the gate and began nosing at the chain link.

Then there was a whooshing noise, and the rabbit jolted to one side. It went stiff and fell flat on the asphalt. A little splash of blood began to blossom around its head, no bigger than a rosebud. The rabbit twitched its hind legs for a few seconds before going completely still.

"I got you," came a voice from somewhere in the trees.

CHAPTER 6

Eliza

A STRANGE WOMAN EMERGED FROM THE WOODS—A WOMAN Astrid had never seen before. The woman noticed them immediately and stopped in her tracks on the sloping embankment. She stared first at Hank and then at Astrid.

Well. That obviously wasn't right.

"There's a lady by the road," Hank said.

Astrid didn't answer him. She didn't even move. Neither did the strange woman. She was rather old, though not as ancient as most of the adults in Goldsport. She must have been about Amblin's age. In one hand she gripped what appeared to be a slingshot, and in the other dangled a canvas sack stained about the bottom with concentric rings of red and brown.

"There's a lady by the road," Hank said again. He must have thought he was whispering. He was not whispering.

"Astrid. Astrid. Do you see her?"

Astrid could only stare. The shocks mounted. The most

obvious one was that the woman was a stranger. Astrid hadn't ever met a stranger before—every single person Astrid knew was a person she had always known. The next was that she was on the wrong side of the gate—she was outside. No one ever went outside. And the final shock, maybe the biggest of all, was that the woman wasn't wearing a bee suit. Instead she had on a mishmash of ill-fitting clothes: rubber rain boots, oversize denim pants, some kind of shimmery blouse, and what looked like a fancy men's jacket. She had nothing on her head for protection but a checkered wool cap with flaps dangling over her ears. But it didn't look like she needed protection. Singers glinted on either side of the road, but none seemed drawn to her.

"Ask her the question," Astrid whispered.

Hank did nothing. She could hear the fabric of his bee suit crumple as his body sank into the metal of the tank.

"Ask her the question," Astrid whispered again.

She was speaking to herself as much as she was speaking to Hank. They had the question memorized. They had practiced the question countless times. And now, somehow, neither Astrid nor Hank could call it forth.

"What do you . . . ?" Hank tried.

"What do you want?" Astrid said.

The woman on the other side of the gate blinked at them, but she made no answer. Like Astrid and Hank, she seemed to be taking a moment to decide whether or not they were real. So Astrid tried again, yelling the question this time.

"What do you want?"

Her voice boomed out across the hills and echoed back against the rim of the valley beyond. The strange woman seemed to jump at the sound of it. But she didn't run away. Instead, she looked Astrid right in the face and smiled.

The question. It had been drilled into Astrid and Hank since they could speak, all but tattooed onto their brains. The question was the first thing they were supposed to say on the slim chance that they should ever encounter a stranger. The only thing they were supposed to say. If their parents were to be believed, the question might as well have been a magic spell.

It sorted the wicked from the true.

A long time ago, back before the wickedness flooded the world, there were better methods. If you suspected somebody of being wicked, you could bring them to any hospital or clinic in the country and be absolutely sure. Doctors would take samples and run them through spinning machines to determine beyond a shadow of a doubt whether or not a patient had been infected. But now there was only the question. Anybody who saw a stranger was supposed to ask them what they wanted. If the stranger was true, they'd give you a normal answer. Like "a sandwich." Or "Who the hell are you? Can you put down that gun?" But if they were wicked, their answer would be straightforward, sincere, and totally terrifying. Like "I want to hold one of your eyes in each of my hands to see which one is heavier." Or "I want to smell you in the brain."

At least that was how it was supposed to go. Neither Astrid nor Hank had ever had to ask the question before.

Again Astrid hollered, "What do you want?"

"I want that rabbit," the woman said. She emerged fully from the woods and stepped up onto the crumbling road. Her movement seemed to loosen something in Hank. He suddenly scrambled, grabbing Astrid by the wrist and pulling them both down off of the tank. Together they took cover on the far side of Mother, peeking out at the woman from behind the tank's massive steel treads.

"You keep away from our gate," Hank yelled. He sounded half choked, like he was having an allergic reaction to his own fear. But Astrid was feeling something very different. They'd asked the question. The woman had answered, and answered right.

She wasn't wicked. And she wasn't wearing a bee suit.

Could this really be happening?

"Don't you try and take my rabbit," the woman said.

Hank started pawing at his bee suit, trying to open the clasp on one of his pockets. But the panic made him all thumbs, his gloved fingers useless.

"Nobody wants to take your rabbit," Astrid called from behind the tank. "And nobody is going to hurt you, either." Hank was still fidgeting beside her, so frantic that you would have thought his bee suit had filled up with singers. Astrid placed a hand on his shoulder to try to calm him down.

"Please don't run away," she called.

"I'm not going to run away," the woman answered.

Her voice was hesitant and brittle. Astrid guessed that the woman hadn't said anything aloud in a long, long time.

"That's good," Astrid said. Very slowly she let go of Hank's shoulder and took a single step out from behind Mother. "What's your name?" she asked.

"God, don't be stupid!" Hank hissed.

Just then Astrid heard the snap of a fastener opening and glanced back to see that Hank had unsealed one of the outer compartments of his bee suit. He shoved his hand inside and pulled out a small revolver. This shouldn't have been surprising—carrying a gun whenever you went beyond the greenway was in the Goldsport community handbook. Hank had been doing it, at his father's insistence, for years now. But the gun basically just lived in that pocket, like a kind of good luck charm. Astrid couldn't remember the last time she'd seen it. She wasn't even used to thinking of it as a thing you could hold like that, a thing you could aim. But that's exactly what Hank did. His greeting to the first stranger either of them had ever met was to point the revolver at her.

"Hank," Astrid said. "Stop it."

She would have snatched the revolver from his hand if she weren't so afraid that it would accidentally go off. The little pistol shook in the air.

"Put it down," she whispered.

"She could still be wicked," Hank said. Then he returned his gaze to the woman beyond the gate and asked her the question again, barking each word.

"What. Do. You. Want?"

The woman glanced at the rabbit, lying dead and bloody at the base of the gate. Then she turned to face Hank, looking right into the little mouth of his wavering pistol. She didn't seem particularly stressed by this turn of events. Maybe the woman didn't think Hank was serious. Or maybe she'd simply seen enough of the world that it took more than a teenager with a six-shooter to rile her up.

"I want something to eat," she said. "I'm very hungry."

"Are you wicked?" Astrid tried, keeping her gaze nice and steady.

The woman cocked her head. It seemed like she was giving the question serious consideration.

"I don't think I am," the woman said.

"Then why aren't you wearing a bee suit?" Hank said, the outstretched gun dipping in his grip.

"Why would I wear a bee suit?" she asked.

"To protect you from the singers," Hank said. "To keep from catching it."

"They don't bother me," the woman said. "I don't think I taste good to them."

Sure enough, the singers were still acting as though she weren't there. Some had gathered above the body of the dead rabbit, and still more had established a dizzy orbit around Hank's head. They tasted the warmth of his breath, gathering around his face expectantly. But for all the humming insects were concerned, neither Astrid nor the woman even existed.

"You see, Hank? She's got to be . . ." Astrid trailed off.

She tried to contain herself, but this was fucking huge. More than just another person in the world, this might be another person like Astrid. When she spoke again, it was directly to the strange woman.

"You're vexed, aren't you?"

"I don't know what that means," the woman said. Again her eyes drifted to the body of the dead rabbit. Suddenly she turned, striding the rest of the way across the road to the base of the gate.

"I said don't move!" Hank shrieked.

"Hank. You didn't actually say that." Astrid put her hand on his wrist and gently pressed down so that the revolver was aimed more-or-less safely at the asphalt. His attention broke, and Astrid cupped the butt end of the gun and pushed it out of his grip. "Get ahold of yourself," she said.

Meanwhile, the woman plucked the rabbit up by one of its hind legs, causing the head to dangle. It seemed stitched to the ground by a thin, unbroken thread of dribbling blood. She must have hit the rabbit square in the skull—no easy feat with a slingshot, no matter how experienced you are. She dropped the limp, puffy thing into her sack.

"I killed that rabbit," she said.

She might not have been wicked, but this woman sure was out of practice at conversation.

"Vexed means 'immune,'" Astrid went on, checking the safety on Henry's revolver before pocketing it. "I'm immune too. My name is Astrid."

"My name is Eliza," the woman said.

"I'm happy to meet you, Eliza," Astrid said. As calm as Eliza seemed to be, Astrid still spoke slowly for fear that she might say or do something to scare her off. "I'm really glad you—"

"She's too old," Hank cut her off. "How can she be vexed if she's that old?"

"Please, Hank," Astrid said. "Please shut up."

"I'm—wait." Eliza held a hand up in the air, as though to shush them both. "You think I'm old?" She sounded genuinely surprised. Astrid found this kind of touching, and sad. "My mom and dad are old," Eliza went on, her wrinkles deepening as she squinted. "But not me. I'm not old."

"Your mom and dad," Astrid said, peering over the woman's shoulder and down at the bog. She could see no trace of other people, but that didn't mean they weren't out there, hiding behind the scrim of trees. "Are they still alive?" she asked. "Are they with you?"

Eliza shook her head, causing her sack to bob up and down in her grip. Some of the rabbit's blood had begun to seep through the burlap. "I'm all alone," she said. "I don't know if my mom and dad are still alive. That's why I came back. My family lives over there." She reached a hand through the chain link and pointed down the road that led back into town.

For a long while neither Astrid nor Hank could conjure up any response to this. They looked at each other and then back at the strange woman.

"You . . . You mean your family lives in Goldsport?" Hank said.

Eliza screwed up her face, looking annoyed for the first time. "I don't know where that is," she said. "That's not what I said. My family lives out there." She pointed again, and it was clear now that her finger was aimed not at their little glass sanctuary, but over it. She was pointing out into the bay. She was pointing at the lighthouse.

"My family lives on that island," Eliza said, "on Puffin Island."

CHAPTER 7

The Question

YEARS AGO, WHEN ASTRID AND HANK WERE LITTLE KIDS, they'd tried to run away together to Puffin Island. It had started out as a game. Astrid had said that they should take one of the lobster boats out. Just, you know, to check out the island for themselves. Hank had said that he knew where his father kept the boat keys. Astrid had suggested that they pack some supplies for the trip. And then, somehow before they knew it, they were actually doing these things. The two nine-year-olds found themselves on the dock in the middle of the afternoon, hoisting a crate of Mrs. Wrigley's canned peaches into the back of one of the lobster boats. If Astrid's father hadn't caught them, they might really have gone through with it.

Amblin Gold was not pleased. Astrid remembered the sight of her father charging down the dock in his bee suit, looking short and enormous all at once. He jumped aboard the boat and threw everything they'd packed over the side and into the blue-black water. The kids scrambled out of the boat as he did this, sensing that a good bout of screaming was about to begin. But Astrid's dad remained deadly silent. He went into the covered wheelhouse, pulled a hammer out of the toolbox, and just began smashing. The boat's little windows blew out, and the instrument panel shattered to shards of rotten wood. That particular boat remained inoperable to this day. It was a side of her father Astrid had never seen before, or since.

It took a whole day for Amblin to calm down enough to try talking with her. When he finally did, he came up into Astrid's room, sat on the corner of her bed, and stared at the floor as he spoke. "I know it's difficult . . . it's actually impossible for you to understand," he said, "because you weren't there when the world fell wicked. But, Astrid, whether you believe it or not, you're probably the luckiest person on earth. You have a home and plenty to eat. You have walls, and you have medicine, and you have friends."

"One friend," Astrid said, not scared enough of her dad to keep her sass in check.

"If he's a good friend, then one is all you need. In fact, one good friend is more than I've got." Her father sighed. "But that's not the point. The point is that your grandpa founded Goldsport so that we could all have this wonderful life, free of the wickedness. He built this place just for us, so that we wouldn't have to worry about being hungry, or cold, or frightened ever again. And yes, sure, maybe it's a little boring here. And I know you wish that there were more kids your age. But, Astrid honey, you can't just take the good parts of Goldsport and leave behind the rest. Without the bad parts, there are no good parts."

With this her father placed his hands atop his knees and pushed himself up into a standing position. He made to leave.

"Dad?" Astrid asked, stopping him on the threshold.

"Yes, honey?"

"Are you . . . ? Did you get so mad because we were going to take the boat out by ourselves? Or because we were going to Puffin Island?"

"I got angry because you were leaving," her father said with a tired smile. "Puffin Island had nothing to do with it."

Even at nine Astrid could tell that this was bullshit. Though, at the time, she'd probably used a different word for it in her head.

"Your family lives on Puffin Island?" Hank asked now. He seemed, at least for the moment, to have forgotten how afraid he was.

"I left a long time ago," Eliza said. This didn't really qualify as an answer, but the strange woman seemed to consider it sufficient. "I hope they're still there," she added, seeming to speak as much to herself as to either of them. "I'd like to see my family again. I really miss my family."

"Do you mean . . . ?" Astrid trailed off. After years of questions, she finally had someone to ask them of. But where to start? "Do you know whether or not they're still on Puffin Island?"

"I don't," Eliza said. "But I saw the lighthouse turn on a few days ago, and I thought that I should check. I remembered that there are boats in Port Emory. I thought I would take one of those boats and use it to go to the island."

At this Hank gave Astrid a look.

"Port Emory?" Astrid asked. "Where's that?"

Eliza gave no answer—she seemed not even to have heard the question. Instead, her eyes wandered. She examined the walls, the watchtower, and the tank. Finally, her gaze settled on Astrid's bulging pocket.

"I saw you put the gun in there," Eliza said. "I saw you."

Almost reflexively, Astrid put her free hand over the pocket. "My friend only aimed it at you because he thought you might be wicked," she said. "He didn't want to hurt you."

"He didn't want to hurt me," Eliza repeated, as though to reassure herself. Her attention lingered on the pocket for a moment before snapping over to Astrid's other hand. "Tell me what that is."

"Oh . . ." She'd almost forgotten. Somehow through all the panic and confusion, Astrid was still gripping the foil-wrapped treat in her left hand. She'd hardly eaten any of it. "It's ice cream," Astrid said.

With these words Eliza's hazy, spacey expression seemed to sharpen. Her eyes brightened, and she grinned, exposing an incomplete set of weathered teeth. "I remember ice cream," she said. "Can we make it so that it's mine?"

"Oh—um . . ." Astrid knew neither what to make of this

request, nor the strange way in which it was asked. There was something about the woman's diction that she found unsettling. But then again, Eliza did live alone, out beyond the walls. Her oddness was perfectly understandable.

"Yeah. I guess . . . Of course you can." She stepped up to the gate and pressed the packet through the chain link.

"Careful!" Hank said, but before he could do anything, Eliza dropped her slingshot and canvas sack and snatched the ice cream through the gate. Peeling the wrapper back, she shoved the entire remaining bar into her mouth, chewing with an expression that turned very quickly from delight to confusion. Meanwhile, the sack splayed open at her feet, revealing not just the rabbit but also a string of red squirrels and a raven. The kills were fresh—they looked alive and floppy as dolls. The rabbit was still bleeding.

"I don't think this is ice cream," Eliza announced, her mouth full and chalky.

"It's freeze-dried," Hank said.

Eliza spat out a jagged glob of rapidly moistening strawberry and rubbed the remainder off her lips. "I've had ice cream," she said. "I've had mint-chocolate-chip, and I've had chocolate-fudge-brownie. I think you must be confused about what ice cream is."

"Sorry," Astrid said.

"It keeps forever," Hank said a little defensively.

"I've never heard of anything that keeps forever," Eliza said. Then she picked up her slingshot and her sack of game. "I'd like to come inside now," she said.

"Oh." Astrid paused. Ever since Eliza had mentioned Puffin Island, Astrid had felt two or three steps behind in the conversation. But this seemed to be a natural next step, didn't it? Now that they knew Eliza wasn't wicked, the next thing to do was to tell somebody who could let her inside. Still, Astrid was hesitating.

Why was she hesitating?

"I mean—yeah," she said. "You should probably come inside."

"We don't have the key," Hank said.

"My father keeps it," Astrid said. "He's the chairman of the board."

"I don't know what chairman of the board means," Eliza said.

"It means he's in charge," Hank said. "He's like the mayor of Goldsport."

"I told you," Eliza said, shaking her head, "I don't know what a Goldsport is."

Again Astrid and Hank glanced at each other. Meanwhile, Eliza simply stood there and waited, patiently, to be let inside.

"Why don't you . . . ? Why don't you go and get my dad?" Astrid said to Hank. "I can stay with her."

She could tell that Hank didn't like this idea. If Astrid was being honest, she had some reservations too. There was something troubling about Eliza. But they'd asked her the question, hadn't they? And she'd passed with flying colors.

"You keep clear of the gate until I get back," Hank said.

"I will." Astrid nodded as he left. "But she's not going to hurt me."

"I'm not," Eliza said.

Astrid couldn't be sure, but for a moment it almost sounded like a question.

As soon as Hank headed down the hill, Eliza's awkwardness began to melt away. Astrid tried asking her once more about living on Puffin Island, and this time her question opened the floodgates. Eliza spoke about her parents and her sister and her sister's husband. She spoke about the lighthouse tower, which was much bigger than Astrid had imagined— it had an engine room and an observation deck, yard-thick storm walls and bathtub-size lenses. Eliza spoke about the great flocks of puffins that nested on the western shore and the pods of whales that passed by every summer on their way into the bay. In fact, once Eliza really got to talking about herself, she seemed unwilling—almost unable—to stop. Her life story tumbled out in a frantic stream, the words "I" or "me" anchoring every single sentence. "I left." "I wandered." "I hunted." Astrid imagined Eliza, alone for all those years. Outside of the walls and away from her island, she had existed to no one but herself. And now that she'd been found, she was suddenly real again.

Eliza had just begun to tell the story of her return to the coast when they were interrupted by a sound on the road below. Astrid turned to see three shapes in identical bee suits running up toward her, each trailed by their own personal swarm of singers. The shortest of them was her father. The much larger, pear-shaped figure beside him could only be Henry Bushkirk, which meant that the person trailing a few paces behind must have been Hank. Mr. Bushkirk had a rifle slung over his shoulder, and even at a distance Astrid could discern the rough outlines of a scowl through the cross-hatched shadows of his mesh veil.

"Jesus," she could hear Mr. Bushkirk exclaim, "she's naked." He meant Eliza—that she was out in the open without a bee suit.

"Get away from the gate, Astrid!" her father shouted.

"You don't have to worry." Astrid tried to calm them, but her words had no effect—they'd begun sprinting. Henry Bushkirk fumbled with his rifle. "She isn't infected!" Astrid hollered, desperate now to stop them. "Dad! Listen to me!"

"I said away from the gate!" Her father reached the crest of the hill first, and he very nearly tackled Astrid. He wrapped his arms around her and pivoted, spinning her away from the shuttered gate and putting his body between her and Eliza. It knocked the wind out of Astrid.

"We asked her the question," Astrid gasped, furious. The first vexed person she'd ever met, and now they were going to scare her away—or worse! Astrid tried to buck out of her dad's grip, but couldn't. She had no idea that he was still that strong.

"Hank," she called out over Amblin's shoulder, "didn't you tell them?"

"I did!" Hank cried out.

Henry Bushkirk snorted. "What the hell do you kids know about the question?" He aimed his rifle at Eliza through the chain link. And just as before, Eliza didn't flinch, or even seem to notice. She had her eyes on Amblin Gold.

"Dad..." Astrid was in a full-on panic, struggling against his grip. "She isn't wicked," she said. "She's vexed, like me!"

"Easy," her dad said. "Henry won't do anything until he knows for sure." As he spoke, Eliza's interest in him seemed to grow. Her eyes widened, and her breath caught.

"Oh, I already know," Mr. Bushkirk said. "I'm only double-checking for your benefit." He stuck his hand up and wriggled his gloved fingers in the air to get Eliza's attention. "Lady," he said. "What do you want?"

Slowly the woman's gaze turned from Astrid's father to Hank's. "I heard him call you Henry," she said. "I used to know a man named Henry."

"It's a common name," Mr. Bushkirk said. "But mine's Dutch. Little different. Hey, speaking of that, what do you want?"

"I didn't like that man," Eliza said. "He came to town when I was a kid, and I didn't like him one bit. His name was Henry and he was rude to my parents."

"Sounds like a jerk," Henry said. "Bet he's dead now. What do you want?"

Eliza blinked for a moment at the dark mouth of his rifle. She seemed not to realize it was a device that with great ease could do her tremendous harm. Then her eyes returned to

Astrid's father. "I want you to say something," she said. "I want to hear your voice again."

"Not how it works," Henry said. "What do you want?"

"I want him to speak to me," Eliza said.

"Tell us what you want," Amblin said.

"What's wrong with you two?" Astrid tried again to escape her father's grip, but there was nothing doing. She'd have to break one of his arms—or one of hers—to get out. "She answered the question!"

"Not yet she didn't," Henry said.

"Tell us what you want," Amblin said again.

At that Eliza tipped her head into the wind and closed her eyes. She looked for a moment like someone trying to recall a piece of music. Then her eyes popped open again, and she grinned. There was still ice cream on her teeth—pink and white and brown.

"I knew it," she said. "I knew it was you. Do you remember me? I'm Eliza."

Astrid felt a jolt run through her father's body.

"That's outstanding," Henry said. "Tell us, Eliza, what do you want?"

"I want something to eat," she said, not missing a beat. "And I want to come inside the wall with you."

"What do you want?"

"I want to talk to my mom," Eliza said. "I want my sister."

"What do you want?"

"I want everything to go back to how it was before,"

74

Eliza said. "I want things to get better. I want real ice cream, and I want to watch TV all day."

God, it was like torture.

"What do you want?" Henry asked again, bored and sadistic all at once.

Now Eliza paused. And she seemed, for the first time, to really think the question over. When the answer finally came to her, she smiled with undisguised relief. "I want you," Eliza said, relishing the word. "I want all your bones. I want to open up your ribs and look at your heart. I want to feel what it's like when you're not alive anymore. I want to fill your skin with sand, and to stitch you closed, and to carry you into—"

She probably would have kept going. But then, Henry Bushkirk shot her.

PART II

PUFFIN ISLAND

CHAPTER 8

The Man in the Tower

THE TIDE WAS GOING OUT ON PUFFIN ISLAND, AND IT WAS getting to be time for Natalie to go and check the traps. Her mom knew it as well as she did, but neither of them spoke about it. Not during dinner. Not as they washed up. Not as Natalie gathered her gaff and nets or as her mother climbed the loft stairs and rolled into bed.

What was there to say?

Four whole days had passed since they'd caught so much as a crab. Two weeks since their last lobster. At this point Natalie was afraid that even thinking about those traps would be enough to jinx her. Her little family couldn't handle any more bad luck than it already had.

She left shortly before dusk, hauling her gear out of the bunkhouse and down the gravel path that led to the western shore. It was a fine evening, and the sea was so flat that the bells affixed to the offshore buoys had fallen silent. A good sign, Natalie hoped. But there she was again, hoping. It was a nasty habit.

Natalie could hear the puffins up ahead, grumbling as they settled in for the night. Their bright orange beaks flickered in the shadows between the rocks. Natalie's path took her right through their nesting grounds, but the birds paid her no mind. They'd grown used to her over the years. It probably helped that her family didn't eat puffin.

At least not yet they didn't.

"Wish me luck," Natalie whispered to the birds as she picked her way between their nests.

Good luck! came their reply. *Bring us back some dinner!*

"Catch your own damn fish," Natalie said.

One of the puffins crawled out of the rocks and shook itself all over. *Rude!* the bird declared.

Of course, the puffins weren't really talking to her. But when you live on an island with basically zero people on it, imaginary conversations are often all you've got. In Natalie's head, the puffins sounded high-pitched and manic. At once sincere and unhinged. Exactly as crazy as Natalie sometimes felt.

The shore lay beyond the nesting grounds, where the outgoing tide had exposed a slick garden of kelp, gasping in the evening air. Natalie edged out across the slippery mess, using her fishing gaff as a walking stick. The kelp popped and hissed under her boots. Then, arriving at the water's edge, she got down on her belly and shimmied out as far as she could. The sea rippled beneath her face. In it Natalie could see her own reflection—her wiry hair and purple eyes. They glowed back up at her from the surface of the water. The eyes of a vexed girl.

From here the lobster traps were just within reach. Natalie hooked one of the marker buoys with her gaff and pulled it in. Then she hauled up the rope, which got darker and more bearded with algae and barnacles as she went. Finally the trap broke the surface, and what did she find but a pair of decent lobsters! Their shells shined in the evening sunlight, and their antennae twirled through the air with buggish confusion. Natalie hooted. She moved the lobsters to her net and hooked another buoy with her gaff. A little more than ten minutes later, her net was brimming. Seven lobsters—the best haul they'd had in months. Good news for Natalie and her family.

Good news for the puffins, too.

Natalie rebaited the traps and then carried her catch back across the kelp and through the rocky nesting grounds. The sun was sinking fast toward the mainland, shining its last rays across Natalie's home. She could see the entire island from here—not that there was all that much to see. It was basically a big pile of rocks, without so much as a single tree to liven up the view. That there weren't any singers out here—the sea winds kept them away—and that it was remote were the only things to recommend Puffin Island as a home. Still, in the early-evening light it was beautiful. The lighthouse glowed orange, looking as though it had just been pulled from a furnace. Natalie ran her eyes up the tower, and when she reached the top she caught a dark twist of movement in the lamp room. She could make out a stooped human shape up there.

It was Natalie's grandfather. He lived in the lighthouse.

Or, to be more exact: It was Natalie's wicked grandfather. They kept him locked up in the lighthouse. For his own good, and for everybody else's.

Natalie froze. She heard her grandpa's voice every day, but it was rare to actually catch a glimpse of him. The old man seemed to be wrestling with the massive ornate lens in the center of the lamp room. He must have been up to his old tricks again—trying to get the lighthouse turned back on. He'd set himself to this task every so often, becoming suddenly obsessed with the ancient lenses and wiring. He hadn't managed to get it working in a long time. A good thing, too. That lighthouse might as well be a dinner bell for the whole wide wicked world.

Here we are! it would shout for all to hear. *Come and get us!*

Natalie approached the lighthouse, craning her neck to get a better view. Her grandpa disappeared from the lamp room and stepped out a moment later onto the gallery—a circular metal walkway fastened about the neck of the tower like a dog's collar. He stood out there for a moment, basking deeply in the day's final light, breathing the fresh air with a look of contentment. For a wicked man, Natalie's grandpa looked pretty good. His skin was pale from all the hours spent locked up indoors, and he was thinner than Natalie liked, but his eyes were clear and his back was as straight as the lighthouse itself. He held a wrench in one hand and went to work on a set of solar panels that were fastened to the railing.

Natalie got closer. She did this without any fear—the gallery was high enough that her grandfather couldn't jump down. And the reinforced iron door at the base of the tower was locked securely from the outside. Up on the gallery her grandpa was busy removing the old solar panels, caked in a film of bird crap. He'd installed those panels to the railing himself some months ago, during a previous attempt to get the lighthouse working again. Now he hauled them back into the lamp room one by one. When he finally noticed Natalie down on the rocks below, he stopped what he was doing, grinned wide, and waved at her.

Despite his illness—or perhaps because of it?—Natalie's wicked grandfather was always cheerful like that.

"Hi, Grandpa!" Natalie called up to him.

"I didn't see you down there!" he called back. He ran the back of his hand across his forehead, blotting sweat.

"Well . . . here I am," Natalie said. She lifted her net of squirming lobsters, still dripping with seawater, so that the old man could get a better look. "What do you think?"

"Lobsters—I love lobsters," her grandfather said with a little laugh. He shifted his weight from foot to foot, like an excited little kid. "I wish you'd give me some. I wish you'd feed me." He paused for a minute, as though thinking this over. "You never feed me anything, do you?"

"That's not true," Natalie said patiently. "I came by at dinnertime, remember? The egg and stuff?" Natalie meant the meal that she'd left on her grandpa's windowsill a few hours ago. All of the lower windows were completely bricked up, save one on the ground floor, in which a sliver of space remained. It was through this gap that Natalie and her mother delivered food and water to the wicked man. It was also how they gave him everything from winter coats to the old magazines and coloring books that they sometimes salvaged on rare trips to the mainland. Dinner that evening had been particularly meager—a third of a hard-boiled egg, a mealy tomato from the greenhouse, and a scoop of coppery crabmeat that they'd tinned the previous winter. But it was no worse than what Natalie or her mother had eaten.

"I suppose?" he said. "I guess it could have been you. Honestly, I don't find you all that memorable." He paused briefly. "Maybe I should break your skull open. Then I would remember you probably." Her grandfather's smile and his open, airy demeanor didn't change a bit as he said these words. To him, promises of violence came as naturally, as irresistibly as his own heartbeat.

Natalie was unfazed. Her grandpa had been like this since before she was born, and she'd long ago accepted that he couldn't help himself. It was the wickedness. The disease claimed you, and it changed you. Natalie could hardly hold that against her grandfather. Though she did keenly regret that she never got to meet the person he used to be.

"I'm out of salt," her grandpa said, as though this thought

were a natural extension of the horrible ones that preceded it.

"I can bring you some with your breakfast tomorrow morning," Natalie said. She tipped her head down for a moment to stretch her neck, which was getting sore. When she looked back up at the gallery, the wicked man had returned to work.

"So. Giving up on the solar panels?" Natalie asked.

"I'm taking them away!" her grandpa called down, sounding less than happy for the first time. He had both hands on the wrench handle. The bolt must have rusted.

"Why?" Natalie asked.

"I don't like them anymore," he said. "They're not doing what I want them to do, and so I don't like them."

"You trying to power up the lamp?" There was nothing sneaky about this question. Natalie knew that she only had to ask and her grandfather would tell her. That was just how the wicked were.

"Of course I am," he said, his body twisting this way and that as he struggled with the bolt. "I hate it," he said. "I hate it when stuff doesn't listen."

With that he suddenly paused, his eyes locked on the wrench. Even from so far below, in the gathering dark, Natalie could see a childlike look of discovery suddenly overtake her grandpa's face. He always looked like that when he was getting an idea—sort of open and surprised and delighted. Like the idea came from elsewhere, an unexpected gift given by a kindly stranger.

Slowly Natalie's grandpa removed the wrench from the

rusted bolt and stood. Natalie had just enough time to realize that she should probably get away from the tower when he chucked the heavy metal thing down at her head. It came close—a rush of air blew across her ear as the tool whipped by. It smashed into the ground, cracking off a dusty handful of granite chunks before spinning away across the craggy surface of the island. Over on the western shore the puffins heard the clang and called out in alarm.

Natalie was so embarrassed by her own foolishness that she nearly dropped her lobsters. If her mother had been awake to see that, she'd have had a fit. Without saying another word, Natalie turned and began walking away from the lighthouse, her cheeks and forehead burning.

"Oh dear, I suppose I didn't think that one through," her grandfather called after her. He sounded embarrassed, too. "I actually still need that wrench. I need it to get these panels off."

Natalie kept walking.

"I—hey!" the wicked man called. He seemed genuinely surprised that Natalie wasn't turning around to help him. It was just a wrench, after all. Such a small request. "Could you bring it back to me, please? Could you just slide it through my window? I still need it is the thing."

Natalie didn't turn around.

"Give me a hand, will you?" He was beginning to get desperate. "I need the wrench to fix the light. I need to fix the light so that people in Goldsport will see us. I need the people in Goldsport to see us so that they can come to the island. So that they can let me out of this lighthouse. So that I can set you and your mother on fire."

The poor old nut had no clue whatsoever that this wasn't a persuasive argument. It was one of the many perplexing symptoms of the wickedness—an inability to imagine, even at the most basic level, what another person might be thinking or feeling. A total collapse of empathy—which is itself an act of imagination. Her grandfather kept talking, explaining just how important it was that he be allowed to do these horrible things. But Natalie simply closed her ears to it. She returned to the bunkhouse, deposited her lobsters into a big tub filled with seawater, climbed the loft stairs to her bedroom, and put her head under a pillow. She tried to sleep.

For a long time, she couldn't.

CHAPTER 9

Lights in the Dark

SOMETIMES NATALIE THOUGHT THAT KEEPING HER GRANDfather locked up inside of the lighthouse was the cruelest thing they could have done to him.

The tower wasn't a horrible place to live. In fact, as prisons go, Natalie guessed that it was a pretty good one. The rooms inside were furnished, and they were warm. The thick walls offered protection from the harsh climate of Puffin Island. On clear days her grandpa could even go out onto the gallery and take in the fresh air. But still, there was something about it that always seemed wrong to her. She felt as though they'd done more than simply lock her grandfather up inside the lighthouse. They'd also imprisoned him within his own disease—locked him tight inside the wicked person he'd become.

Natalie knew that this was an ugly thought, but it still occurred to her from time to time. It wasn't as though they had any real alternatives. If they let the old man live with them in the bunkhouse, they might as well just count the hours until someone got stabbed. If they dragged him off to the mainland, he probably wouldn't make it six months before starving or freezing to death. Even if her grandpa did survive, with time he might find his way to Goldsport. That was the town he'd been raving about—an old fishing village that sat just opposite them on the mainland. According to Natalie's mother, none but the wicked lived there.

They didn't know how many there were, but it had to be at least fifty. Possibly much more than that. At dusk they could often see lights twinkling. If they paddled close, they could just make out human figures wandering this way and that through the strange glass tunnels. Even from a distance, it was obvious that the wicked men and women of Goldsport were living together in complete harmony.

This was the cruel irony of the disease. The wicked would attack literally anyone—from a sleeping baby, to an armed soldier, to even a mildly convincing scarecrow— except for another wicked person. It had something to do with the virus in their brains, some mechanism that kept it from feeding upon itself. Natalie had even read some old reports about people voluntarily exposing themselves as a way to stay safe. This was in the early days before the vex, back when the epidemic looked more like a war. Back then whole families were known to walk out into the woods together and let the singers infect them. At least that way, the thinking was, they'd still be together. Wicked husbands and wives. Wicked mothers and daughters. Arm in arm, laughing together, forever safe from fear and from one another. Just like the people in that odd glass village.

That was why they could never allow Natalie's grandfather to go to Goldsport. If he ever made it there, it would be only a matter of time before he led a smiling mob right back to Puffin Island.

And what about the other option—the unspoken one?

What about simply putting the old man out of his misery?

Natalie wasn't proud that this thought had occurred to her, but it had. Obviously it was out of the question. Besides, it didn't even seem like her grandfather was miserable. Actually, he enjoyed almost everything about his life.

At least that made one of them.

These familiar thoughts kept Natalie up for hours. Then, just as she'd finally begun to drift into sleep, a blinding flash of light filled up the bunkhouse, followed by a long howl of delight.

Somehow, her grandfather had turned the lighthouse on.

"Here I am!" he called into the night. "It's me!"

Natalie stayed in bed for a minute, hoping that the lamp would sputter out by itself. Light flooded and drained.

"I'm so happy," her grandfather screamed. "Oh my gosh, I'm so happy!"

Natalie forced herself out of bed and down the loft steps. Her mother was already awake, standing before the big window that overlooked the bay. She was bracing her weight on the broad stone sill, one hand placed under her bulging stomach. It seemed like every time Natalie looked at her mom these days, she was more pregnant than she'd been a minute before. Another pulse of light outlined her brilliantly.

"Any activity in town?" Natalie asked.

"A few lights." Her mother sighed, repositioning her weight. "No movement in the harbor, though."

She turned from the window, and in the darkness of the bunkhouse Natalie could see her own purple eyes reflected back at her. Natalie's mother had the vex, too. She might have been the oldest vexed person in the whole wide world. But then again, Natalie knew of only the two of them, so that wasn't necessarily saying much.

"Have a look," she said, holding out the binoculars.

Natalie took them and focused on the distant village. Goldsport looked like a heap of enormous glass bottles littered across the shore. Natalie could detect a few points of light—windows, probably. Though at this distance, there was no telling if anyone was looking out of them.

"I'll go outside and check for boats," Natalie said, stepping into her unlaced boots, which stood beside the front door. This was a part of their routine. Whenever there was a disturbance, they had to check to see if anybody had noticed, both in town and in the wide ocean beyond.

"Take a jacket," her mother said.

Still bleary, Natalie grabbed a coat off the peg and stepped out into the black morning. It was only after the wet, salted wind hit her in the face that she realized she'd mistakenly taken her father's coat. He'd forgotten it here when he'd up and left some two months ago. It still smelled like his sweat. Natalie had to fight the urge to take the thing off and fling it down upon the rocks.

"I know you're down there!" her grandfather called from his tower. "I know exactly where you are, sweetheart!"

Natalie trudged around to the far end of the bunkhouse. The bay yawned to her left, digging darkly into old Canada. To her right the black water opened out into the Gulf of Maine, and beyond that the Atlantic Ocean. Natalie brought the binoculars back up to her face and scanned the horizon.

No lights. No boats.

She went back inside and saw that her mother had slipped some driftwood into the stove and put the kettle on. Her mom was usually strict about supplies, but she'd been relaxing her grip a little in recent weeks. Natalie had no problem with this—her mother deserved a hot drink whenever the damn hell she wanted one. Natalie watched her lower herself onto one of the solid wooden chairs at the dining table. It seemed a delicate operation, as though her mother's body were a great ship and she, the pilot.

Natalie took over the job of making tea. "Nothing in the bay," she said.

"Good," her mother said. She began working her knuckles into the small of her back, her expression at once pained and satisfied. "So," she said, "I see that you had some good luck last night."

"What?" Natalie glanced back at her.

"With the traps." Her mom nodded at the tub, where the lobsters were trying in vain to climb up the slick porcelain rims. The tiny commotion produced a faint, unsettling clicking. "That's awe-some," Natalie's mom said, actually singsonging the word. God—only her mother would be able to focus on those lobsters at a time like this. The lighthouse was blazing, her husband had run off, her own father wanted them all dead, and in another week or so she'd be having a baby on a barren rock in the ocean. And somehow, despite all this, she could still see the glass as half full. Who was Natalie kidding? It was, like, 5 or 10 percent full, at the most.

Natalie busied herself with the tea, steeping some loose peppermint leaves in the still-bubbling water. Outside, they could hear her grandfather coughing. Or maybe laughing? It was hard to tell.

"Thanks," her mother said, accepting the offered mug of steaming tea. Natalie sat across from her. In the darkness, the purple light from their two pairs of eyes was almost enough to illuminate the table.

"Oh, it's good!" her mother said, sipping from the mug.

Natalie shrugged. "It's totally normal tea."

"Well . . ." Her mother closed her eyes, savoring. "Normal tea is good."

The conversation that they weren't having loomed over them like smoke in the rafters. How were they going to get the light turned off? Natalie's grandfather had pulled this stunt a few times before, and over the years her parents had developed a pretty solid routine to deal with it. The problem was that the routine had two parts, and her father's was central. Now he was gone.

"Can't we just shoot the lens out?" Natalie asked.

"The windows up top are reinforced," her mother said. "We'd only waste bullets."

"Then maybe . . ." Natalie paused, trying to gauge her approach. "Maybe I should be the one to lead Grandpa outside?"

"Honey," her mother said, glancing at her through the steam rising off her tea. "That is a terrible idea."

"Okay." Natalie looked at her for a moment. "Do we have any better ones?"

Her mother made no answer to this.

"Could we just . . . ?" Natalie paused. "I mean, what if we just left it on? The wicked people in Goldsport might ignore it. They've never bothered us before."

At the mention of the word—Goldsport—Natalie's mother shuddered.

"You mean they've never bothered *you* before," she said. "No. One way or another, that light has to go off."

CHAPTER 10

The Iron Door

NATALIE WAS PRETTY SURE THAT SHE COULD PINPOINT THE exact moment her father had decided to abandon them. It had happened six months ago, right at the crest of winter. The family was gathered in the common room of the bunkhouse, listening to an old episode of *The First Voice* on their shortwave receiver. It was one of the last in the series, featuring a dramatic reading from *The Tempest*, an incomprehensible debate about the best actor to ever play Batman, and a rapid-fire series of obsolete news bulletins. The voices on the radio talked about how the singers had been pushed back to the far rim of the Rocky Mountains. They gave an update on efforts to reestablish contact with Beijing and Paris and spoke about promising early test results for the vex. The lady announcer was simply overjoyed as she shared the news. It had come to nothing, of course. The woman had no doubt died before Natalie was even born. But there was her voice, crackling out of the radio, her hope preserved like an extinct bug in amber.

As the show ended, Natalie had gotten up to deliver breakfast to her grandpa—dried mackerel and some of the peas they'd canned the previous autumn. He had snatched the meal off of his windowsill, talking while he ate.

"Sometimes I like to pretend that I have bread," her grandfather said, sounding wistful.

"I hear you," Natalie said. She'd had bread before—bread was a hell of a thing.

"I bet we could make some," her grandpa said, his mouth full of mackerel, words jellied by the fatty skin and softened bones. "I remember that they have flour in Goldsport. I remember that they have it treated and packed in special vacuumed bags and stacked in stacks in an underground room. They have enough to feed me, and you, and everybody we know, for as long as we know them. I think we should go there and take the flour and make bread. I think we should make waffles, and French toast, and beer batter, and blintzes."

The old man had gotten well into the realm of things that Natalie had never heard of. What on earth were blintzes? But whatever—if they were made of flour, then they were probably delicious.

"And if anybody over there tries to stop me," her grandfather continued, "I will strangle them and I will roast them, and I will eat them on the bread."

"That sounds great, Grandpa," Natalie said, ignoring the business about the strangling. "But you know we can't go to Goldsport."

"I can go to Goldsport!" he snarled, his teeth threaded with silvery strips of mackerel. "I can go wherever I want, whenever I want!" This was demonstrably false, but saying the words at least seemed to calm him down. He fell back to chewing, once again happy as a clam, his sudden craving for bread forgotten. "I love breakfast," he said. "I love eating in the morning. I could eat breakfast every morning."

"You do eat breakfast every morning," Natalie said, smiling slightly.

At this her grandfather stopped chewing. "Lucky me," he said. He sounded really, just profoundly delighted by this.

Not at all a bad interaction with the old man, as far as those went. Natalie had returned to the bunkhouse feeling cheerful. But the moment she stepped into the common room she realized that in the few short minutes she'd been gone something had transpired between her parents. *The First Voice* was over, but neither of her parents had switched the shortwave off. It sat between them on the broad dining table, crackling with empty static. Natalie's father's eyes were closed. His arms were at his sides and his hands gripped the wooden bench so hard that they looked drained of blood to the wrists. Natalie's mother held her husband in her gaze, scrutinizing him in that way that Natalie knew he hated.

"It never works," Natalie's father said, pitching the words down at the tabletop. For a moment Natalie thought he could be talking about the shortwave—but no, that wasn't right.

"It has worked," her mother said. "At least twice. You've got two examples standing right in front of you."

"Okay." Her father's eyes were still closed. Natalie could tell that he was trying, very hard, not to have a tantrum. Her father's screaming fits did not occur frequently, but when they did, they were embarrassing for everybody. He took a breath, swallowing it down like a gulp of water. "Yes. The vex has worked. Shall we count the times when it didn't? Do you even remember their names?"

"I know you're angry, but that's beneath you," Natalie's mother said. "Of course I remember. But it worked with Natalie. And it'll work with the next one." Then she glanced at her daughter, frozen in the frame of the bunkhouse door. "You can come in, honey," she said. "We aren't keeping any secrets."

Natalie stayed where she was. It wasn't unusual to find her parents arguing about the vex—it was the oldest, most ragged wound between them. There were no singers on the island, and so a few days after Natalie was born her mother had stolen her away in the middle of the night, sailing them to the mainland. There she'd sat with Natalie in the woods and waited until the singers descended, perching one by one atop her bare skin and drinking their fill. Natalie's dad had been dead set against this, and he'd never forgiven her for doing it in secret. He wasn't interested in the fact that the vex had worked—that it had made Natalie immune, just like her mom. He stayed fixated on what could have happened. What should have happened, given the odds.

But why were they talking about it now? And what the hell did her mother mean when she said the next one?

On some level Natalie knew before she knew.

"How can you possibly think this is a good idea?" Tears began to collect in her father's pinched eyes. Whether they were tears of rage, sadness, or self-pity, Natalie couldn't tell. "I don't know how you could have let this happen."

"As I recall, you had something to do with it," her mother said.

"That's not what I meant," her father said.

"Isn't it?"

"You're pregnant," Natalie said. She immediately regretted how horrified she'd looked when the words came out of her mouth. Her father seized on it like a fish on a lure.

"You see?" he snapped, jabbing a finger in the direction of his daughter. He gave a barking, jagged, desperate laugh. "Even the kid knows it's a shitty idea."

"Well," her mother said with a sigh. "It's a lot more than an idea right now."

There could be no doubt that was the reason. That was what caused her father to disappear. By the end of the spring thaw, he was gone.

It wasn't the first time he'd departed Puffin Island in a huff, after some blowout fight with Natalie's mom. But the longest he'd ever stayed away before that was a full night. It had been two months now, and he hadn't come back. Honestly, Natalie was still working out how she felt about it. Often it seemed as though she was able to put her dad's disappearance out of mind entirely. Whatever feelings she had about it were still there, she guessed. They were probably just working themselves out under the surface without her being completely conscious of it. Like a pot left to simmer out of watch. Or maybe more accurately like a stick of dynamite—who could say how long the fuse was? Once or twice, when Natalie was alone in the loft, she'd uttered the words "I fucking hate you" aloud. They escaped her unbidden, like a hiccup. And then, just as quickly, even as she was feeling embarrassed about talking to herself, she would mutter, "I'm sorry."

So, yes, it was fair to say that Natalie was not dealing super well. But at least this business with the lighthouse had given her something tangible to feel. It allowed Natalie to miss her dad for really solid, practical reasons. It allowed her to wish that her dad were still on Puffin Island to help them turn the lighthouse off. It would have been so much easier with him there.

"You need to remember that your grandpa is faster than he looks," Natalie's mother said as they gazed out the bunkhouse window, waiting for the morning fog to burn away. "And he's stronger, too. I want you to keep your distance. You should be just close enough that he follows you, and no closer."

"Okay." Natalie nodded.

"It's important to keep him talking," her mother went

on. "Remember that your grandpa doesn't want to hurt anybody. At least not until the idea strikes him. So it's important to change the subject as often as you can. If he gets it into his mind to pick up a stone, you should pick one up too. Make a bet about who can throw it farther. Make it a game. He loves games."

"Got it." Natalie fidgeted, glancing from the shoreline up to the spinning lamp atop the lighthouse tower. She was eager to have this over and done with.

"Try to stick to the paths wherever you can," her mother said. "And definitely stay away from any kelp or seaweed."

"I'm not going to fall, Mom," Natalie said. Her hands were clammy, and her feet felt hot in her boots.

"I know you're not, honey," her mother said, squeezing the nape of her neck. "It's for your grandpa. Please don't forget that he's very, very old. If he slips and falls, he could really hurt himself. I want everyone to be safe. Even him."

"Everyone will be," Natalie said, willing the words to be true.

"That's my girl," her mother said, giving her neck one last squeeze.

A short time later they decided that the fog had cleared enough for them to begin. Natalie headed for the lighthouse tower. She unlocked the dead bolt on the big iron door, swung it wide, and immediately backed off. Some minutes passed, and then her grandfather appeared in the arched stone doorframe, blinking in the morning sunshine.

He seemed happy, but not surprised, to find himself outside again for the first time in ages.

"I think this is outstanding," he said. He sucked in a long breath and then let it out with a full-body shiver of satisfaction. He stretched, elbows and knees popping. "I mean, for my money, this is a whole lot better than being cooped up inside."

"Totally," Natalie said, taking a cautious step back and then another. "I can see how that'd be true."

Then, rather slowly, her grandfather began to approach. "Can I eat breakfast outside today?" he asked.

"Don't see why not," Natalie said, still backing away. She took a long breath, hoping to steady herself. "How about we go down by the western shore?" Natalie asked. "That way we can watch the puffins."

"I think that sounds great," her grandpa said, still grinning with contentment. Natalie continued to walk backward, keeping her distance as she led him away from the shining lighthouse. She stuck to the main path, giving herself room to run in case things went bad. Though it appeared that they wouldn't—if this was a chase, it was the slowest chase in history. Her grandpa ambled with his hands on his hips, gazing out across the landscape of boulders and stones. There was a small cemetery near the southern shore, and when he caught sight of it, he stopped walking.

"That's were my wife is," he said.

"Yes, it is," Natalie said, stopping as well. Her grandma

had died shortly after the family relocated to the island, and Natalie had never had the chance to meet her.

"I'd like to go visit my wife," her grandpa said. Then, lest this sweet sentiment be allowed to stand on its own, he added: "So that I can dig her up."

"Maybe in a bit?" Natalie said. She caught sight of her mother in the distance, slipping out of the bunkhouse and making for the open tower. Her mom was carrying the big fireman's ax that they kept in the common room. Natalie forced herself to look away. Everything was riding on her ability to keep her grandfather's attention. Everything depended upon her. Natalie had thought she was ready for this.

She didn't feel ready.

"How about we . . . ? Let's go and . . ." Her voice fell to pieces before she could finish the sentence. Again Natalie forced down a long breath. She crossed her arms over her chest so that they'd have something to do other than shake.

"I bet she's just a bunch of dumb white bones by now," he said, still gazing lovingly toward the cemetery. "I wonder how many we can find."

"Maybe the puffins first?" Natalie asked, backing another step down the trail. "We can dig up Grandma after that."

Her grandfather scrunched up his nose. He seemed unconvinced.

"I bet the puffins will try and fly away from us," Natalie offered.

That was the clincher. The old man beamed. "I won't

let them," he said. "I've got an idea—I'll break their little wings."

And so together they continued, Natalie walking backward to the nesting grounds with her grandfather sauntering after. Soon the air grew heavy with the stink of fish and droppings. The nesting puffins grumbled as Natalie approached.

You keep that crazy man away from us, one of the birds scolded.

Natalie couldn't turn it off, even when she wanted to.

"I used to eat their eggs," her grandfather said, reminiscing now. "Before we got the chickens. Your mother would steal their eggs, and I would eat them."

"For real?" Natalie asked, pulling the biggest surprised face she could. "Are puffin eggs any good?"

Over at the lighthouse she could see that her mother had made it all the way up to the lamp room. She lifted the fireman's ax over her head and brought it down onto the ornate spinning lens. The lighthouse beam switched off all at once, but in the bright morning light you couldn't tell unless you were looking right at it. Astrid watched out of the corner of her eye as her mom's shape disappeared back down the stairs.

"I was hungry," her grandpa said with a shrug. "I ate them up."

As if in answer to this, the birds decided that they'd finally had enough. They burst from their nests, flying with quick little wingbeats, a cackling cloud of black and white and orange. Natalie's grandfather beamed up at the puffins as they flew.

"I see you up there!" he called to the birds. "Don't think I don't see you!"

The flock wheeled over their heads in a kind of synchronized panic. He turned to watch them, and in doing so he caught sight of the extinguished lamp at the top of the lighthouse. All at once his childlike enthusiasm vanished.

"I thought I left that on," he said, suddenly annoyed.

"No . . . I'm pretty sure you didn't." Natalie was hoping to stall him. For some reason her mother still hadn't emerged from the lighthouse.

Her grandpa shot Natalie a look over his shoulder. "I will yank out your lying tongue," he said. "Remind me to do that later, please." Then he headed for the lighthouse. The old guy was moving a lot faster now than he had been before.

For a moment Natalie didn't know what to do. It would have been simple enough to run up behind her grandfather and push him down onto the jagged rocks. That'd stop him, no doubt. But it could also be enough to break his hip. Natalie didn't want to do that until there were no other choices left. So instead she raced toward the lighthouse, giving her grandpa a wide berth as she passed him by. When she got there she found her mother in a heap at the foot of the spiral staircase in the engine room. Her face was bright pink, slick with sweat. For an awful second Natalie thought she might be about to have her baby. But then she saw her mom's ankle—inclined and twisted on one of the wooden steps. She must have fallen on her way back down.

"What are you doing here?" her mom said, wincing with pain.

"He saw that the light is out," Natalie said, rushing to her. "He's coming."

She propped her mother up, and together they hobbled three-legged to the door. Her grandpa had already made it back to the center of the island. He was sort of speed-walking now, knock-kneed and jaunty. He looked so terrifyingly happy to see them. He threw both arms up and flapped them about in the air, like a castaway calling for rescue.

"Don't start without me!" he called, his voice carrying across their empty island home. "I'm almost there!"

Her mother's grip suddenly tightened on Natalie's shoulder. "We can't leave him the ax," she said. Natalie glanced back and saw that the fireman's ax was still lying across the spiral steps, where her mother had fallen. Natalie left her braced against the doorframe and rushed back to grab it. But by the time she returned to the tower door, her grandfather was only fifty yards away.

"I can't make it to the bunkhouse," her mother said.

More than anything, she seemed surprised that their plan had gone so very, very poorly. Natalie was surprised too. She felt her mother's hand return to her shoulder, but this time instead of grabbing for support, she was pushing. "You can still get there," she said.

"No way," Natalie said, pulling them both back into the lighthouse. "Not a chance, Mom."

Natalie shut the big iron door and quickly used her mother's keys to lock it from the inside. The engine room went dark as soon as the door closed, and for a moment there was nothing but silence. Then they heard the low gong of knuckles on the metal door.

Knock-knock.

"Guys, it's me," her wicked grandfather called. "Can I come in?"

CHAPTER 11

Knock-Knock

NATALIE'S GRANDFATHER REMAINED JUST OUTSIDE THE LIGHThouse. "Can I come in?" he called, knocking gently on the locked iron door. He sounded so sweet and innocent. Like a child who knows that it's important to be on his very best behavior. "I'd really like to come inside with you."

Natalie and her mother said nothing.

They remained absolutely still.

"Can you even hear me in there?" Her grandpa's breath puffed across the hinges, and his voice echoed about the enclosed space of the engine room. "If you can hear what I'm saying, clap twice."

He clapped to demonstrate.

Natalie shut her eyes. It seemed as though the room were shrinking all around her. A strange thrum ran through her chest, sort of like a hiccup. Natalie's breath was catching the way it did when she was about to cry. Or scream. In the darkness, her mother's hand found hers. It squeezed tight.

"I'm waiting," her grandfather called, ever hopeful.

"Mom," Natalie said. The word just came out of her all on its own. She couldn't tell if she'd yelled it or whispered it. She wasn't even sure that any sound had come out of her at all. "I'm scared," she said.

"I am too," her mother whispered back. "Let's just take our time. It'll pass."

Natalie opened her eyes again, blinking in the muggy darkness. She could just make out a concrete platform, upon which sat a pair of antique generators that dominated the engine room. Beside that was an ancient air compressor for the foghorn. But there was nothing else—no desk, no furniture, not even a chair. No place to sit.

Natalie caught herself—no place for her mother to sit or lie down. That was a nice, solvable problem.

"Can you make it upstairs?" Natalie whispered.

Her mother didn't answer for a moment. Her whole body was wedged against the doorframe, bad leg jutting out to one side. She was sweating—even in the darkness, Natalie could see it. Her mom shifted her weight, and her eyes bulged. The light in them seemed almost to swell, filling the room with the faintest purple glow. Somehow, she managed to keep from hollering in agony.

Once her mother had regained her composure, she simply shook her head.

"I know that you two are in there," her grandfather singsonged from outside the iron door, still rapping away. "I know that you can hear me!"

As carefully as she could, Natalie threaded her mom's arm over her shoulder. Then they hop-hobbled to the center of the circular room, where she helped her down onto the edge of the machine platform. Between leaning on Natalie and holding up her own bulging belly, her mom accidentally shifted to her bad leg. And now there was no stopping it—she shouted out in pain. Her face shut tight, squeezing tears from her eyes like water from wrung cloth. Outside, Natalie's grandfather hooted with delight.

"Wait for me!" he hollered, still tap-tap-tapping on the door. "Don't kill her without me, please."

The tapping went on for hours.

At one point it stopped briefly. Natalie strained her ears and heard the icy crumble of gravel outside. There was a faint scratching on the storm walls, and a dark shape passed across the open food slot. Her grandfather was circling the lighthouse, looking for another way inside. You'd think that if there were another door he'd have found it years ago. But those sorts of calculations didn't interest the wicked. Natalie's grandfather took his time, testing the concrete blocks for give. When he found no secret passageways, he returned to the iron door and recommenced his knocking.

The light pouring into the engine room sharpened as the day got away from them. Natalie and her mother had kicked off this ill-fated scheme in the mid-morning, so it must have been late afternoon by now. Eventually Natalie decided it was worth the risk to try to head upstairs, to see if she could find something that would make her mom more comfortable. She took the spiral staircase slowly, but the stairs still creaked with every step.

The second floor was slightly smaller than the first. It was also darker, owing to the fact that the windows up here were entirely covered. It was the kitchen—what was left of it, at least. Natalie's parents must have hauled away anything that a wicked person might have used to hurt himself or someone else. A gap in the countertop was the only clue as to where the electric stove used to be. The cabinets had been stripped of their doors and emptied of plates and cutlery. The only thing inside the refrigerator was a plastic mug holding a bouquet of disposable forks.

At this moment an unsettling thought struck Natalie. There was nothing to eat in the lighthouse. More than that, there was nothing to drink. Everything that sustained her grandpa came through the slot on the ground floor. Every mouthful of food. Every sip of water. Even as Natalie realized this, she suddenly became aware of a dry ache in the corners of her mouth. Neither she nor her mother had had anything to drink since the tea they'd shared that morning, waiting for the fog to burn off. Their plan had gone poorly, but it was only now that she understood just how poorly.

They had to figure out a way out of this tower.

A little shaky now, Natalie continued up to her grandfather's bedroom on the fourth floor. There a shaft of summer light nearly blinded her. The bedroom windows hadn't been bricked over—it was too high to jump—and it made a huge difference. Sunlight shimmered through the thick, warped glass, illuminating dust motes in the air. Natalie stood there for a moment, her eyes readjusting. A full-size bed sat in the middle of the round room, covered in a nest of quilts. There was a large couch oozing stuffing, as well as a shelf stacked with adventure books and picture encyclopedias, all salvaged from the mainland. Natalie could remember passing many of these books through the food slot, into her grandpa's happy hands. One of them—a giant wildlife encyclopedia—lay open in the middle of the bed. Her grandfather had torn some of the pages out and had stuck them to the walls of his bedroom. Color photographs of a rooster, a bear, and even a puffin all gazed down at the bed. They looked very nearly alive.

It was a strange sensation, to be standing in her grandfather's private space. It felt almost like she were peeking into his head. Natalie often wondered about the person that her grandpa used to be, before the wickedness forever changed him. But her mother was useless on the subject. "What matters is who he is now," she'd always say. "If I hadn't let go of who your grandpa used to be, I wouldn't be able to care for the person he has become. If I hadn't let go, I might have started hating him. And I don't want to hate him. He's my dad." So then, based on this bedroom, what kind of person was her grandfather now? It certainly didn't seem like a dangerous man lived here. No, this was more like the room of a boy. A kid who loved animals, who treated his possessions with care, and who hated making his bed.

Natalie was so lost in her thoughts that it took some moments to realize that the knocking on the lighthouse door had stopped. She inched toward the window and peered down at the rocks below, hoping to see that her grandfather had wandered off. Even if he'd gone only as far as the grave-yard, that would still give Natalie and her mom enough time to slip out of the tower and back to safety.

She couldn't find him anywhere. Natalie looked to the bunkhouse and saw that the door had been flung wide on its hinges. Some of her mother's clothes lay splayed across the rocks in the front yard. As she watched, her grand-father emerged from the bunkhouse doorway. He held their crank-powered shortwave radio in his hands, lifting it up into the sunlight with a look of rapt curiosity. Then he dropped it. Natalie winced as the radio crashed upon the stony earth. So much for listening to *The First Voice*. So much for talking to the outside world—you know, if the outside world ever became safe and sane enough to talk to.

Natalie became overwhelmed by all the other damage her grandfather might do. But that wasn't a problem she could solve right now. Natalie forced the thoughts out of her head, pulling some broad cushions off of the couch. She carried them down the spiral staircase. Down in the engine room her mother was still breathing heavily from the pain. Her ankle had nearly doubled in size.

"I think your grandpa left," her mom whispered.

"I saw," Natalie said. She arranged the couch cushions end-to-end on the floor, forming a makeshift mattress. Then she helped her mother roll onto them.

"Thanks." Her mom lay back, exhausted.

"Do you think it's broken?" Natalie asked.

"It's bad, but it's just a sprain," her mother said. "Just a sprain," she repeated, as though willing the words to be true. But she must have known they weren't. Natalie knew it, and she couldn't even feel the pain. Again there was a tug at the back of her tongue. She swallowed spit.

"Did you see where he went?" her mother asked. "Can we make it to the bunkhouse?"

Natalie paused, but there was no point in withholding the truth. "He's in the bunkhouse."

Her mother closed her eyes, breathing deeply as the news settled in. The bunkhouse was the worst possible place he could have gone. There were knives in there, and if he searched hard enough he might even find their rifle. But that wasn't the scariest thing—it was far more unpleasant to imagine what he might do to their food stores or stock of seeds. To their greenhouse or hen coop. Their life and comfort on this barren little island had already been hanging by a thread, and now Natalie's grandpa was on the loose. And he had scissors.

"Shit," her mother finally said.

"Yup," Natalie agreed. She hesitated, knowing that her mom wouldn't like what she was about to suggest. "He seems pretty distracted," she finally said. "I think I could get to the front door before he even knew I was—"

Her mother shook her head before Natalie had even finished. "Too dangerous," she said. "You don't know what he's found. Better to wait until he falls asleep. Otherwise, one of you could get hurt."

"Mom." Natalie tried to keep her rising frustration out of her voice. "You need to drink now. Besides, one of us is probably going to get hurt either way."

"You don't know that," her mother snapped, a look of sharp disapproval cutting through the pain on her face. "That's something your father would say."

There was a pause, and they were both quiet.

"That was mean," her mother said. "I'm sorry. Your dad did the best he could."

"His best was awful," Natalie said.

Her mom didn't argue the point.

As evening approached, Natalie's mother fell into a restless sleep. She tossed and turned, crying out softly whenever her swollen ankle shifted. The sea winds whistled through the hinges, and it grew cold. Natalie retrieved a quilt from her grandpa's bedroom upstairs and draped it over her mother. Then, careful not to wake her up, she placed a hand on her forehead. Her mom was running a fever, and her skin felt tight and dry under Natalie's fingers.

Natalie went to sit below the food slot. From there she could keep an eye on her mother while also keeping track of the jabbering and footsteps outside. The moment her grandpa wandered out of hearing range, Natalie meant to sneak out to the bunkhouse to get some water. But she wasn't going to wait forever. Natalie decided to give it an hour—two at most. After that she was going outside no matter where her grandpa was. Even if he was waiting for her on the other side of the iron door.

Even if it meant going through him.

CHAPTER 12

The Rifle

NATALIE SAT THERE IN THE DARK ENGINE ROOM, STEWING. She felt bad for arguing with her mom. Even worse that the subject of her missing father had come up. It had been a long time since they'd spoken of him.

That was Natalie's fault, mostly. She'd never worked up enough courage to tell her mother that she'd seen him steal away from Puffin Island. Not just seen it coming. She'd actually watched her father leave.

It was only two months ago. Natalie had thought that the fight between her parents had fizzled out by then, that her dad had finally accepted the inevitability of a new baby. But obviously she was wrong. One night she stumbled out of bed to go to the toilet and was startled to find her father down in the kitchen, fully dressed. He was wearing a backpack, and an oil lantern dangled from each hand. The moment she saw him, Natalie knew what was happening.

Neither of them said anything for a long time. When her father finally opened his mouth, it was just to whisper the words: "Can you hand me one of those?" He nodded in the direction of the lobster traps, stacked against the far wall and looking like a heap of rotting bones. In a daze, Natalie picked up one of the traps and passed it to him. He balanced it across his forearms.

"I'm only taking one," her dad said. His eyes fell to the flagstone floor of the bunkhouse. "I'm leaving all the rest for you."

Okay.

Did he want to be thanked for this?

They were quiet for a while. Then, without another word, her father trundled over to the front door and bumped it open with his hip. Natalie followed him, not bothering to put on proper boots, or even a coat. They walked in silence across the barren surface of Puffin Island, heading for the windward shore. The family kept their lobster boat back there, hidden in the shadow of the lighthouse. The tide was up, and in the moonlight Natalie could see one of their sea kayaks bobbing in the shallows. Her father's bee suit had been stuffed into the kayak, alongside bottles and clothes and other supplies. This obviously wasn't just a little trip to blow off steam.

"Nat . . . ," her dad said. He seemed not so much to be having trouble finding the right words as to be struggling with the physical act of speaking.

"You're leaving?" Natalie asked. That her father meant

to abandon them was clear, but Natalie still wanted to make him say the words out loud.

"I have to," her dad said.

Not. True.

Natalie breathed. She looked her father right in the eyes. "I need you to wait for a second," Natalie said.

Her dad shook his head. "I've said everything I have to say to your mother."

"It's not that," Natalie said. "If you're too scared to face her, I won't make you." She felt weakness sneaking through her and paused to force it out. She had never spoken to her father like that before. Neither of them seemed to know how to react. "I need you to wait while I check something," Natalie finally said.

Her dad raised an eyebrow. "What?"

Natalie stepped past him and, still in her slippers, waded right into the frigid ocean. She grabbed at the towline for the kayak and yanked, pulling the craft up onto the beach. Once it was ashore, she tipped it over and began to inspect what her father had packed. From the supplies she pulled a small cardboard box that rattled with batteries of different shapes and sizes.

"Not these," she said.

Her father cocked his head, taking Natalie in. "I need them," he said. "That's less than half."

"We need them more," Natalie said. "Besides, batteries all come from the mainland. Isn't that where you're going?" She shoved the box into her pocket. It hardly fit, sticking up above the waistband of her pajama pants. But just let her father try to take them back. "You can forage for more when you get there."

Natalie continued to dig through the supplies. Her father had packed a compass, canteens, a fishing rod, and wire snares—all of which they could spare. And nobody on Puffin Island would miss the bee suit—she and her mother were vexed, and of course her wicked grandfather had no use for the thing. The kayak itself would be a big loss, but they had a spare. Not to mention the lobster boat, which still more or less ran. So they could do without the kayak. Just like they could do without her father.

"The rest is fine," Natalie said, straightening up. "But you can't take the rifle."

She meant their .308-caliber hunting rifle, the only gun they had on the island that still fired. She could just make out the stock sticking out from inside her father's pack.

Her dad waited a long time before answering. "I'm taking it," he said.

"We need it more than you do."

"Nat . . ." He trailed off. "I might meet the wicked out there."

"You might," she said, hardening herself. It had been more than a generation since the world had fallen to the wickedness, and no one really knew how many of the wicked were left. But the infested town of Goldsport was proof that the number was definitely something more than zero. Proof that the wicked could thrive over the years, feeding themselves and clothing themselves. Waiting for new friends to arrive.

"Of course you might," Natalie said. "You're going where they live, after all."

"And what about hunting? I can't catch deer with rabbit snares." A kind of sad exhaustion overtook her father. This was such an absurd conversation, made more absurd by the fact that it would be their last.

"You're one person," Natalie said. "We're three. Four," she corrected herself. "You don't need to hunt for deer. And you don't need that rifle."

Natalie's father nodded, as though thinking this over. Then he dropped his pack down onto the beach. He loosened the straps and pulled the hunting rifle free. "All right, then," he said. "You're right."

Natalie took the rifle from him, as well as a small satchel of rounds. Then she just stood there, clutching it awkwardly as her dad repacked his kayak. He seemed to want to try to hug her before leaving, but was smart enough not to attempt it. Instead, he just shoved out into the shallows and planted himself in the seat.

"When the baby comes, try to talk your mother out of bringing it to shore." Her dad wedged his paddle against the rocks beneath the water, making ready to push himself away from the island. "I don't care what she says. The vex isn't worth the risk."

"It was for me," Natalie said.

"Just because you were lucky doesn't mean your baby brother or sister will be." Her father winced even as he said it. Given what was happening, he must have known that "lucky" was the wrong word for his daughter. The wrong word for any of them. He remained there for a moment longer, anchored by his paddle to the rocks below.

"You could come with me," he finally said. "I guess that you . . . you probably don't want to. But you can."

To this, Natalie had only one answer. At the time it had felt righteous, and brave. But it wasn't either of those things.

"Don't ever come back."

Natalie didn't realize she was falling asleep until she woke up again. She found herself on the cold floor of the engine room, palms flat against the concrete, blinking and blind. Night had come. She could hear her mother's deep, steady breathing from somewhere nearby. Natalie pushed herself up into a sitting position and immediately felt dizzy. She waited for it to pass before trying to stand. Her thirst greeted her as a sensation that most closely resembled physical pain. Her spit was thick as glue in the back corners of her mouth. The insides of her nostrils ached.

What time was it? Surely her grandfather had to be asleep by now. Natalie climbed the spiral staircase, pawing her way from one step to the next. Up on the fourth floor her grandfather's bedroom was all aglow, starlight gleaming across the glossy animal pictures on his walls. She went to the window and looked down at the bunkhouse. The doors and windows were all flung wide, but the house itself remained dark.

Natalie continued up the tower, through the service area and then out onto the open-air gallery. She gripped the railings. The gallery seemed much higher off the ground from up here than it ever had from the rocks below. Once her vertigo had passed, Natalie scanned the length of the island. It was a beautiful night. The sky was cloudless, and the stars were out in swarms. She could make out the ragged contours of the western shore. But there was no sign of her grandfather.

Then a cry of "I see you up there!" caused Natalie to jolt so hard that the catwalk shook beneath her.

She stepped to the edge and looked straight down. There, sure enough, was her grandpa. He had hauled the master bed out of the bunkhouse and dragged it—frame and all—to the base of the tower. Now he lay sprawled out atop the mattress, legs spread and hands clasped behind his head.

"Do you remember when I threw that wrench at you?" he asked. "I was standing right where you're standing now!" At this her grandfather giggled, the coincidence too fabulous to bear.

Natalie said nothing. She knew she should go back inside and wait for him to fall asleep. But thirst kept her on the gallery. Her eyes returned to the bunkhouse. One of the outer walls was lined with rain barrels. The sight of them made her throat ache.

At this point anything was worth a try.

"Grandpa," Natalie called out, hoarse. "Can you see the barrels lined up against the house?"

"Yes, I can," he said, still chuckling about the whole wrench business. "I'm not blind yet, you know."

"That's great," Natalie said. "What they are is rain barrels, and—"

"You know, I was wondering about that," her grandfather said, bopping himself on the forehead with the palm of his hand. "That's what I drink, isn't it?"

This was more progress than Natalie had hoped for. "That's right," she said. "Do you think you could bring us some of that water? We're really thirsty in here."

"Of course I can," her grandfather said.

Natalie waited, but he stayed exactly where he was atop the bed. It really seemed as though he'd understood the request—or, at least, each of the individual words in the request.

"Grandpa?" Natalie tried again. "The barrels open up from the top."

"Do you know what I found?" her grandfather called up brightly, already on to the next subject. "I found something really good. I mean—really, just, wow."

Natalie sighed and let her head droop. Her jaw pressed against the cool metal of the gallery railing. "That's great, Grandpa," she said.

Her grandpa didn't pick up on much, but he did pick up on how underwhelmed his granddaughter sounded.

"Did you even hear me?" he called, annoyed. "I want you to look. I want you to look at what I've got. Then just try to tell me it's not super good."

Exhausted, Natalie lifted her head. Her grandfather was holding something in the air. Something long and skinny and blackish. Natalie blinked in the dark, and the shape grew familiar.

He had found their rifle.

Time seemed to slow to a crawl. Natalie's eyes stayed locked on the gun. She felt a strong urge to pull away from the gallery—to dive back into the lamp room, behind the cover of the storm glass. But she resisted, holding tight to the railing. She knew that she couldn't panic. Showing fear would only get him worked up. Her grandpa was like an old bear in that way. He might not realize that he wanted to eat you until he saw you running away. It was the flight that begged the chase.

"You're right," Natalie called. "That is super cool." Her fingers flexed on the railing, the metal sharp in her grip. Her feet went shifty beneath her.

"I know," he said, proud as could be.

Fighting every impulse she had to do the opposite, Natalie leaned over the edge of the catwalk and made like she was trying to get a better look at the rifle. "I can't tell from here," she called, "but . . . is that the big one?"

To Natalie's own ears, her voice sounded utterly stilted, and false. But her grandpa was oblivious. "I don't know," he answered, turning the gun over in his hands. "Nobody told me you had more than one!"

"Of course we do," Natalie said, as offhandedly as she

was able. "We keep some on the second floor of the—" She caught herself. There were far less dangerous places to send her grandpa than back into the bunkhouse. "I mean the second, um—we have a second box of guns. We keep it down on the western shore, for emergencies."

"Sounds like a good idea to me," he said.

Natalie waited, but he made no move to get up off the bed and go investigate. Instead he turned the wooden stock of the rifle into his shoulder and lined up the sights. He arced the gun wide, aiming at the sky above them, like he meant to have some target practice with the stars.

"Well," Natalie said, lowering her hands from the railing. "I should probably get some sleep." She stretched, inching back into the shelter of the lighthouse. It was only after she was safely inside the lamp room that she called out again. "Good night!"

"I'll see you tomorrow." Coming from a wicked man, this sounded just as much like a threat as it did a simple statement of the facts. He was still pointing his gun up at the sky, shifting his aim from star to star.

"You know," he called, "I'm actually pretty sure this is the big one." Then, without any further warning, her grandfather squeezed off a round. The gunshot exploded over the island, rippled out to the far shores, and echoed back as the sound of a thousand angry puffins. He leapt to his feet, standing square in the middle of the bed.

"I think I got it!" he hollered. "Did you see how I . . . ?"

Natalie's grandpa never made it to the end of that

sentence. Firing the rifle must have reminded him that rifles could, indeed, be fired. And so, as though it were the most natural thing to do in the world, he turned his aim toward the lamp room and shot again. The reinforced storm glass immediately in front of Natalie's face made a wet, sucking sound. It blossomed with ice-blue cracks.

"Hey," he called, "did I kill you?"

Natalie felt as though she'd been physically struck— winded. Grabbing at the wall for balance, she returned through the service area and down the spiral staircase. As she crossed her grandpa's bedroom, another shot rang out, and one of the windows exploded. A spray of bottle-thick shards shredded the air just behind her, smashing into the opposite wall and tearing up the decorative animal pictures. Who knew that her grandfather was such a marksman?

Down on the ground floor her mother had heard the shots and was calling for her. "Natalie! Where are you?" She was beyond frantic.

"I think she's dead," her father answered joyously from outside. "I'm pretty sure I got her that time."

"I'm all right!" Natalie hollered down.

"I think she's all right!" The wicked old man corrected himself without missing a beat. "I thought I killed her, but I was wrong."

Natalie continued downstairs, stumbling through the office and kitchen, all but crashing into the engine room. There was just enough light down there to see that her mother had crawled off of the couch cushions and taken cover on the far side of the generator. Natalie could see her luminous purple eyes, huge in the darkness.

"Honey," her mom hissed, "get back upstairs!"

"Can you walk?" Natalie asked.

"I can't," her mother said. "Upstairs!"

From just outside came the crunch of footsteps, and a long shape darkened the partially open window. "You guys," the wicked man said, "I think that today is the day. I think everything is going to finally work out for me." Then, to Natalie's horror, he shoved the narrow mouth of the rifle through the food slot and fired off another round. The sound in the enclosed space was deafening, and sparks burst here and there as the bullet ricocheted around the room. Natalie just stood there. She could feel the bullet in the air as it traveled around her in a jagged, angular orbit. Now passing by her ear. Now bouncing beside her foot. It seemed like the first bullet hadn't finished its flight before her grandfather fired again, and again, blindly, pinging shots between the generator and the air compressor. Her mother was screaming for Natalie to move, but somehow she couldn't. She stood frozen in the center of the room, locked in a moving cage of sparks and metal. She was going to die—Natalie was as sure of it as she'd ever been of anything. She was going to die when she'd hardly lived a fraction of a life, and all of it on this tiny heap of rocks in the sea. She wanted to close her eyes, but she was too frightened to even do that. What a bitter last feeling this was to have. The surprise to learn that you're a coward.

Suddenly Natalie's mom was on her feet, her bad ankle bent oddly beneath her. She grabbed Natalie by her shirt and pushed her down upon the concrete behind the generator. Then she threw herself on top of her. It would have winded Natalie, if she'd had any wind left in her. The shots kept coming. They whistled and pinged about the engine room like a swarm of angry singers. One of the bullets bounced to a stop right in front of Natalie's nose, lying there on the floor hot and spent. Then, just as abruptly as he'd started shooting, her grandfather stopped again.

"How about now," he asked, "did I kill either of you?"

CHAPTER 13

Hello!

NATALIE AND HER MOTHER STAYED HUDDLED AND SILENT behind the generator for the rest of the night. Her grandfather remained outside for a time, calling their names. But as dawn approached, his attention drifted, and he wandered off.

"I'm so sorry," Natalie said, her voice hoarse with thirst.

"This was my stupid idea," her mother said. She shifted her weight to one side. "I'm the one who should say sorry."

"I just froze."

"You didn't—" Her mother caught herself. "You won't next time."

She really sounded like she believed it, which made it easier for Natalie to believe it too. Off in the distance they began to hear a sharp, brassy clang. Her grandpa had returned to the bunkhouse. He was fussing with their pots and pans.

"Your ankle is broken, isn't it?" Natalie said.

"It is," her mother said.

They were silent. Nothing much else to say about that.

Morning light poured through the open window. Slowly but surely the stagnant air began to warm again. Despite that, Natalie had stopped sweating. Her mother had too. She was also panting, even though she hadn't moved in hours.

"There's a breeze upstairs," Natalie said. "Can you make it?"

Her mother thought it over for a moment. "We'd probably better try," she agreed.

She was able to get upright easy enough, but walking was more complicated. The slightest press of weight on her broken ankle was agony. Carefully Natalie led her mother up the spiral staircase, supporting her weight as she hopped from one step to the next. The skin of her mom's palms felt swollen and tight. If going this long without a drink was hard on Natalie, she could hardly imagine how it must feel for a pregnant woman.

"Do you know how many he used?" her mother asked as they made their way slowly through the dark kitchen. "I lost count."

"How many bullets?"

"Yeah." Her mother bumped into the fridge with her hip as they passed by, and the plastic forks inside chattered like teeth. "I'm pretty sure . . ." She trailed off, lips smacking. "Well, you tell me first."

Natalie had to think it over. Her grandfather had fired a shot at the stars, a shot at the storm glass, and a shot through the bedroom window. But then . . . how many into the engine room? Six maybe? Seven? The sound had drummed and doubled against the walls, so she couldn't be sure.

"About ten altogether?" she guessed.

Her mother frowned. "I'd hoped it was more than that. We can't go outside until he's used them all up." Only ten bullets fired meant that there were still at least ten more to go. Natalie found something about this thought grimly funny. For the first time in the history of their lives on Puffin Island, they were looking forward to running out of something. The way things had panned out, Natalie would have done better to let her useless dad take the rifle after all.

At least it was getting cooler as they climbed. A fresh breeze greeted them in her grandfather's bedroom, blowing in through the shattered window. "That's the stuff," her mother said, sighing deeply as she lowered herself down onto the mattress.

They could still hear him chattering on the rocks below. His voice burbled up, carried on the wind. "I know you're in there, my little darlings," he said. "I know that you're hiding from me." Strange—he sounded too far away to be talking to them. A moment later Natalie heard a creaking, metallic crash, followed by a terrified squawking. Her grandpa must have been talking to the hens. He'd found their hen coop, and the precious, scrawny little chickens inside. She rushed for the window to get a look.

"You stay away from there," her mother snapped.

"We should at least try to stop him," Natalie said. It was

horrible. She could hear the tin roof of the hen coop groaning and the wire walls scraping loudly across the rocks. The chickens wailed from inside. Her grandfather giggled. "If he sees me, he might get distracted," she said. "Maybe some of them will get away."

"We're not reminding him that we're in here," her mother said firmly.

Natalie didn't have time to argue before she heard a metallic snapping. Then there was a scramble of wing beats and squawking. A few more shots rang out from the rifle, and the birds fell silent.

"I'll huff and I'll puff!" her grandpa sang out from below. "And I'll pull out your little lungs." From the sounds that followed, it seemed like he was doing just that.

Natalie slumped down to the floor, her back pressed against the wall. Those hens meant more than just eggs to her. Next to the puffins, they were the only company her family had on this horrible little island.

"There are more out there," her mother said from atop the bed. "It's a big world. Plenty of chickens left in it."

Natalie found her optimism nauseating. "Well, that's good," she said, regretting her sarcasm immediately. Still, she couldn't help it. "If that's the case, then everything will work out super for us."

"Glad you see it my way," her mother said, ignoring her tone. She blinked, her eyelids pale for lack of water.

Not a minute later, she was asleep.

• • •

They didn't have time to sit around and wait for Natalie's grandpa to run out of bullets. Her mom, and the baby inside her, needed water now. Who knew how much longer they could go until permanent damage set in?

Natalie moved quietly. She scooted along the tower wall and peered out the window. Her grandfather had wandered down to the little cemetery, where he tried unsuccessfully to yank out the gravestones. Then he went to the greenhouse and busied himself digging holes in the vegetable beds. Finally, when he tired of this, he wandered off to the western shore. The glass village of Goldsport was faintly visible on the horizon, and her grandfather began waving his hands in the air in some kind of hopeless attempt to get their attention. He began hollering a name—Henry. Natalie had heard her grandpa use it before, but she had no idea who Henry was supposed to be. For all Natalie knew, he could be alive or dead, real or imaginary, a person or a puffin or a moose.

"I'm right here, Henry!" he was calling. "If you can hear me, clap twice!"

Natalie wasn't likely to get a better chance than this. She snatched the lighthouse keys from her mother's pocket and headed softly downstairs. There she cracked open the iron door and slipped out of the tower and into the sharp midday sun. Locking the tower behind her, she approached the bunkhouse. The scene that greeted her there looked like the aftermath of a flood. The bed lay out in the open, its coiled blankets rigid with dirt and dew. Clothes were scattered everywhere, carried from the bunkhouse and dropped once her grandfather had grown bored of them. The hen coop lay mangled on its side. Bright splashes of dust-crusted blood were only clues as to where the hens themselves had met their ends. A single, giant word—HELLO!—was painted in jam across the greenhouse wall.

With her head ducked low, Natalie crossed the yard, stepping over the remains of their shortwave radio and into the bunkhouse. The situation was even worse than she'd imagined. It seemed as though, in just one day of freedom, her grandfather had been able to ruin every single thing they owned. Fishing poles lay snapped in half, tools had been scattered willy-nilly, and candles had been stomped into crumbling smears of wax. Natalie's lobsters had been put into a large pot set atop the stove, where they clicked their claws angrily. Grandpa had either forgotten what the next step was in preparing food, or else decided at the last minute that he wasn't hungry. The only evidence that he'd eaten anything at all was an open sack of sugar on the dining table, surrounded by handprints in white crystals.

But there was no time to take stock or obsess over their losses. Quick as she could, Natalie picked up a pair of large jerricans and brought them outside. Twisting open the spigots on the rain barrels, she grabbed a quick mouthful of water for herself—she had to fight the urge to put her lips right on the spigot and just lie down beneath it—and then set the cans to fill. Meanwhile, she ducked back into the bunkhouse, made a pouch of her shirt, and stuffed it with as many cans of crab and mackerel and peas and fruit as she could carry. When she went back outside again, the jerricans had filled. Natalie screwed on their caps, closed the spigots, and hauled her bounty back to the lighthouse tower, depositing everything on the concrete floor of the engine room.

Her first instinct was to run upstairs with one of the jerricans and wake her mother for a drink. But when Natalie peeked back through the iron door, she saw that her grandpa was still down on the western shore, hollering at distant Goldsport. There was no telling how long it would be before Natalie found another chance to raid the bunk-house. So once again she locked the iron door behind her and raced across the stony yard, into her home.

Now that she'd salvaged the essentials, Natalie was more deliberate. She hooked up another jerrican to the rain barrels outside—they couldn't have too much water—and while it filled she conducted a thorough search of the bunk-house. On second inspection, the damage didn't actually seem so bad. Her grandpa had made a mess, but he hadn't broken all that much. Their stock of dry goods remained mostly untouched. The lobster traps had been stacked into a whimsical, teetering pillar, but they were also undam-aged. And while he had wrecked their shortwave radio, he hadn't discovered the chest of batteries, copper wire, and spare parts. Best of all, Natalie found that the knife block was right where it should be in the kitchen area. All of the knives were accounted for.

Natalie picked one of their mesh fishing nets up off the

floor and used that as a sack. Into the net she stuffed clean clothes, a crank lantern, and their full supply of disinfectant. She was just about to head back to the tower when she remembered the box under her mother's bed. It was where her mom kept all of Natalie's baby stuff. She hurried up to the loft and was relieved to see that her grandpa hadn't found it. Natalie pulled out her old bottle, a tiny blanket with little felt bears on it, and a few vacuum-sealed packets of dehydrated baby formula. The stuff was ancient, but it was probably still okay. Every once in a while her father used to tear open a packet and mix it with powdered cocoa to make hot chocolate. Speaking of old stuff—that reminded Natalie to grab the prenatal vitamins from her mother's nightstand. The pills dated back to the world before the wickedness, and they'd crumble to chalk between your fingers if you weren't careful. Still, her mom took them every morning as an act of faith—optimism in action.

Natalie finished loading her net and headed back down into the common room. She was just about to leave the bunkhouse when a sound in the kitchen brought her up short. It was a rather feeble scratching, coming from an open cupboard beneath the sink. Natalie bent down and peeked inside. A fluffy, round shape stood cowering in the darkened cubby. One of their hens had survived! The bird was shaking all over, but she seemed unhurt. Natalie's joy took her by surprise. She picked the hen up and squeezed her to her chest. She pressed her face into the downy tuft of feathers on the hen's nape.

"Good girl," Natalie whispered.

"Hey, you haven't seen my book, have you?" Natalie froze. Her grandfather. His voice was clear as a bell. He was just behind her, standing in the open doorway of the bunkhouse. Blocking it.

Stupid.

So, so stupid. How had she not heard him? Carefully, Natalie set the hen down on the floor, where she scurried back into the open cupboard. Then she turned to face her grandfather. He still had the rifle, but it was slung across his back. With any luck, he'd forgotten that it was there. With any luck, the fact that he wanted to murder her had slipped his mind.

But when had Natalie ever had that? She cursed herself—she shouldn't have spent so much time inside. She should have been smart enough not to need luck.

"Your what?" she asked, smiling for all she was worth.

"My book." Her grandfather's eyes went from Natalie to the mess he'd made. "I couldn't find my book anywhere."

"Your book," Natalie repeated. She took a half step backward and slipped one of her hands behind her. Her fingers found the edge of the countertop and then walked their way up the side of the knife block.

"Of course," Natalie said. "If you tell me what book you're reading, maybe I can help you look for it."

"Not my book for reading," he said, dismissing the idea with a scowl. "My book for writing. My diary book."

"I see," Natalie said. Her fingers closed on the handle

of one of the knives behind her back, and she waited. If the fancy struck him, how long would it take for him to unsling that rifle? Could Natalie get to her grandfather in that amount of time?

And even if she could, then what?

"I've had a great day!" he carried on, gazing over the tumult in the bunkhouse with satisfaction. "I want to write it all down. I always forget stuff, and I don't want to forget any of this."

"Yeah, you probably should write it down, then," Natalie said. Her fingers grew damp on the knife handle. The lobsters scuttled about on the cold stove, sloshing water out of their pot. From inside the dark cupboard, the chicken clucked.

"Well." Her grandpa sighed. "Be sure to tell me if you find it." And with that he turned and dissolved back into the sunlit yard.

Natalie nearly collapsed. She counted her grandfather's paces as he walked back in the direction of the little graveyard. As soon as she judged him far enough away, she dumped the knife block into her net, snatched the surviving hen, grabbed the overflowing jerrican, and raced to the lighthouse as fast as her legs could take her. Her grandpa noticed and watched her go.

"I could give you a hand with that!" he called.

"No, thanks!" Natalie hollered back.

Then she arrived at the lighthouse, went inside, and locked the iron door behind her. She fell right down onto the concrete floor, her back up against the cold metal of the door. She was either catching her breath or hyperventilating. The tears in her eyes were either from relief or embarrassment or panic.

Pull your shit together, the chicken said, looking up at her with disgust. *You've got to do better next time.*

CHAPTER 14

Sister

IT TOOK A LONG TIME TO WAKE HER MOTHER UP. LONGER than Natalie would have liked. She had to grab her by the arms and pull her up into a sitting position just to get her eyes open. But once her mother had swallowed a few careful sips of water, she perked up. Natalie watched her mom's face change as she looked from her favorite tin mug in her own hand to the full jerrican sitting on the floor beside the bed, as she reasoned how any of these things possibly could have made it into the lighthouse. For a moment she seemed on the brink of scolding Natalie for her recklessness. But instead her mother only asked, "Did anyone get hurt?"

"No," Natalie said.

"That's good," her mom said, pausing to drink again.

The two of them sat there silently for a long time. Natalie kept refilling the mug, and they traded sips on the edge of the bed. She brought up a jar of cooked crab apples, and they shared it, bite for bite. Natalie could almost feel the sugary syrup trickling into her blood. The sweet, cooked apples somehow even made the water taste wetter.

"Honey," her mother said. "I think you should prepare for the fact that you might have to go out there again."

Natalie just blinked at her. This was not the reaction she expected. "I've got a lot more food and water down in the engine room," Natalie reassured her. "I think we can just wait Grandpa out."

But her mother shook her head. "That's not what I'm talking about. I mean . . . when your sister comes. And believe me, she's coming soon. . . ." She trailed off. Natalie considered asking about that word, "sister," but decided against it.

"What I'm saying is, I don't know if my leg will be better by then. I don't even know if I'll make it through the—"

"Mom." Natalie was having none of this. She wanted her mother's intolerable optimism back. "You're going to be fine."

"I am," her mother said. "I am," she repeated. "But listen. If I'm not, you're going to have to take your baby sister. And you're going to have to bring her to the mainland."

She paused, letting it sink in.

"Natalie," her mother went on, "I need you to do for your sister what I did for you. Whatever happens to me, you need to make sure she gets the vex."

PART III

QUARANTINE

CHAPTER 15

The Wicked Always Return

ASTRID STOOD AT THE GATES OF GOLDSPORT, BOUND UP IN her father's arms. Her heart pounded in her ears. The sound of the rifle echoed out through the trees. The wicked woman lay dead beyond the chain link, bleeding on the road. Her blood flowed into the still-wet glob of ice cream that she'd spat out, and turned pinkish. Astrid couldn't bear to watch. She twisted her face into her dad's arm.

Meanwhile, the adults were discussing what to do next. Specifically: how to break the news to everybody in Goldsport. Just a few days ago the old folks had thrown a tantrum at the very mention of the vex. And now they'd have to be told that, after years of silence, the wicked had finally returned. They were going to lose it.

"I think it should be you," Mr. Bushkirk said, looking at Astrid's dad. "Bad news sounds better coming out of your mouth than it does mine."

No arguing with him on that one.

"Besides," Mr. Bushkirk went on, "you are the chairman of the board. Burdens of leadership and all." He grinned through his mesh veil. If the fact that he'd ended a woman's life a few minutes ago had any effect on him, it was hard to tell. "Junior and I will deal with this," he said, nodding his bonnet down at the body as though it were no more than a heap of unwashed laundry. "No sense putting it off."

"You two will manage all right by yourselves?" Amblin Gold asked.

"We always do," Mr. Bushkirk said, nodding at his son. Hank didn't even look at him. Like Astrid, he appeared to be in shock. "We manage great."

And so it was decided. The Golds would return to the greenway to break the news to everybody, while the Bushkirks would remain behind at the wall. There they would gather up firewood, build a pyre, and burn the wicked woman's body.

No—Astrid caught herself—burn Eliza's body.

Eliza, who'd said she missed her mom.

Eliza, who'd wanted real mint-chocolate-chip ice cream.

She'd been shot to death, and now they were going to set her on fire. Astrid's mouth felt dry, and she still couldn't get her breathing right.

"You shouldn't have done that," Astrid's father said, breaking the silence as they returned to town. He reached out and rested his gloved hand on the nape of her neck, as though to reassure himself that Astrid really hadn't been hurt. He sounded too relieved to be properly angry. "You should never have stayed up at the gates," he said.

"We asked her the question. . . ." It was all Astrid could manage.

"Even so," her dad said. "Even if it turned out that the lady wasn't infected. True doesn't necessarily mean good." At this Amblin Gold fell silent for a moment and pulled his hand back. He seemed lost in ugly memories.

"The second you noticed a stranger at the gate," he finally continued, "you should have come back to town to tell me. Or Mr. Bushkirk."

Together they reached the western hatch and passed through the quiet room. Astrid's father sterilized his bee suit and began the arduous task of stripping it off.

"Did you recognize her?" Astrid asked. It had taken the whole trip back to town for her to work up the nerve.

Her father didn't answer at first. He pulled his legs free of the bee suit and then took his time turning it right-side in. "What?" he said, making like he hadn't heard.

"The woman. Eliza." Astrid paused. "She said she knew who you were."

Amblin shook his bee suit out and hung it onto a hook affixed to the clear greenway wall. "Yeah. That was weird, wasn't it?" He turned to face Astrid. There was something about his expression that didn't sit right. "Not the weirdest thing I've ever heard the wicked say, though."

"Oh . . ." Astrid fell silent, uncertain of where to go from here. She was positive that her father had reacted when Eliza spoke. In fact, he had all but jumped out of his skin when she'd said her name. Could it be that, in the heat of the moment, Astrid had simply imagined it?

She didn't think so.

"So, Eliza didn't even look familiar?" Astrid asked as casually as she was able.

"Nope," Amblin said.

Yeah. That was definitely a lie.

Together they headed down the glass shunt, directly to the plaza. On the way they ran into Mr. Collins, wrapped in a silk dressing gown and wearing a pair of snakeskin boots. His glasses were askew, and his breath smelled of mint and sherry. He must have come from the weekly bridge tournament hosted by Missy Van Allen. Few people ever left that party sober, or fully dressed.

"Did I hear a . . . um, a gunshot?" he asked, scratching the back of his head. His dressing gown opened as he did so, revealing coils of silver chest hair. His boxer shorts had pictures of martini glasses on them.

"That you did," Amblin said.

"Didn't know there was a hunt scheduled," Mr. Collins said, smiling at the thought. "Not a bad idea, though. It's been a while since we've had anything but seafood for commemoration."

"It wasn't a hunt," Amblin said, squeezing past Mr. Collins and continuing down to the plaza. "There was nobody at the west hatch," Amblin called back. "Do you know who's supposed to be on duty?"

"Oh dear." Mr. Collins fell in after them, clutching his dressing gown closed to keep it from fluttering behind. "That would be me, I suppose." He straightened his glasses and smiled sheepishly. "But here I am, aren't I? On the case."

He must have been going for a laugh, but Astrid's dad gave him nothing. They came to the final junction, where the greenway opened out onto the cavernous plaza. The dome was deserted, dotted with litter from the picnic. A half-made sandcastle crumbled silently. Amblin headed to the little stage. There, he powered up the Goldsport PA system.

"So," Mr. Collins said, peering at them both through his little golden bifocals. He'd finally realized how upset they were. "If it wasn't a hunt . . . ?"

Amblin made no answer and instead toggled the PA on and off a few times. Then he brought the microphone to his lips and delivered the news straight.

"This is an all-call announcement from the chairman of the board," he said. "A wicked woman has been discovered and killed just outside the gates." Amblin paused, maybe to allow this to sink in for everybody. Mr. Collins let slip a stream of surprised obscenities, and the PA microphone picked up a few of them. Moments later they could hear his curse words echoing through the greenway, rebounding down the crystal halls. Astrid's father scowled at him but continued.

"I repeat, the wicked woman is dead. All investors are requested to come to the plaza immediately for more information. Thank you."

All across Goldsport, people must have dropped what

they were doing and raced to the plaza. Mr. Gregory was the first to arrive, dressed in long underwear and the top half of a tuxedo—he must have been at the bridge tournament too. He was followed moments later by the Abbitt twins, Missy Van Allen, Mr. and Mrs. Bishop, the extended Pratt and White families, and even Klara Bushkirk, wandering through the entrance with a puzzled expression on her face. Soon nearly the whole town was squeezed into the plaza—just under a hundred lucky souls.

There wasn't an immediate panic. Rather, when they heard the news, the Goldsport investors mostly just seemed sad. They fell into silence, avoiding eye contact and shifting their weight. Mr. Gregory sat down on the damp sand, worrying the shining lapels of his tuxedo jacket between his thumb and forefinger. He was the first to speak.

"I guess . . . I guess I'd started to hope that they'd all . . ."

He didn't even have to complete the sentence. There was an immediate general nodding of agreement. "That they'd all died out," Mr. Collins finished for him.

"Or starved to death," Mrs. Bishop said.

"Or killed each other," offered Missy Van Allen.

"Don't be dumb," snapped Mr. Pratt. "The wickedness doesn't work that way."

"That we know of," said Mr. Bishop. "Who knows what the wicked will do when there are no true people left?"

Then the gathered crowd slipped back into silence. They stared off into nothing, all lost in their own personal versions of the vanished world. Astrid didn't have the heart to tell them that, based on how Eliza had killed that rabbit, they could definitely rule out the hope that the wicked would simply starve to death.

Eventually, Amblin cleared his throat. "Well . . . ," he said. "We know that there was at least one more out there."

"So she was alone?" Mr. Gregory asked.

Amblin nodded.

"You're sure?"

"Not completely. It'll be a good idea to search the woods beyond the wall. But we can talk about that more when Henry gets here."

"Was anybody hurt?" Klara asked from the back of the plaza.

"Nobody," Amblin said. Though, of course, that didn't count what had happened to Eliza herself. "The wicked woman never became violent. But she failed the question. Henry took care of it."

At this there was a great, collective sigh. The crowd seemed to be taking a moment to give thanks for the existence of Henry Bushkirk. Klara, for her part, seemed not to recognize the name.

"Any guesses as to where she came from?" Mr. Collins asked.

At this Amblin Gold only pursed his lips and shook his head. But there was something in his expression that seemed to say: *not now.*

"Eliza told me she'd been traveling up the coast," Astrid offered.

"Who?" Mr. Gregory blinked up at her from the sand.

"The wicked woman," Astrid said. "Her name was Eliza. She told me that she saw the lighthouse turn on, and that she was on her way to check it out."

"Honey." Her dad put a hand on her shoulder. "Let's just give it a rest about the lighthouse. This isn't the best time."

"But that's what happened," she said, pulling out of her father's grip. "Eliza told us that her family lives on Puffin Island."

Now there was a very different kind of silence. Astrid scanned the faces in the crowd, looking for some hint of recognition. But nobody, not even Klara, would meet her gaze. Amblin closed his eyes and pressed his fingers against his bushy temples.

"That she did . . . ," came a voice from the entryway. "No use denying it."

It was Henry Bushkirk. Everybody turned to see him standing at the plaza entrance. He must have sprinted all the way back to the greenway, because he was struggling for breath. He hadn't even bothered to change out of his bee suit yet. Astrid could see Hank standing just a few paces behind him. He, too, was still in his bee suit.

How had they both returned so quickly?

"Not that it's any excuse—" Mr. Bushkirk was brought short by a sudden fit of coughing. He doubled over, flecks of phlegm snagging on his mesh veil. When he finally spoke again, he seemed more or less to have recovered his wind.

"Excuse me," he said. "What I was saying was, that isn't

any excuse for the way you handled things, Amblin."

That made no sense at all. Astrid glanced at Hank to see if he knew what his father was talking about, but he wouldn't make eye contact.

"What do you mean?" Amblin said. "How did I handle things?"

"Oh, come on," Mr. Bushkirk said. "Are you going to make me spell it out?"

"Yes," Amblin said. His face hardened, and for a moment his eyes seemed to blaze almost as brightly as Astrid's. "I am."

"Very well." Mr. Bushkirk sighed, his disappointment false as a wax apple. "What I mean is how close you let the wicked woman get. To you. To all of us."

"My dad didn't go anywhere near Eliza," Astrid said. She must not have been speaking very loudly, because no one seemed to notice.

"I was no closer to her than you were, Henry."

"Amblin! We both know that isn't true!" Mr. Bushkirk threw his arms out, making like he was shocked.

"Yes, it is," Astrid said. Again, it was as though no one could hear her. The entire population of Goldsport had their eyes and ears locked on Henry and Amblin.

"And I must say that I don't approve of this, either." Mr. Bushkirk pointed his gloved finger about the plaza. "I don't think it's smart for you to be in here with everybody else. Especially before we know whether or not you got yourself exposed."

At this Mr. Gregory leapt up off the sand. "What are you talking about, Henry?" he asked. "What do you mean 'exposed'?"

"Of course he didn't get exposed!" Astrid must have been shouting this time, because now people finally took notice. For the first time since he'd entered the plaza, Mr. Bushkirk looked right at her. There was a wet shine, a glimmer of a smile in his eyes. But his lying mouth betrayed nothing.

"You can't know that for a fact, honey," he said. Then, to Amblin: "Did you really not tell them yet?"

"Tell us what?" Missy Van Allen asked.

"Dear me." Mr. Bushkirk wagged his head from side to side. "Listen up! Everybody, for your own safety, I'd like you to all move away from Amblin Gold."

"He didn't get exposed!" Astrid shouted again.

It made no difference—a frantic shuffle had already begun. Everybody pressed themselves up against the curved glass dome, leaving Astrid and her father stranded at the center of the plaza. A few people even pinched at their shirt collars, pulling them up over their noses and mouths, to avoid breathing the same air as her father.

"There's no need to get too worked up," Mr. Bushkirk went on. "It's really just a precaution at this point."

"But my dad was wearing his bee suit!" Astrid shouted. "And he didn't even touch the lady." As everyone knew, singers weren't the only way you could catch the wickedness. The virus also spread from person to person. Just a handshake with the wicked, or a fist to the nose, or even an unfortunately aimed sneeze could be the end of you. But that was pretty rare. Most of the time, if an infected person got close enough to touch you, it ended with them stabbing or strangling you.

"Hank!" Astrid wheeled around on him. "Tell them!"

Hank did nothing. He just stood there at the entrance to the plaza with his eyes on his boots. She knew that he was afraid of his dad, but this was just ridiculous.

"Honey, please, there's no need to get excited." Mr. Bushkirk patted the air with his gloved hand. "No one is saying your dad touched the wicked lady. But he did get close to her. Much too close, if you ask me. Though I guess most of us here can understand his reasons. . . ." Mr. Bushkirk paused. Then he let out a long, world-weary sigh, dragging out the silence.

"The wicked woman was one of them," he finally said. "She was one of the people from Port Emory."

This name set off a whole chorus of huffs and gurgles from the crowd of investors. At first it meant nothing to Astrid, but then she remembered—Eliza had used it too. She'd said that she'd been on her way to Port Emory, to take a boat to Puffin Island.

"Now, none of us," Mr. Bushkirk said, "are proud of what happened between our community and the folks in Port Emory. And I know, Amblin, that you took it real hard." He turned now, once again addressing Astrid's father directly. His voice had taken on this pleading, friendly, I'm-on-your-side quality. "But, Amblin, that just can't excuse how careless you were today. I don't have to tell you this, right? You've got to know that you should never have let her come inside the walls."

Now, finally, the crowd was seized with real panic. People gasped, and shouted, and grabbed one another by the shoulder.

"I didn't do that," Astrid's father said through clenched teeth.

Astrid said it louder, her mind racing faster than her words could keep up. "He didn't . . . No! He didn't do that! No one came inside!"

Henry Bushkirk ignored them both. "It's a lucky thing my boy came and got me when he did," he said, speaking over the commotion. "I found the two of them right outside the greenway. I asked the lady the question, and unfortunately she failed it, so I had to shoot her. But like I said, I don't feel very comfortable with how close she was to Amblin. You all know how easy wickedness catches. And more important, I'm not too happy about the decision making at play here. He just opened up the gates and let her—"

Fuck no—Astrid went ballistic. She was not about to let this happen. Her dad seemed paralyzed by Henry's words, frozen and gaping, so she climbed up onto the little stage and grabbed the PA microphone. "That's bullshit," she said, interrupting Mr. Bushkirk. Her words boomed through the plaza. "Everybody, Henry Bushkirk isn't telling the truth."

That got to him. He spun on Astrid, eyes narrowing with undisguised menace. "I most certainly am," he said, "though I can't blame you for trying to cover for your dad."

Astrid couldn't believe the man. He'd just shot a woman through the head, and now here he was shamelessly spitting lies out of his smiling mouth. If he was capable of all that . . . well, who knew what else he could do. But she didn't back down. She met Henry's gaze, then very deliberately pressed the microphone up to her lips, so close that it almost went inside her mouth.

"You are a liar," she said.

The word echoed down the empty halls of the greenway. It rebounded back at them, as though the sanctuary itself were speaking it. "Hank," she said, turning to her one friend. "You were there—tell them! Eliza never came inside. My dad never got anywhere near her. You know it's true!"

Everyone in the crowd turned to face him, but Hank only shrank under their gaze. Still, he said nothing. What a . . . What an utter coward he was. And her father! He wasn't saying a damn peep to defend himself. He just stood there staring daggers into Mr. Bushkirk. As though that meant anything to the traitorous old shit.

"Hank!" Astrid hollered, so loud that the feedback stung her ears, the whole town flinching as her voice exploded against the dome above. "You know your dad is lying. Tell them the truth—"

Just then her father leapt onto the stage and unplugged the PA, cutting her off. Astrid gawked at him, wild-eyed.

"You're not helping," he whispered.

"Listen . . . nobody has to take my word for it," Mr. Bushkirk said, grinning victoriously. "Though I'd hope that after so many years of service, my word would be enough. By all means, do go and see for yourselves. The body is out by the western hatch, right where I shot her. Though if you haven't had brunch yet, I'd skip it."

Even before he'd finished speaking, the investors rushed out of the plaza and down the glass shunt, toward the junction. They became nothing but a blur of color through the layers of glass. Soon only Mr. Bushkirk, Hank, Amblin, and Astrid remained in the plaza. There was no point in following—they knew what they'd find there. Astrid knew. Henry would have arranged everything just right to incriminate her father. There'd be a staged scene, with Eliza's body twisted and bloody on the doorstep of the greenway. A horrifying sight, more convincing than anything Astrid could possibly say. Especially with Hank refusing to back her up. A new thought occurred to her just then. Mr. Bushkirk was a big man, but could he have dragged Eliza down from the wall that fast all by himself? Was it possible that Hank had actually helped him? He'd kept his eyes on his boots this whole time, unable to look Astrid in the face. But now that the plaza was empty, he finally found his voice.

"Astrid, I'm—"

"I never want to hear you say another word again."

"Ouch." Mr. Bushkirk chuckled. "A little harsh, no?"

158

"You shouldn't have moved the body," Amblin said.

"Moved her?" He winked. The pig was having a grand old time. "Gosh, what an imagination you have!"

"You know it isn't sanitary," Amblin went on. He sounded exhausted, like he'd already accepted defeat. "Especially with how she was bleeding."

And at this Mr. Bushkirk cracked a sly smile. He held his hands up in the air and wriggled his fingers. "That's what gloves are for," he said.

"You're an awful person," Astrid said. She wasn't on the attack anymore. As soon as the crowd found Eliza's body, it would be over. Astrid realized that. But she couldn't help saying this aloud for them all to hear.

With the other investors out of earshot, Mr. Bushkirk didn't mind being stood up to. He dismissed her with a wave of his hand. "You have no idea how lucky you are, kid, to live in a world where this is your idea of awful."

Down the greenway, they began to hear more shouting. The panicked crowd had found Eliza's body.

"You'd better burn that bee suit, just to be safe," Amblin said.

"Agreed," Mr. Bushkirk said. "But no biggie. Plenty more where this one came from. And speaking of that, you might want to put your own bee suit back on." Again, he smiled. It didn't even seem that mean anymore. "I'm sure everybody is going to feel a lot safer once you head on outside."

CHAPTER 16

The North Shore

THE BOARD OF INVESTORS CALLED AN EMERGENCY VOTE ON the spot. They immediately suspended Amblin Gold as chairman and sentenced him to a full ninety-day quarantine. After that time, if he remained true, he'd be allowed to return to the greenway. Then, by a unanimous show of hands, they elected in Henry Bushkirk as acting chairman. It all happened so quickly. Only minutes ago Amblin had called them all to the plaza to announce the news. And now he was bundled up into his bee suit, exiled from the town that his own father had built and had died defending.

Astrid's blood was boiling, but there was no use fighting anymore. One look at the faces of her terrified neighbors was enough to tell her that she was beat. They were too scared to listen—too scared to even think. What a nest of babbling cowards. Astrid couldn't bear to be near them for even a second longer, so when her father left, she did too. Mr. Collins and Mr. Gregory came along as well, each struggling under the weight of plastic tanks of quiet strapped to their backs. They escorted Amblin away from the greenway as though he were some kind of prisoner.

The quarantine house stood at the far end of the north shore—the portion of their sanctuary that had been destroyed by the wicked all those years ago. To get there they had to cross a desolate wasteland of fire-blackened homes, with giant shards of greenway glass strewn among the tide pools. Only Astrid's recluse of a mother lived out here. Mr. Collins and Mr. Gregory glanced about nervously. You could tell they didn't have a lot of practice being outside.

"You were real stupid back there," Amblin said, speaking low so that only Astrid could hear. She didn't know what she expected her dad to say, but that wasn't it.

"What?"

"Getting in Mr. Bushkirk's face like you did. Insulting him in front of the investors. In front of Klara and Hank."

"He was lying, Dad."

"He was. And you said so. That's not what I'm talking—"

"Somebody had to say so," Astrid snapped. "I can't believe you just let him—"

"Hey!" her father snapped right back at her, loud enough that Mr. Collins and Mr. Gregory jumped in their bee suits. "You want to keep having a tantrum, that's fine. But I'm your father, and you do not yell at me. Understood?"

Astrid could only nod.

"I'm not talking about telling the truth. Which, by the way, I did. I'm talking about antagonizing him. I'm talking about you telling him he's an awful person. Maybe I'm missing how that's helpful." He tilted his bonnet toward Astrid, letting her see just how furious he was. "Care to explain your strategy there?"

"I didn't do it to be helpful," Astrid said, defiant. She'd just stuck up for her dad in front of the whole town, and now she had to defend herself to him? "I did it because Mr. Bushkirk is an asshole."

Her dad breathed through his teeth. She'd never seen him like this. "Astrid. I've been neighbors with the man for most of my life. I've been running this town, with him in it, for all of yours. You really think I don't know what kind of person he is? No. You need a better reason than that."

"I was angry."

"And I wasn't? Wrong. Try again."

"But . . . if you were angry, then why didn't you say anything?" she asked, careful not to yell this time. "I mean, you just folded over. You didn't even try."

Her father quickened his pace. He splashed through a tide pool, getting the legs of his bee suit all wet.

"Try to what?" he asked.

"Try to stop him."

"Astrid." Her dad took a long breath. "I know you've got a good brain in there, and I'd like you to start using it, please. How do you think it would have gone if I'd called Henry a liar? How do you think it would have gone if it were his word against mine? And meanwhile, just outside, you've got the wicked woman's body bleeding all over the place. Would every single person have believed me? Would every single person have been rational? You saw for yourself how frightened they were. Take it from me. A big group of frightened people can get real stupid, real quick. No, there are things you stop, and things you get out of the way of. This was the latter."

Together they crested a dune, and laid out before them was the great ruin of the north shore. The old firehouse, reduced to nothing but a single crumbling brick wall. The swimming pool, now a muck-filled home for crabs.

"You also need to consider how much trouble Henry went to," Amblin said. Now that he'd slipped into a lecture on leadership, he seemed to calm down a little. "It couldn't have been easy to drag her body all the way down the road. You have to ask yourself, in a situation like that: If he's willing to go that far, then how much farther might he go? Sometimes you just have to let him have it."

Let him have it?

Astrid didn't want to fight anymore, but she couldn't help herself. "He tried hard? That's why you let him get away with it? That's why you let him win?"

"It isn't about winning or losing," her father said. "This is about what's best for Goldsport. Henry has wanted to be chairman for a long, long time. If this is the only way he can make that happen, then why not just let him get it out of his system? Besides . . . it's not like there's all that much to the job. And he'll have good, smart people around him— the board and the other investors. So let him hold the little wooden hammer at the meetings. Let him sit at the head of the table. Let him be stuck organizing the commemoration. Believe me, Astrid, he could do a whole lot more damage trying to get the job than he can actually do in the job. This one just wasn't worth the fight."

"It would have been to me," Astrid said. "You're going to be stuck out here, by yourself, for three months."

"I'm not saying I'm happy about it. But for someone who's never seen a real fight, you're awfully eager to have one."

Astrid didn't know how to respond. She was shocked. Who was this person walking beside her? She was used to her father's cheerful, constant-optimist routine. The man who was the smiling beacon of Goldsport. Like the lighthouse out on Puffin Island, he shined every way he looked. But maybe deep inside there had always been a harder version of her dad. An Amblin in the dark, working the buttons and levers. Keeping the lights on and the lamp spinning.

"I'm not looking for a fight," she said. "I mean, at least . . . I'm not looking to start one."

This must have been the answer her dad was waiting for. He nodded at her through the mesh veil. "Good."

By that point they'd begun to approach Ria's big beach house—the only truly livable structure left on the north shore. It was a beautiful property, skirted with verandas and topped with a turret that overlooked the bay. If not for the fact that it was in this wasteland, unconnected to the greenway, it would have been one of the most sought-after homes in Goldsport. Astrid scanned the windows and saw a shape behind the heavy mosquito screen. Ria must have noticed them crossing the shore.

"You're going to have to explain to your mother what happened," Amblin said. "In fact, you might want to stay with her for a few days."

"Of course." Astrid had already decided as much for herself—she had no intention of returning to the greenway.

"It'll give Henry a chance to cool off," he said. "I don't think you know how mad you made him back there."

Only minutes ago Astrid would have had a smart-ass response to this, but who knew? Maybe her dad was right. She glanced behind them and saw a thin, tar-black tendril of smoke curling up into the sky from the far side of the sanctuary. Eliza's body burning. Meanwhile, up ahead, the quarantine house emerged from the scattered ruins. It looked like a tiny fortress, with windows boarded up and a halo of concertina wire ringing the roof. The door was barred with a solid crossbeam and locked from the outside. The foundation sat half buried in the sand.

Quarantine was a rare event, but the rules were always strictly enforced. Guards in bee suits would be posted on rotation, twenty-four hours a day. They would bring Amblin his meals, take his temperature three times a day, and keep a logbook of any symptoms. Visitors, even immune ones like Astrid, would be allowed to come no closer than twenty feet. Which meant that once her dad was locked up in there, they probably wouldn't have a chance for even a semi-private conversation for three whole months.

"Dad . . ." Astrid didn't know how to bring it up, but they were running out of time. "Mr. Bushkirk told everybody that Eliza . . . that the wicked woman was from someplace called Port Emory."

"Well, he probably just meant—" Her father caught himself and took a breath. Maybe he realized that there was no point pretending anymore. "Yes. He did say that."

"Eliza also mentioned a place called Port Emory."

"Did she?" Amblin seemed genuinely surprised.

"Yes. When I was up there alone, talking to her. She said that she was on her way to Port Emory to get a boat. How did Mr. Bushkirk know?"

Her dad didn't answer for a long while. The quarantine house drew nearer.

"Because Henry recognized her," he finally said.

"You did too," Astrid said. "Didn't you?"

"Yes."

They both let the admission just sit there for a moment.

"I'm sorry I lied about it," he said.

Astrid dismissed this with a shrug. On the scale of lies told just this morning, that one was puny. "Where did you know her from?"

"From the world before," her father said. "But not very well. We were kids. I used to see her in the summers. Some summers. Sometimes."

"Were you two friends?"

"We were kids," Amblin repeated. From the crack in his

voice, Astrid knew not to go down that road any farther. "I didn't know she'd fallen wicked," he continued. "I guess I just assumed that she had died."

By now they had reached the quarantine house. Mr. Gregory approached the front door, unspooling the nozzle from his tank. He sprayed quiet all over the door. The blue liquid frothed in the air and sent the singers recoiling back toward the tree line.

"It didn't look all that bad," Astrid said at last.

Her father glanced at her, puzzled.

"The wickedness," she said. "Eliza didn't seem to be in pain. She wasn't scared, or upset. She probably had it for a long time. But I don't think she was suffering."

Now he had to look away. The mesh veil meant that he couldn't wipe his face. "You're a good kid," he said.

Mr. Gregory had finished treating the door. He lifted the crossbeam, opening the quarantine house and revealing the grim interior. A paunchy sofa and card table sulked in the darkness. There was a lantern on the table, and an oilcan. A spare bee suit hung from a peg on the far wall, looking like a faded pelt in the shape of a man.

"Sorry, Amblin . . . ," Mr. Collins said, butting shyly into their conversation. "Could you put your arms up, please?" He unspooled the nozzle from his tank. "Don't want to take any singers in there with you," he said.

Without a word, her father raised his arms into the air.

Quiet burst out of the spray nozzle in a fine blue mist, running down Amblin's bee suit in hissing streams. It gathered in a sizzling puddle on the sand below. Some also floated back in Mr. Collins's direction—he hadn't thought to stand upwind—speckling his veil and even his bifocals underneath with little droplets of blue.

"Good enough," Mr. Collins said, coughing and gagging.

Amblin gave him a cold nod, then turned back to Astrid. "I'd hug you, but . . ." He held his arms out, still dripping. "I should get inside before this wears off."

"Do you want me to bring you anything?" she asked.

He stepped into the darkened doorway, and Mr. Gregory began to swing the door closed.

"You visit me," Amblin said, "and I'll have everything I need."

CHAPTER 17

The Coward

AFTER THAT, ASTRID HEADED STRAIGHT FOR HER MOTHER'S place. She flung open the front door and banged through the entry hall—which Ria had made into a little do-it-yourself quiet room—and into the den.

"Mom!" she called. "I need to talk to you."

There was no answer, but Astrid could hear something bubbling away in the kitchen. She kicked off her shoes and stomped across the hardwood.

"Mom, are you—"

What Astrid saw brought her up short. Dinner was well underway in a big steel crock atop the gas range. Onion skins and carrot ends slumped in a wet mound on the counter, beside a tin of freeze-dried beef threads and a half-emptied glass of red wine. But Ria herself wasn't there. Instead, sitting at the round kitchen table was Hank. He still hadn't changed out of his bee suit. His gloved hands rested flat on the table. His chin was on his chest, and his bonnet drooped forward. He didn't say anything when Astrid stormed into the room. He didn't even look at her.

Just the sight of him brought every bit of her rage flooding back.

"What the hell are you doing here?"

"You're right to be angry at me." The words leapt out of his mouth.

"You think I need you to tell me that?"

"Of course not," Hank said.

"Like, I need your permission?" Astrid approached Hank. She pressed her fist into the table, and the wood seemed to compress under her knuckles. "You helped him lie about my dad. You lied about my dad."

Hank kept his eyes down. "I'm really sorry, Astrid."

"Sorry?" The word could have been a knife, a snake, and still she'd have tossed it right back in his face. Astrid didn't want an apology. She wanted to leave bruises. "Sorry doesn't get him out of quarantine. Not unless you want to go back to the greenway and tell everybody what your father did." Astrid leaned over the tabletop, trying to look him in the eyes. But she couldn't see anything under his crumpled bonnet.

"I wanted to say something . . . ," Hank pleaded. "He said that if I told, he'd—"

"He'd what? Yell at you? Kick you out? Gosh, Hank, I already knew you were a coward, but that's just something else."

Wow, that was mean. Astrid cringed even as it came out

of her mouth. But she could hardly stop—she was furious. Not just with Hank. She was furious with Mr. Bushkirk for being a lying piece of trash. Furious with the investors for being so easily herded by fear. And maybe most of all, furious with herself. Astrid never should have stayed up there with Eliza. The second they saw a stranger at the gates, she and Hank should have run right to the greenway. Astrid had been so obsessed with finding somebody else in the world like her that she'd endangered them all and had gotten her dad locked away in the process.

"He said that if I didn't keep quiet, he'd do something worse," Hank said. "He threatened Amblin. And he threatened you."

That knocked Astrid back for a moment, but she shook it off. "Come on. You know he wouldn't do anything. Your dad might be an asshole, but he's—"

As Astrid spoke, Hank lifted his gaze up from the kitchen table. Half of the veil that hung from his bonnet was caved inward. Beneath it, his face was a swollen, bloody mess. Hank's left eye was sealed shut, the eyelid puffy and almost entirely black. Astrid could even see the pattern that the mesh veil had left when it had been smashed between Hank's cheekbone and his father's fist. The steel threads had broken his skin, leaving behind a checkerboard of square cuts and gashes. Astrid held back a gasp.

Hank's dad hadn't hit him in years. And never, ever like this before.

"He's what?" Hank said.

Astrid just stared. The next voice was her mother's. She walked into the kitchen carrying a tackle box filled with first-aid supplies, her plaid shirt rolled up to her elbows. She wore a pair of rubber gloves.

"Honey," Ria said. "I could hear you being a brat from all the way up in the attic."

"I'm sor—" Astrid started.

Hank cut her off. "Don't say sorry. I'm sorry."

"Yes, yes," Ria said, banging the tackle box down. "Everybody is sorry and everybody is friends again. Scoot over." She hipped Astrid away from the table, sat down next to Hank, and began to root through her supplies. She pulled out a little bottle of peroxide and a packet of gauze.

"There's a fresh block of ice in the icebox." Ria directed her words to Astrid without looking at her. "Break me off some."

Astrid did as she was told. She took up a screwdriver affixed by a magnet to the icebox door, opened the tray, and chiseled off a few shards. These she wrapped in a tea towel. Meanwhile, her mother unfastened Hank's veil and lifted his bonnet. She took his chin lightly in her fingers, inspecting his face in the fading daylight.

"Your dad hit you more than just once," she said, eyebrows raised.

Hank hesitated, then nodded. "Yes, ma'am."

Ria shook her head as she unscrewed the peroxide, pouring it liberally into the folded gauze. She also doused her own gloves in some of the stuff before patting the gauze on

Hank's bruise. He winced. The gauze loosened up the dried blood, coming away red.

"Tell me . . . ," Ria asked, "did it happen before or after he moved the wicked lady?"

"Before," Hank said. "Because I wouldn't help."

"That's good," she said. "If your father got anything on his gloves before he hit you . . . well. You can't be too careful about that kind of stuff."

Obviously Hank had filled her in on what had happened. But if Astrid's mom was shocked by the return of the wicked, or by the little coup that Mr. Bushkirk had orchestrated, she was hiding it well.

"And your father?" Ria said, turning to Astrid and extending her hand to take the ice chips. "How's he holding up?"

"Dad seems . . . all right," Astrid said. "I think he's trying to stay positive."

"That's my Amblin," Ria said in a voice that sounded neither the least bit affectionate nor particularly annoyed. She finished cleaning Hank's face and pressed the ice-filled towel against it. Again he winced.

"And this wicked woman," Ria went on. "Eliza. Was she what you expected?"

Astrid and Hank looked at each other. Nobody had yet thought to ask them this question. Hell—the woman hadn't been dead for a full three hours, and in that time so much else had happened. Astrid hadn't had time to think about it.

"No," Hank said.

"Not at all," Astrid agreed.

"She seemed like . . . I don't know."

"Like a child," Ria finished for them. "Like a little kid crushing flies. If you ever meet one again, you shouldn't forget how dangerous they can be. But they're not . . ." Ria trailed off. She handed the ice pack to Hank and peeled off her gloves. "They're not bad. To be really bad, you have to understand that what you're doing is wrong. And you have to do it anyway."

A silence settled over them, filled only by the bubbling pot on the stove. Through the screened-in kitchen window, they saw smoke from Eliza's body, still rising.

"Did you know her too?" Astrid asked.

Ria's answer was only to tilt her head back and throw Astrid some side-eye.

"It's all right," Astrid said. "Dad already told me that he knew Eliza from years ago. From the world before."

"I don't know what your father did or didn't tell you," Ria said. "But if you want to dig, do it somewhere else. That isn't my secret to tell. So I'm not going to tell it."

Astrid and Hank briefly made eye contact. "But you're admitting that there is a secret, then?" she pressed.

"Of course there's a secret," Ria said. "Don't play dumb. You've known that there was for a long time. You both have."

With that she pushed herself up from the kitchen table and headed over to the stove to see to the soup. Some of it had burned to the bottom of the pot, and Ria began to scrape at it with a wooden spoon. "It's probably a good idea if Hank sleeps here for a few nights," she went on. "At least until everybody cools down. But I don't want you two thinking you'll be staying together. You can flip a coin to see who takes the couch downstairs."

Hank blushed, though you could tell only from the side of his face that wasn't all banged up.

"Mom," Astrid said. "Obviously."

"Don't give me 'obviously,'" Ria said, pausing to take a big gulp from her red wine. She studied what remained in the glass for a moment before upending it into the soup. "I know you two are just friends these days. But, honey, you're sixteen. He's sixteen. You're a girl who likes boys. He's a boy who likes girls. I'm sleeping with my door open tonight. Anybody who tries to go up or down those stairs after dark"—she turned here to point at them with the dripping wooden spoon—"will get themselves sent right back to the greenway."

Then Ria brought the spoon up to her nose and sniffed it. Her sudden bout of mothering was over as quickly as it had begun. "I don't think this'll be very good," she said. "But let's see."

CHAPTER 18

The Archives

A FEW DAYS PASSED BEFORE ASTRID AND HANK COULD BRING themselves to return to the greenway. Even when they did head back, they were careful to go early in the morning, sneaking in through the seldom-used harbor hatch. Astrid wanted to reduce their chances of bumping into anybody. She'd calmed down a little, but she still didn't trust herself not to say anything horrible. As for Hank, he just wanted to avoid his dad.

The search for clues about Eliza and Port Emory had hit a dead end. Ria remained steadfast in her refusal to talk about it. The bee-suited guards wouldn't let Astrid get close enough to the quarantine house to have a real conversation with her dad. And, of course, interrogating the investors was out of the question on account of all of those mean things Astrid was convinced she'd shout in their faces. So the only thing left for them to do was search the Goldsport archives.

The archives. It was a rather grand name for the dark, rickety old building that sat at the far end of the south shore—the closest thing that Goldsport had to a town library. Back in the world before the wickedness, it had been a church. But the investors had no need for one of those, so they'd hauled out the pews and the pulpit, turning the space into a storehouse for old papers and documents. If you peered out through the stained-glass windows, you could still make out the shapes of the old church furniture, rotting at the rim of the forest.

"Where should we start?" Hank asked as they stepped across the threshold, kicking up a cloud of dust.

"I don't know," Astrid said. "Isn't there supposed to be a map somewhere?"

"I think so," Hank said.

The old building was crammed with bookshelves and filing cabinets, making the open space into a sort of labyrinth. Together they threaded the narrow, improvised hallways. At the back of the archives they found what they were looking for—an enormous canvas map hanging across the metal ribs of the old organ. WELCOME TO NEW ENGLAND was written across the top of the map. The map itself covered everything from Boston to Halifax, with the entire state of Maine looming large in between.

"Well," Astrid said. "If Port Emory is a real place, it's got to be on there somewhere."

As they got closer, Astrid and Hank could see that there were strange marks all over the map. The entire thing was covered in a constellation of stickers, pushpins, and paint. A hand-drawn key helped them decipher what these symbols meant. Their village of Goldsport was marked with a solid yellow oval—YOU ARE HERE. Other safe areas were also dabbed with the same hue of yellow paint. Red pushpins indicated the locations of potentially useful equipment, such as abandoned trucks or salvageable boats sitting in dry dock. Black pushpins, on the other hand, indicated encounters with the wicked. These were scattered in thick handfuls in the woods beyond Goldsport. Once you got as far as the city of Bangor, the pins were replaced by a single stroke of black paint. This must have meant, more or less: too many wicked to count.

"I wonder how long it's been since they updated this?" Astrid asked. It had been ages since anyone from the sanctuary had gone out on a scouting trip.

Hank flicked the map with his index finger, and dust showered down from the top of the frame. "A while," he said.

Astrid found a little bench beneath the organ, pulling it out so that they could climb up and get a better look.

"Any idea where it might be?" Hank asked.

Astrid just stared for a moment. The level of detail was as fine as a pinhead, and the map stretched high above their heads. Somehow, the difficulty of this task was only just sinking in.

"I don't know," she said. "Somewhere on the bay, I guess?"

Hank raised an eyebrow at her.

"*Port* Emory," she said.

"Oh. Right."

They started with the coastline around Goldsport, scanning every cove and inlet. When that turned up nothing, they moved the bench and searched farther afield. Astrid ran her fingers over droplets of purple paint—breeding grounds for singers—and through little forests of pushpins. She lingered over Puffin Island, no bigger than her pinky nail, before crossing the bay to search the western coast of old Nova Scotia. At one point Hank got the bright idea that a place called Port Emory might not necessarily even be on the ocean—it could also be on a lake or a river. And so, with sighs, they set about investigating those as well.

As they were working, Astrid snuck glances at Hank. His bruise had settled into itself over the last few days, shrinking and deepening. His cuts had scabbed over, and his eyelid had finally opened—though the eye beneath was still cloudy and red, laced with burst veins.

"Your dad doesn't . . . ?" Astrid trailed off, giving Hank a chance to stop her if he wanted to. They'd spoken very little about what Mr. Bushkirk had done. "He doesn't hit you often, does he?"

"No," Hank said. "Not anymore."

"He used to," Astrid said.

Hank nodded. "But not for a while. Not since I was ten or so."

"I remember."

"I do too." He made a go at a grim chuckle but couldn't manage it. "He wouldn't actually punch me. As least not back then. He'd use stuff around the house. Leather gloves. A coat hanger—one of the plastic ones. Now, those—those hurt. But they'd break easy too." Hank fell silent. Astrid felt as though she might tumble off of the organist's bench. It was so awful.

"I'm sorry that happened—happens—to you," she corrected herself. "I wish I could have—"

Hank cut her off. "Thanks. But don't be stupid. Of course you couldn't. Nobody can. It's just who my dad is. The only way to fix it is to not be around him."

"Did you ever think about leaving?"

"I didn't think there was anywhere to go," he said. "And also, you know. He's still my father. Even if there weren't any singers, or wicked people . . . Even if there weren't a wall or a greenway. I still wouldn't have known that leaving was a thing I could do."

With that Hank stepped up onto the organ so he could search higher on the map. The keys depressed beneath his boots, but no sound came out of the pipes. All of his attention seemed focused on finding Port Emory. But just as Astrid began to think that their conversation was over, he spoke again.

"You've always known it, though. You've always known you could leave this place. And you've always wanted to."

Astrid wasn't sure how to respond, but it didn't matter. Hank went on without giving her a chance.

"At first it was to go to Puffin Island," he said. "But then later, once you got older, it seemed like it was just . . . just anywhere, I guess. Anywhere that wasn't here. I never really understood that. I used to ask myself: What's she got to run away from? I mean, yeah, your parents were split up. But they both loved you. Neither of them would ever lay a finger on you. For a while I started to worry that it was me. Maybe there was something wrong with me. But that was before we . . . well, you know."

"Yeah." Astrid kept her eyes locked on the map.

Hank did too.

"But anyway. I think I understand you better these days. I realize—"

"I think you do too," Astrid cut in. She didn't know that this was true necessarily. But she hoped so.

"Astrid." Hank sounded suddenly exasperated. "I'm not going to snap in half or anything. You don't have to be so nice all the time. I mean . . . it's starting to weird me out. Anyway, what I was about to say is that I realize now that you weren't trying to escape. You weren't running away from anything. You were just running ahead. It might have been Puffin Island. Or it might have been just anywhere outside of the greenway. But the point is that you were looking forward. You always have been."

Again, there was a long pause.

"Anyway," Hank said. "I think that's pretty cool."

"Thanks." Astrid stepped up onto the organ as well, grabbing at the base of the pipes for balance. "But listen," she said, "if that's your way of subtly flirting with me, you should know that it's not going to work. I mean, I don't feel that sorry for you."

Hank laughed. "That's better," he said. "That I can deal with."

CHAPTER 19

The Monster Inside

IT WAS EVENING BY THE TIME THEY FINALLY FINISHED SEARCH-ing the map and could say for sure that there was no place called Port Emory anywhere on it. But Astrid and Hank were undaunted—they returned to the archives the very next morning and set about examining the maze of bookshelves. These were stacked with dusty newspapers and magazines, as well as printouts from old websites.

Astrid rifled through them, lingering over an article about the first outbreak of the wickedness. She knew the story well. It was legendary in Goldsport. Back then the scientists had called it the Western Cape Virus, because the first known case was an American tourist in South Africa. He'd come down with something that looked like a bad cold and had gone on to kill eight other patients in his hospital wing by strangling them with a stethoscope. It caused a global panic. All travel to South Africa was banned, even for doctors and scientists who wanted to study the virus. No one had known then that the disease didn't even come from South Africa. No one had understood that the tourist hadn't caught it on vacation, but rather had brought it there with him. And so the wickedness spread, slowly but surely, behind a world of turned backs. By the time they realized what was happening, it was too late to stop it.

All it takes is one crack. That was the moral Astrid was supposed to take from this story, just like every other story told in Goldsport. But even when she was a little kid, she figured that the investors had it wrong. America and the other rich countries of the world had locked their doors and barricaded them. They'd shut their windows, turned off all the lights, and pretended not to be home when people outside called for help. But their walls and locks didn't save them. The monster they were hiding from was already inside. Maybe, if there had been a few more cracks, they'd have gotten out.

The bookshelves were a treasure trove of interesting relics like that article. Astrid paged through arguments about whether or not the United States and Europe should have closed their borders, instructions for how to irrigate a home garden, and a hilariously useless recipe for all-organic mosquito repellent. Hank found a box of records from the year Goldsport was founded, including old incident reports and inventory receipts. There was even an original blueprint for the greenway. But the one thing they didn't find was any mention of a place called Port Emory. Not a single clue pointing them in the direction of Eliza.

They had just finished when a voice rang out from the atrium behind them. "There you two are!"

Astrid and Hank shot to their feet. Two figures stood on the opposite side of a bookshelf. The first was Abigail Lee, the vice chairwoman—they could just make her out through the gaps. The second, rather surprisingly, was Klara Bushkirk. Both women wore beautiful summer dresses and brightly patterned silk scarves. A chunky pair of bejeweled sunglasses sat atop Mrs. Lee's head, shining even in the dim light of the archives. Klara wore a wide-brimmed sun hat. These were picnic clothes. Astrid had completely forgotten that it was Sunday.

"We missed the two of you this morning," Mrs. Lee said, cheerful as could be. As though there hadn't just been a coup, exiling Amblin to a shitty little dungeon on the north shore. As though Astrid would actually consent to attend the picnic and watch Mr. Bushkirk, the man who'd exiled him, play chairman in front of everybody. Watch him preen and strut like he didn't have a heart made of garbage and mud.

"We've been busy," she said.

"I can see that," Mrs. Lee said, smiling broadly at them through the bookshelf. Her deeply red lips and white teeth looked like they belonged on a different face. Meanwhile, Klara said nothing at all. She seemed to not even be looking directly at them.

"Do you mind if I ask with what?" Mrs. Lee continued brightly.

"Looking for Port Emory," Hank said.

"Want to save us the trouble?" Astrid asked. "You could just tell us where it is."

"I'm sorry," Mrs. Lee said, her smile stiffening. "I don't know what you mean."

There was a long and awkward silence. Eventually, it was Klara who broke it. "If there's anything Amblin needs while he's . . ."

Mrs. Lee dove in. "Absolutely! I was just thinking that with the commemoration coming up, we should put together a nice care package for Amblin. I'll even have Mr. Collins bring up some lobsters and corn on the day. And speaking of that . . ." She rubbed her hands together, pleased as punch to have found a graceful segue out of this unpleasant business. "Could we ask for your help with something? Klara and I could use some strong young backs for a moment."

"Help with what?" Hank asked.

He'd directed the question to his stepmom, but of course it was Abigail Lee who answered. "Oh, nothing serious. Just a little party prep. It won't take a minute!"

With that the vice chairwoman hooked her arm around Klara's waist, marching her around the bookshelf and deeper into the archives. Astrid and Hank exchanged a quick glance before following. Mrs. Lee seemed to know exactly where she was going, weaving between the shelves and cabinets. She turned into a little chapel and stopped, tapping her chin a few times.

"Now, Klara, do you happen to remember where . . . ? Ah,

never mind. There it is." She pointed up at a large rectangular box sitting atop a repurposed mahogany dresser. "If you two could get that down for us, that would be splendid."

"What is it?" Hank asked, grabbing one corner of the box as Astrid took hold of the other. Together they slid it off the dresser and lowered it to the dusty floor.

"Just some decorations for next week," Abigail said, kneeling down to flip back the cardboard flaps. Inside was a neatly packed row of framed photographs—pictures of commemorations past. Every year the townsfolk would gather at the beginning of the party to take a group photo. It was tradition to hang some of the old photos off of the crystal walls. As though the people of Goldsport needed another reminder that time was passing. Astrid pulled the most recent one out of the box.

"Oh, that was a lovely time, wasn't it?" Abigail said. "Klara, dear, I remember that meringue you made. Bliss!"

Astrid examined the photograph. She found herself and Hank off to the side of the gathering, wrapped tightly in each other's arms. They wore frantic expressions of panic and delight. This picture had been taken at the peak of their relationship. Just an hour prior, the two of them had snuck off to the gardens with a stolen bottle of champagne and made a whole bunch of mistakes. Beside her, Hank flushed. He snatched the picture out of Astrid's hands and passed it to Abigail facedown.

"How many of them do you want?" Hank asked, his voice flat.

"Oh, the last ten years should be perfect," Abigail said.

Hank began to leaf through the pictures, not saying another word. With each one he pulled away, everybody in the frame grew younger. Astrid looked on as she and Hank became nothing but friends again. They grew shorter. Their faces filled with baby fat. Astrid watched as her dad's hair returned. She watched Mr. Bushkirk grow slim and Klara's posture straighten.

"Well, now," Abigail said, gathering up her ten pictures and clutching the stacked frames to her chest, "that does it. Would you two mind putting the box back for us?"

"No problem," Hank said.

"And you both . . . You're going to come, aren't you?" Mrs. Lee asked. "To the commemoration, I mean."

"Of course they aren't," Klara snapped. "Abigail, please stop being ridiculous."

This took them all by surprise. Abigail blinked so hard that it looked like she had a bat caught in her eye. "That's . . . Well, that's silliness," she said. "They simply must come. It's commemoration!" She looked from Astrid to Hank, giving them her most forceful smile. "Do say you'll come."

Neither of them answered. Klara, too, remained silent. She only stood there, examining Hank's bruise.

"Yes, of course you will!" Mrs. Lee all but shouted. "It's settled, then. We'll see you at the party. If not sooner."

And with that she again hooked a bony arm around Klara's waist, and the two beat a hasty retreat out of the archives.

• • •

Hank watched them go. Once the ladies were safely out of earshot, he said, "You know, she's the only person in this place that I feel sorry for."

Astrid only nodded. She didn't think Klara had done much to earn her stepson's sympathy. The woman had always been useless when it came to getting between Hank and his father. Worse than useless—she had made herself blind to it. Though it was hard to tell how much of that was her fault. And if Hank could forgive Klara, who the hell was Astrid to hold a grudge against her? He was the one with the busted face.

Hank squatted back down on the floor and continued to leaf through the pictures Abigail had left behind. He and Astrid became ever younger in the photographs, shrinking from little children, to toddlers, to babies. There was a younger version of Klara, gazing down at Hank, frail as a bundle of sticks in her arms. Then he turned over another photograph, and there were suddenly more kids. Eleven little people, swaddled up in fleece and held close by beaming parents. There was Hank's twin sister. There was his older brother, sitting atop Mr. Bushkirk's shoulders. It was the generation that could have been but never was. By the following commemoration, the vex would have killed all but Hank and Astrid. He lingered over this shot for a moment.

"Damn," he said.

"Yup."

"They had no idea what was coming."

"Nope."

Nothing else to say. Astrid reached into the box as well and turned to the photo from the previous year. Then she, Hank, and most of the other children disappeared altogether. Another year into the past and even his older brother vanished. Only their parents remained, clutching champagne flutes in the same outstretched hands that would later hold children. His mother was there. His father looked truly happy. They all beamed for the camera.

"Simpler times," Hank said.

"You mean before us?"

"Sort of," he said. "Before *The First Voice* told them about the vex. Just look at them here." He pulled the picture all the way out of the box and held it close. "They're not hoping for much more than a full belly, a walk in the gardens, and maybe a game or two in the afternoons. That's the definition of a good day." Hank snorted.

Slowly his expression soured.

"Not that anything has changed," he said. He slotted the picture frame back into the box, setting it down so hard that the glass cracked.

"What do you mean?"

"I mean it's the same today," he said. "Why do they even bother holding the commemoration? Or the Sunday picnics? It's not like those days are much different from other days. It's all just eat, drink, and relax. Experience as little displeasure as possible while they all get one day older. One day closer to dying."

Astrid couldn't say she disagreed. Still, she was surprised to hear the words come out of Hank's mouth. She reached out and took him by the shoulder.

"That's not really fair," she said. "You're forgetting about sleeping in. And badminton. And the book club."

"And lobster cookouts," Hank said, rising somewhat out of his anger.

"Lobsters, totally. With rehydrated butter."

"God, I hate that stuff."

"Of course you do," Astrid said. "On account of it tastes like snot."

Idly, she reached into the box and flipped back another photograph and another. The investors grew ever younger. "I don't think they actually like it either," she went on. "They just eat it so that they can remember real butter."

"Real butter must have been pretty great, then," Hank said.

"Real ice cream, too," Astrid said.

She continued looking through the frames, going further and further back into the history of Goldsport—getting closer and closer to the world before. It was actually kind of mesmerizing, watching all of her neighbors age in reverse. Watching her own parents fall back in love. There were Ria and Amblin in the center of the gathering, clutching hands and mashing faces. There were Ria and Amblin clinking glasses with arms interlocked. There were Ria and Amblin, awkward flirty teenage friends standing slightly apart. There were Ria and Amblin, little more than children themselves, ketchup on their pointed chins, held lovingly about the shoulders by their own parents.

And then, suddenly, Ria disappeared.

Astrid had come to the last picture. She pulled it out to get a better look. Still, she couldn't find her mom. Actually, as Astrid investigated the picture, she realized that she could hardly find any of the investors in the gathered crowd. There was Ronnie Gold, her grandpa. And there was Klara, looking beautiful and severe in an evening gown. But where was Mr. Collins? Where were Abigail Lee and the other investors? And who was that little sandy-haired girl grinning gamely beside a young Amblin? The more Astrid searched, the more she realized the entire photo was filled with unfamiliar faces. It was as though Astrid's whole town had been replaced by a group of strangers.

"What the . . . ?" Hank, too, was puzzling over the picture.

Astrid held the beginnings of a thought in her mind. It was in that place before you can even recite the words to yourself in your own head. She stood up from the floor, knees shaky, and traced her way through the dusty aisles. Hank followed her. They returned to the giant map tacked up above the organ. Goldsport glowed—a bright circle painted in the most hopeful shade of yellow.

Astrid climbed back up onto the organist's bench and ran her fingers over Goldsport. She could feel the subtle elevation of the paint. She worked her thumbnail under the raised edge, and the yellow circle began to crumble and bend. It came away in dusty flakes. There were letters beneath the paint. Words. Astrid knew what they would be before she could even spell them out.

Port Emory.

CHAPTER 20

Thank the Investors

AT FIRST ASTRID FELT BLANK.

Her legs carried her out of the archives and down the glimmering greenway. She and Hank passed through the dairy gardens, where the milk goats were bleating in their cages. They crossed the plaza, where Abigail and Klara had rejoined the commemoration committee to hang up the old photographs. Hank yanked on his bee suit, and together they stepped out of the harbor hatch, through the stinking curtains dripping with quiet, and back onto the north shore.

Minutes later they were at Ria's house. Astrid opened the door, and it clattered loudly against the inner wall. She hadn't meant to slam it.

"Mom!"

There was no answer. Astrid checked the pegs on the wall of her mother's quiet room and saw that her suit and waders were missing. She returned to the veranda and scanned the tidal flats. Ria was out there in her bee suit, digging for

clams in the shallows. A few singers circled about her, trac-
ing streaks of purple light across the water, skimming like
dragonflies.

Astrid and Hank headed for the flats, wading into the
outgoing tide. Ria heard their splashing and straightened up.
She must have realized that something was wrong, because
she dropped her spading fork and bucket, which bobbed
like a little boat upon the water.

"Astrid," she called. "What happened? Is it your father?"

"Eliza used to live here," Astrid said.

"What?"

"The wicked woman," Astrid said. "The woman Henry
Bushkirk shot. She used to live here." Astrid had reached
her mother. The outgoing tide soaked through her jeans,
pulling her gently toward the open water.

"Used to live where? What do you—"

Astrid cut her mother off, throwing a hand back in the
direction of the greenway. "This is Port Emory. Goldsport
is Port Emory."

Even as she put this into words for the first time, it dawned
on Astrid how obvious it should have been. The ruined fire
station, the vacant church, the antique houses, their quaint
little fleet of lobster boats. These could only be the bones
of an older town, upon which the flesh of Goldsport hung.
The glass, the gardens, the pressure-ventilated underground
grocery—these were nothing but adornments. How could
Astrid not have seen this before?

"I don't know what you're talking about, but . . ." Ria

trailed off, apparently unable to finish her sentence. She seemed to crumple within her bee suit, as though somebody had pulled a plug and let out her air. Then she gave her head a hard shake. "Sorry," Ria said. "Old habits."

"Is it true?" Hank asked.

"It is," Ria said. For a moment she offered nothing more than that. Then she reached down beneath the water and groped about for her spading fork. When she found it, she straightened and retrieved her floating bucket. "Who told you?" she finally asked.

"Nobody," Astrid said, flicking the word at her mother like a dart. "We had to find out in the archives."

"I would have," her mother said. "I wanted to, a few years ago. But your father thought it was too early."

"But . . . why keep it a secret at all?" Hank asked.

Ria stared into her bucket, as though the right words might be down there with the shining clams. "Everybody in town would rather forget about Port Emory," she finally said. Her voice was so small that it was almost drowned out by the singers. Astrid had never in her whole life heard her mom sound like that.

"Why?" Astrid pressed.

Ria looked up at her with an almost dumbfounded expression. "Because we are ashamed. And we don't like feeling ashamed," she said, as though this were the simplest thing in the world. "It's not a story that we look good in. So we don't tell it." Ria's gaze fell back down upon the outgoing tide. "Or, at least . . . we don't tell all of it."

"What are you even saying?" Astrid felt as confused and disoriented as she had a few minutes ago, back in the archives. She couldn't imagine what her neighbors—what her parents—could have done that they needed to feel so terrible about. They might have annoyed Astrid out of her skull 70 percent of the time, but they weren't bad people. They were clever, and thoughtful, and diligent. They had taken responsibility for themselves, and worked hard, and made a home after the end of the world. These were the exact kind of people who were supposed to look good in stories.

It was Hank who finally put it into words. "We stole it from them, didn't we?" There was a kind of quiet dawning in his voice, as though suddenly everything made complete sense. But to Astrid, things had never made less sense.

"*We* stole it." Ria tapped her chest with her free hand. "You two didn't steal anything. You weren't even born when it happened. Tell me . . ." She looked from Hank to Astrid. "How much of it have you figured out?"

"We don't know," Astrid said.

"All right," Ria said. "I'll start from the beginning, then."

Together the three of them waded out of the shallows and returned, dripping, to shore. But rather than lead them all back to her house, Astrid's mother instead headed for a long snarl of driftwood that jutted from the sand. She sat, motioning for Astrid and Hank to join her. From there they had a view of the entire harbor, with Puffin Island glinting in the distance. The shattered north shore extended off to their left, while the glass-covered south shore lay to their right. At their backs rose the forested hills, the crown of the watchtower just visible above the treetops.

"All of this," Ria said, stretching a gloved hand from the north shore to the south, "used to be called Port Emory. That was before the wickedness fell and before any of us lived here. I'm afraid that I don't know much about what it was like back then. It used to be a real fishing town. But that was a long time ago. By the time the wickedness came around, Port Emory was really just for tourists. People— rich people, mostly—who would come here for a few weeks in the summer and rent out the grand old houses."

Here Ria paused, her face going sour beneath her bonnet. "Ronnie Gold, your grandpa," she continued, "was one of these tourists. So was your father, though he was just a little boy at the time. They used to come here every summer."

"But Dad was born here," Astrid said, almost defensively.

"He wasn't," Ria said, snapping her head from one side to the other. "None of us were. Other than you and Hank, I mean."

Again she reached out to point from one end of Goldsport to the other. "You see how the beach is shaped like a crescent moon? You see how"—Ria turned, pointing behind them—"how the hills stretch all the way from the north shore to the south? That's what sold your grandpa on Port Emory. On one side you've got a quiet ocean, with a hidden little harbor. And on the other you've got steep hills and a bog filled with mosquitoes. Your grandpa Ronnie decided that this would be a good place to try to ride it out. So he started calling up rich friends of his, to see if they wanted in. To see if they could help him build what he needed—if they could help him invest."

Ria bit down hard on that last word, as though she meant to damage it. She stayed like that for a moment, teeth clenched. When she spoke again, her voice took on a new edge. "My parents were two of those investors. I was very young, but I remember. We shopped around, visiting a few sanctuaries. We went to one high in the mountains, outside of Denver. We went to one built underground, in New Mexico. It was almost like shopping for a vacation house. But in the end my mom and dad decided that Port Emory was the best of the lot. The only problem was that the town was already full of people. But that was minor. Getting rid of them wouldn't be nearly as complicated as digging the grocery or finding the right kind of glass for the greenway."

"That doesn't make any sense," Astrid said. "You can't just steal a town."

"Can't you?" Ria asked, her voice sharpening more and more. "Says who?"

Astrid hesitated. "This was before the wickedness," she said, less certain. "There were supposed to be rules."

"Of course there were rules," Ria said. "Books upon books of them." With each breath, Astrid's mom seemed to be slipping out of sadness and into a well-worn bitterness. "Rules written by people like your grandfather. People like

Mr. Bushkirk. By them and for them. The rules didn't stop it. The rules helped."

At this point Ria had gotten herself worked up enough that she stood. But there wasn't anywhere to go, so she just stayed there, boots cratering the wet sand. "At first the investors tried to buy up all of the houses," she said, turning to face Astrid and Hank. "Nobody wanted to sell, but they tried all the same. They offered more than the houses were worth. Your grandpa . . . He always used to remind us of that. Whenever we would fight about what happened, Ronnie Gold would trot it out. 'We made them a generous offer,' he'd say. As though that made it all okay."

Ria's boots dug deeper into the sand and came upon something hard. She kicked at it, revealing a chunk of greenway glass about the size and shape of a piece of pie. The edges were rounded, and the glass itself had turned opaque. Ria reached down and grabbed it. She gripped the glass tight in her gloved fist.

"In the end Ronnie Gold offered to share the town with them. The people of Port Emory were frightened too. Everything on the news was so terrifying, and the idea of Ronnie Gold swooping in and paying to build a great big wall and a bunch of glass domes and tubes sounded good to them. So they signed over everything. The agreement was that as soon as construction finished, they'd be allowed to come back."

"But then the wickedness fell," Hank said.

"Yes," Ria said. "Quicker than anybody thought was

possible. When the people of Port Emory tried to come home, they found the wall that they'd been promised, only they were on the wrong side of it. And there was a tank guarding the gates. In the old world, they could have gotten their homes back. The courts promised to help them sort it out, in a year or two. But the old world was already slipping away. The courts themselves didn't last a year. By then Port Emory was already gone."

"But how did they—" Astrid stumbled, not just over the sentence but also over the thoughts behind it. They seemed too horrible to consider all at once. "Where did those people go?"

"Different places," her mother said. "A few headed across the bay and into Canada. Others tried moving inland, up toward Baxter, to make a stand in the forest. And the rest settled on Puffin Island."

"Eliza's family," Hank said.

"Maybe," Ria said. "Probably." Then she fell silent. It seemed to Astrid that, for the first time since they'd cornered her mother out on the tidal flats, Ria was once again debating whether or not to say something.

"What is it?"

Her mother only shrugged. "They did this," she said.

"What do you mean?" Hank asked. "Did what?"

"This," Ria said, holding up the piece of greenway glass still clenched in her gloved fist. She cast her free hand in a circle, indicating the entire ruin of the north shore. "The attack," Ria said. "It wasn't the wicked. It was the people from Port Emory, trying to come home. And it was us, trying not to let them. It was us, trying to keep what we'd stolen. It was us, being worse than wicked."

With that Ria wheeled back and chucked the piece of greenway glass out across the beach. It landed in the shallows, slipping in almost without a splash. Astrid felt the cold chunk of glass settling down into her own stomach. Pressing at her insides with hard, rounded edges. She couldn't shake the image of the sandy-haired girl. The child grinning beside Amblin in that old photograph. Eliza. Eliza who had been put out of her home. Eliza who had fallen wicked. Eliza whom they'd shot and burnt to cinders. Which of the investors had taken her house? Who was sleeping in Eliza's bedroom today? It may as well have been Astrid—the theft spread quick as wickedness, infecting everybody who touched it. There was no immunity from this.

Astrid stood bolt upright from the driftwood. Her skin felt hot.

"Are any of them still out there?" Hank asked. "On Puffin Island?"

"I don't know," Ria said. "I didn't think so. A lot of them died in the attack, and the ones who didn't wanted to get as far away from here as possible. But then the lighthouse turned on, and . . ."

"You don't think it's just old batteries?" Hank asked.

"I don't know," Ria repeated. "It might be."

Astrid took a single step forward. Her legs felt amazingly solid beneath her. "Then we have to go and see," she said.

PART IV

THE VEX

CHAPTER 21

The Baby and the Book

THE NEXT TWO DAYS PASSED SLOWLY FOR NATALIE AND HER mother. They stayed locked in the lighthouse the entire time, safe for now behind the storm walls. They ate sparingly, drank all they wanted, and spoke hardly a word—holding out hope that Natalie's wicked grandfather might forget that they were in there. Though he never did. And by the time the baby came, it didn't matter anymore. Even the puffins on the far side of the island could hear her mother screaming.

It happened on the morning of the third day. Natalie's grandfather danced about the lighthouse walls, reveling in the sounds. He understood what was about to happen. "I'm going to be a grandpa!" he chanted, perhaps forgetting that he already was one. "I'm going to live forever!" The old man sang himself hoarse, and it was to the sound of his voice that the baby was born.

A baby sister.

"Eva," their mother named her. Natalie couldn't tell if she'd been thinking of this name for a long time, or if it came to her on the spot.

Other than the fact that they were locked up inside the lighthouse, everything went as they'd rehearsed. This seemed a miracle to Natalie—both the birth itself and the fact that nothing went wrong. She wiped her new sister dry and cleaned out her tiny mouth and nose. She cut the umbilical cord with a pair of shears salvaged from the bunkhouse. Then she draped Eva across her mother—across their mother—and pulled the duvet up around them both. It was everything they'd prepared for.

But there were other things—things you couldn't prepare for. Surprises big and small. The way Eva's skin felt on Natalie's fingers. Or the way her arms and legs were all curled up, like pink fiddleheads. Or the striking strangeness of her features—her little nose, and lips, and eyes. It was only the fifth face Natalie had ever seen in real life, counting her own reflection. An entirely new face. An entirely new person. Natalie found herself overwhelmed by the thought. She felt as though she might float away on it.

It wasn't an entirely pleasant floating. It was a light-headed, dizzy, nauseous floating. "She isn't really here yet." Natalie whispered the words out loud, trying to pull herself back down to the floor. Trying to calm herself. "This isn't permanent until she has the vex." Her own feeble attempt to keep from getting attached. After all, there was a real chance that Eva wouldn't make it. The vex could very well kill her.

Just because their mother was in denial about this didn't mean Natalie was. And if Eva didn't survive, how could the two of them possibly go on?

As if in answer to this, the baby began to cry. Tiny as she was, she had a set of lungs on her. She wailed so loud that their grandfather stopped singing.

"Oh—oh—oh," he called from down below, "can I have her, please?"

How he guessed that the baby was a girl, Natalie couldn't say.

Natalie's mother got stronger over the following days. The more she ate, the more her appetite came back. Soon she was licking clean tins of salmon and peas and chugging water straight from the lip of the jerrican. The baby, too, seemed healthy and strong. Whenever Eva wasn't screaming, or sleeping, or blazing through their dwindling supply of cloth diapers, she was nursing with an intense, squint-eyed abandon. It might have been Natalie's imagination, but the baby looked bigger on the second day than she had on the first. Bigger still on the third.

But her mom's ankle wasn't getting any better. The bruise had spread down the foot and up the shin, like a horrible purple mold. They tried fashioning a splint out of chair legs and torn strips of bedding, but still the ankle would bear no weight. It soon became clear to them both that walking wasn't in her mother's immediate future. Not tomorrow. Not in a week. Maybe, depending on how the broken bones healed, not ever again. Meanwhile, if Eva didn't get the vex within the next few days, she'd miss her chance. Natalie knew without being told that she and her sister would be heading to the mainland alone.

"There's a place where your father and I used to go," her mother said. "A little cabin about five miles up the coast from Goldsport." She grabbed a worn notebook off of the nightstand, flipped it open, and began sketching out a rough map. "It's safe. You can't see the cabin from the water, but there's a jetty," she said, marking the location with an *X*.

"Is it deep enough for me to tie off?" Natalie meant their lobster boat, which sat rusting in the shadow of the lighthouse.

"It is, but I don't want you to take that boat," her mother said. "Your grandpa will hear the motor, and he still has that rifle. The people in Goldsport might notice it too. Better use the kayak. You can come and go quietly."

The word "quiet" must have been offensive to Eva's ears, because it was at this moment that she tumbled out of her nap and into a full-throated fit of bawling. Seconds later her grandpa began to harmonize from down below, screaming his own head off. Natalie's mom lifted Eva up and began to comfort her. Then she thought better of it. She held the screaming baby out for Natalie to take.

"You do it," she said.

Natalie hesitated. Holding the baby still felt vaguely unnatural to her.

"Go on," her mother said. "You're going to need the practice."

So she took Eva. She rocked her, and bounced her, and made little kissing sounds. None of it worked. The baby only screamed louder. From outside, her wicked grandfather laughed. "Okay, okay, you win—I can't get that high!" he called.

"I think she's hungry," Natalie said. She made to pass the baby back to their mom.

"What?" Her mother had already turned her attention back to the notebook and the map that she was so carefully sketching. "No, honey. I won't be there to feed Eva when you two are on the mainland. Better figure out a bottle."

She meant the old formula that Natalie had salvaged from the bunkhouse, vacuum-sealed in a heavy-duty plastic bag. Her parents had found it on the mainland years ago. The formula inside was specially treated to last for years, and her dad had drunk it a few times without getting sick. All the same, Natalie hesitated.

"Is it still good?"

"Try it," her mother said without looking up. "If it's turned, you'll know."

So, with Eva screaming herself purple, Natalie set about mixing up a bottle. She tipped the white powder into some water and shook it vigorously. She held it under her armpit for a few minutes to warm it. Natalie gave the formula a taste and found it sweet, and distinctly gross. But it wasn't rancid. She tried putting the rubber nipple up to her little sister's mouth. Eva latched on to it at once, and a little bit of the formula spilled out at the corners of her lips. Then she pulled away, coughing and smacking her gums. She'd hardly swallowed any.

"You two will get the hang of it," her mother said, entirely unconcerned. She finished the map, holding it up so that Natalie could see. It showed the entire coastline in surprising detail, from the south shore of Goldsport up to the old Canadian border.

"This is Highway 191," she said, tapping on a double-edged line that ran inland, parallel to the coast. "It's pretty beat-up, but you can't miss it. If you reach the highway, that means you've gone too far. Turn around and look for the cabin again. I don't want you straying from there. The woods out back will have all the singers you need. And if you get delayed for any reason, you'll have a place to spend the night."

With that her mother closed the notebook and tucked it into Natalie's bag. "That's where I brought you," she said. "When you got the vex."

It seemed like she meant this as a kind of encouragement. But Natalie didn't find the thought of herself as a baby, covered in bloodsucking singers, to be all that comforting. "How did you know?" she asked.

"Know what?"

Natalie hesitated. Somehow she'd never been able to ask this question before. But now she had a practical reason to. Now the occasion finally demanded it.

"How did you know the vex wouldn't kill me?"

"I—I didn't know," her mother stammered. "I believed

that you'd survive. But I didn't know for sure. How could
I have?"

"Dad thought it would kill me. He said—"

"Well, it didn't," her mother snapped. "Your father was
wrong."

For a time the only sound in the lighthouse was Eva
finally, half-heartedly, gumming the bottle. Natalie's mother
closed her eyes. When she opened them again, they seemed
to glow all the brighter.

"There's a chance you might see him out there," she said.
"Your dad."

"I know," Natalie said.

"If you do . . ." She trailed off. There were so many ways
the sentence could have ended. Like: *Tell him I never want
to see him again.* Or: *Tell him to come home.* Instead, her
mother simply said, "Hide."

It was only later, as Natalie studied the map drawn in the
notebook, that she realized what she was holding. She turned
a page and found, to her surprise, that it was filled with
writing. The penmanship was careful, precise. She turned
another and found more still. Then it struck her. This was
her grandfather's diary. This was his "book for writing,"
the one he'd seemed so desperate to find back when she'd
raided the bunkhouse.

What an odd thought it was. Her wicked grandfather
keeping a diary. Settling down to write about his day every
night before drifting off to sleep. Natalie had been sure at

the time that his rant about the book was nonsense. But here it was, sitting open in her hands. The entries were strange. Some were simply descriptions of the meals her grandfather had eaten. Others were about interesting things he'd observed from his high windows. For one of the days, all he'd written was: "I saw a whale!" The rest of that page was filled with nothing but carefully etched exclamation points. Another entry contained a surprisingly beautiful drawing of a puffin, while still another included a list of people the old man intended to kill. Natalie's entire family appeared on the list, along with about a hundred other names that she didn't recognize. For all she knew, those people were already dead. Or maybe they'd never even existed.

It didn't feel right to keep the diary from him. Natalie tore out the map and folded it up for safekeeping. Then she grabbed the pencil and wrote an entry of her own.

> Dear Grandpa,
> I found your book for writing. I want to give it back to you, so that you can keep it up. I hope you don't mind, but I read some of the entries. I'm really glad that I found it. I hope you're okay down there. I love you.
>
> > Your granddaughter,
> > Natalie

She thought about it a moment more before adding something at the bottom. A warning. Natalie didn't know if her grandfather would be able to understand it, but still, it was only fair to tell him.

> Please stay out of my way, Grandpa. If you
> see me outside of the lighthouse, please keep your
> distance. I don't want to hurt you. But I will if I
> have to.

When she was done, she carefully edged toward the shattered window and tossed the diary outside. The cover opened in the breeze, and the pages fluttered. It seemed to glide for a moment. Then the diary fell straight down, like a bird shot out of the sky.

CHAPTER 22

Across the Bay

NATALIE SET OFF THAT AFTERNOON WITH A BAG OF SUPPLIES over her shoulder and Eva in her arms. It was a rushed departure—they'd planned to leave the following morning, but the conditions became too good to pass up. A heavy fog fell upon the island, thick and dark as a thundercloud. And Eva had nursed herself silly, falling into a deep sleep. It meant that Natalie would have places to hide and at least a temporary guarantee that the baby would stay quiet. Her odds weren't likely to get better than that.

She crept down the spiral staircase, pausing for a moment by the iron door to listen. The last she'd heard of her grandfather was an animated, one-sided conversation coming from somewhere around the cemetery. Now there was nothing but silence.

"Grandpa," she whispered.

No answer.

Natalie unlatched the iron door as quietly as she could

and slipped outside. The fog was wet as a damp towel upon her skin, so thick that it was almost hard to breathe. Natalie blinked into the white emptiness. All she could see were the stones immediately around her, merging into the fog. She stayed still, listening. She heard only the waves and a distant murmur of nesting seabirds.

Natalie locked the door behind her and tossed the keys inside through the food slot. No going back now. They kept their last remaining kayak down there, hidden in a nook between the boulders. No one else would ever have been able to find it in this weather, but she'd memorized every inch of Puffin Island. She stepped deliberately, avoiding patches of gravel and wobbly stones. Her boots felt weightless, and she moved without making a sound.

Then something made her stop.

Natalie couldn't be sure if she'd actually heard a noise or just felt one. But there was something—an unsettled quality to the air. She looked all around, but she couldn't see so much as a shadow in the fog. Had she just imagined it?

"I see you out there!"

Her grandfather's voice shattered the silence. It seemed to come from far away, faint in the thick fog. He must have still been down by the cemetery, talking to the birds, or the graves, or the rocks.

"I found you!" he called again. "Don't go anywhere until I get there!"

Natalie felt her panic rising and had to force herself not to sprint back to the lighthouse. She remained completely still, locking her knees to keep them from shaking. *It's impossible*, she told herself. *If you can't see him, then he definitely can't see you.*

"Natalie, please tell me that you brought the baby," he said. "Which of us do you think can throw her farther?"

Shit.

Frantic, she searched the fog again. Natalie began to hear the jagged crunch of little stones—somebody in the distance, moving toward her. But it made no sense. How could he possibly see her from so far away when all she could see was a wall of milky fog? The wicked man was ancient, and her eyes were much better than his.

Her eyes.

What an idiot—she might as well have been walking around with a pair of purple lanterns. Natalie shut them, sealing herself up in darkness. In an instant the sound of footsteps stopped.

"Oh my," her grandfather said, awed. "I was looking right at you, and then you disappeared!"

Natalie listened. With her eyes closed, it was easier to tell exactly where his voice was coming from. Her grandpa was about fifty yards ahead of her, on the path that ran the length of the island.

"You have got to teach me that, Natalie," her grandpa called. "I want to be invisible too. No one will ever see me coming!" He giggled at the thought. "Think of all the fun I'd have."

For a moment Natalie considered rushing him. She'd

have to open her eyes again, but it might not matter. If she set Eva down, she could probably get to the old man before he managed to take a shot. Though even if she did, then what? Instead, she quietly knelt into a squat and placed her free hand upon the ground. She groped around, plucking up a stone about the size of an egg. Natalie stood, turned her body a few degrees, and threw the stone as far as she could. Seconds later it landed with a sharp *clack*.

"I love this game!" her grandfather said, clapping. "How did you get behind me?"

With that he began to scramble around, no doubt swiping at the fog in search of her. Natalie turned her back to the sound and opened her eyes a crack. When she was sure that he couldn't see her, she doubled back in the direction she'd come, circling around to the kayak the long way. She could still hear her grandfather when she reached it.

"You need to give me a hint, at least!" he pleaded. "The rule is that when I say 'Marco,' you have to say 'Polo.'"

Natalie shifted the baby to her left arm, silently begging her not to wake up. Eva only dipped her chin, snuggled deeper into her coil of blankets, and sighed. Natalie grabbed the front of the kayak and dragged it into the water. She pulled her compass from the supply bag, stashing everything else in the day hatch. Then she lowered both herself and her sister into the cockpit. It was a one-person kayak, so Natalie had to prop Eva between her legs.

She pressed the blade of her paddle against the rocks below and pushed off. The kayak glided out across the water, away from Puffin Island. The shore disappeared into the mist behind them. Natalie used the compass to set a course northeast across the bay and paddled out blindly into the fog. Within moments she was riding the rough channel current. Eva's eyes blinked open as the kayak began to bounce across the choppy sea. One of the waves hit them at a bad angle and sent a splash of cold water crashing into the cockpit. It soaked Natalie's pants and landed square on Eva's little forehead. The baby was wide awake in an instant, coughing and sputtering. For a moment she just stared, dumb with shock. Then, clear as a bell, Natalie heard her baby sister's imagined voice in her head.

Oh. Oh, hell no.

Eva began to scream. Natalie pulled the baby to her chest, trying to comfort her. But Eva would not be comforted. She was wet, and she was cold, and she was a baby.

"I can hear you out there!" their grandfather called merrily from the unseen shore. "Why didn't you tell me you were leaving in a boat?"

Natalie didn't answer. She just set Eva back down and began to paddle. The baby screamed the whole time.

"I want you to come back," their grandfather called, "and take me with you! I could bring you into town. I could show you where our family used to live!" He fell silent for a little while, racking his brain for a winning argument.

"I bet the people in Goldsport could help us shut that baby up!" he offered, his voice bright with hope.

Natalie ignored him. Puffin Island fell farther and

farther behind them, and as it did, her grandfather's shouts faded to nothing. With time, even Eva quieted down. But she wouldn't go back to sleep.

It took hours to cross the bay, and by the time Natalie finally spotted the jetty it was nearly dusk. She was numb, seasick, and chilled through with sweat. Eva wasn't doing so well either. The infant had emptied one of the bottles of formula on the trip over and had then made a surprisingly horrifying mess of her swaddling blankets. Unlike her first few bowel movements, this one stank. There'd been no changing her in the kayak, so the first thing Natalie had to do after tying off was sort out the mess. She rinsed the soiled blankets in the shallows and pulled a fresh set from the day hatch. All the while, Eva seemed to glare up at her reproachfully.

"None of this is my fault," Natalie told her, exhausted.

And what, it's my fault? There was Eva's voice again, ringing in Natalie's imagination. It sounded high-pitched, alive with fury.

"Nobody said that."

Well. You implied it.

Natalie smiled. It wasn't exactly a choice—hearing her baby sister's voice in her head like this. She'd been doing it her whole life with the puffins and seals and terns on her island. Now the voices sort of just came whether she wanted them to or not.

She wrapped her baby sister in a clean blanket. Eva

squirmed, blinking up at her. It struck Natalie, in that moment, that if the vex worked, this would be one of the last times she'd see the true color of her sister's eyes. Soon they would turn purple, just like Natalie's, pulsing with little shards of light. But for now they were a glossy dark brown. They looked like wood after a rainstorm.

And if the vex didn't work?

Natalie chased the thought from her head.

"Come on," she said, tapping her sister's well-wrapped tummy. "Let's go find those singers." She grabbed the rest of her supplies from the day hatch and headed down the jetty with her sister. Just as her mother had promised, she found an overgrown path that led to a little cabin. The building was about the same size as her bunkhouse back on Puffin Island, though it was in much worse shape. It was rotten and half swallowed into an ocean of dead ferns and brown moss. The door stood stiffly ajar on rusted hinges, and greasy tarpaulins hung over the broken windows.

Better be careful, Eva whispered.

Good advice. Natalie approached one of the windows and listened for sounds of movement inside. Hearing nothing, she continued to the open door and peered through. All she saw was a dark, empty room. The walls were covered with pen-and-ink graffiti of travelers come and gone. There were boot prints on the floor, but they looked old. For all Natalie knew, they could have been left by her own father, months ago.

Eva began to fuss. Could she be hungry again already?

"Cool it," Natalie said.

Of course, this had no effect.

"All right," she said. "Go crazy. Nobody's here anyway."

With Eva writhing in her arms, Natalie began to poke through the rest of the cabin. She found a bedroom with an old stone fireplace and a pair of metal cots with gummy mattresses. She found a bathroom with a shattered porcelain sink and a roll of petrified toilet paper still hanging from the dispenser. Other than that, the cabin was totally empty and silent. Come to think of it, everything was totally silent.

That was strange.

Natalie carried Eva back outside and stood in the forest. According to her mother, these woods should have been teeming with singers, but now that Natalie was listening for them, she couldn't hear anything. Not a single note or hum. And it wasn't just singers. Natalie strained her ears, but there was no birdsong. No squirrels. Not even the rustle of wind passing through leaves. Natalie looked at the canopy and saw that the trees above stood bare as winter, their branches sickly and brittle.

Had there been a fire? She walked slowly around the cabin, but she couldn't see any sign of burning. Besides, a forest fire would have burnt the cabin itself to cinders. Instead it looked like everything around her had simply wilted and died. She tried heading out even farther, but after several minutes of walking she still hadn't discovered a single living plant or heard even one singer. It was almost funny. First their plan to turn off the lighthouse had gone remarkably bad, and now she couldn't even find singers on the infested mainland.

"You must be bad luck," Natalie said, brushing her finger across the very tip of Eva's nose.

Sure, her baby sister said. *Because everything was so perfect before I was born.*

"Fair."

Natalie stood there in the woods for a moment, considering her options. If she walked far enough, she was sure to find a swarm, but it was already getting late. She didn't know this coast and didn't like the idea of trying to read a compass in the dark by the light of her own purple eyes. So she decided to return to the cabin for the night. First thing the next morning, she and Eva would go out and hunt for singers. With any luck they'd be back on Puffin Island by lunchtime.

The sooner the better, Eva said. *I'm starving and I hate you.*

"You sound like our grandpa," Natalie answered.

CHAPTER 23

Reggie

IT WAS A ROUGH NIGHT. NATALIE WAS IN AND OUT OF SLEEP, waking more times than she could count to the sound of Eva's crying. One time the baby wanted to eat, finishing up a half bottle of hastily prepared formula before drifting off again. Another time she needed to be changed—Natalie tossed the dirty cloth diaper into the far corner of the bedroom, too exhausted to go through the work of washing and drying it. And a few other times it seemed as though Eva simply wanted to practice her hollering. So it was a relief when Natalie finally awoke the next morning to warm daylight and the soft, soothing sound of her father's voice drifting in through the window.

No.

That wasn't right.

She lay motionless on the cot, blinking at the mold on the ceiling. Was this a dream? She'd never had one before—a side effect of the vex—so she couldn't tell. It took a moment to remember exactly where she was—on a cot, in a cabin, on the mainland. Eva lay nestled beside her. And outside, someone was speaking. Not her father, as she'd first imagined, but a stranger. No, wrong again—strangers. They were standing just outside.

"I don't know what your problem is. Let's just junk the battery."

"My problem is that the battery is fine."

"Miranda agrees with me that it's not."

"Well, two people can be wrong about the same thing."

Natalie sat up. She glanced down at her sister, lying in a shallow divot atop the mattress. Eva was wide-eyed— terrifyingly awake. Her mouth opened and closed. She was a little alarm bell that could go off any second. Outside, the two men were still talking, splitting the air to pieces with their strange voices.

"Miranda!" one of them hollered.

"What?" cried a woman from a short distance away.

"What do you think is wrong with the disperser?"

"Battery!"

"Miranda is an entomologist," grumbled one of the two men.

"Reggie thinks that you're full of shit, Miranda!"

"That's not what I said!"

Natalie's heart was pounding so hard that she was actually swaying back and forth. She slipped off of the cot as slowly as she could to keep the springs from creaking. Then she scooped up Eva and crept toward one of the draped windows. Pulling back a corner of the tarp, she saw a pair of tall figures standing in the wilted yard behind the cabin. They were wearing the strangest bee suits Natalie had ever seen—bright yellow and shiny like wet rubber. The suits were capped with boxy, octagonal bonnets and black-tinted visors. She couldn't make out either of their faces.

"Listen, you can fiddle with the disperser all you want," one of them was going on, "but if it isn't back up and running by noon, I'm putting in another battery. The singers are getting closer, Reggie. I saw one back at the road."

"One? Well, we don't have any time to spare, then."

There was a sudden banging on the front door. Every muscle in Natalie's body tightened. She quickly dropped the tarp back into place and pulled away from the window.

Another person in an identical yellow bee suit and tinted bonnet stepped into the cabin. This must be the woman—Miranda. She had a backpack slung over her shoulder and a belt hanging low on her hips. Attached to the belt were a utility knife, a square radio-looking thing, and a holstered pistol. Natalie couldn't tell, through that tinted visor, if the stranger had noticed her yet.

"Don't be an ass, Reggie," the woman called out, scraping mud and dead leaves off of her boots. Then she turned to the wall and began to hang up her gear, unfastening the snaps on her tinted bonnet. She peeled it off and shook her head in the air. Her hair was buzzed short, save a long pony-tail sprouting out of the back of her skull.

"Just fix it, would you, please?"

Natalie took a sliding step toward the back of the bedroom, out of view of the doorway. It was a small miracle that they hadn't been noticed yet. It was an even bigger miracle that Eva was staying quiet—she must have worn herself out from her night of hollering. But if Natalie had learned anything in the last few days, it was that tired babies can be the loudest babies. She had to get them out of here now.

There was a second window in the back of the room, opening out onto a patch of dead ferns. Natalie kept her movements slow and smooth, grabbing her backpack, sitting on the windowsill, and turning so that both legs dangled out. Then she and Eva slipped through the window and into the yard. On her way down Natalie remembered the dirty cloth diaper that she'd thrown into the corner of the bedroom. But that mistake was written in stone now—there was no going back for it.

Meanwhile, out front, the strangers had begun to raise their voices.

"I always fix it," the man named Reggie protested. "When the hell do I not fix it?"

Natalie pressed her back against the cabin wall. It was all happening so quickly, her brain had yet to catch up with the rest of her. How long had she been awake? Ten minutes? Fifty seconds? Inside of the cabin there were now more voices—four or five, by her count. Natalie heard boots on the hardwood and a general commotion of complaints and sighs. The cot springs squealed as somebody sat down in the bedroom, right where Natalie had been only seconds before.

Would they be able to feel the warmth in the mattress?

Would they see, or even just smell, the diaper?

Would they hear the tremendous, deafening sound of her heart?

"I hate it here," someone said.

"Life of a searcher," Miranda answered. "Look on the bright side. We have just five more months before we can go home."

There was a quiet, depressed smattering of laughter.

Natalie scooted along the wall, toward the water. She peeked around the corner of the cabin and saw that it would be impossible to make it to the kayak. Two bee-suited strangers were sitting out there on the stoop. One had removed his helmet and was smoking some kind of pipe. He had a big purple tattoo of a singer climbing up out of the collar of his bee suit and across the meat of his neck. Natalie pulled her head back. Eva's mouth smacked open and closed.

"You are being so, so good," Natalie told her sister, her lips moving but no real sound coming out. "I love you so much."

Don't screw this up, Eva answered.

Natalie bent low and hurried through the ferns and into the dead woods. None of the strangers in the cabin noticed. Their voices faded. She glanced back to see if she was being followed, which almost made her lose her footing. She grabbed at a dead blackberry bush for balance, tearing her hand up on the thorns. Almost instantly, the cuts began to bleed. They looked like they should hurt, but Natalie, numb with terror and adrenaline, didn't feel a thing.

Up ahead was a low hill. Natalie rushed for it, climbing over the crest. But as soon as she reached the other side, she realized that this had been a mistake.

Someone was down there.

It was a man in a yellow bee suit—one of the two who had been arguing outside of the cabin. He was down on his knees, examining a generator-like contraption. It was about the size of an oven, with an aluminum pole sprouting out of the top, reaching high into the trees. At the end of the pole was a rotor, crusted with some kind of blue gunk. The man had his back to Natalie. All of his attention seemed focused on the device.

"You know that this won't go any quicker if you watch me," he said, not bothering to turn around. He must have heard her come up the hill and assumed she was a member of his group.

Natalie froze.

Eva squirmed, opening her mouth in a cranky yawn.

The man went about his work. He pulled the front panel off of the device and reached one of his gloved hands inside. Natalie's eyes fell on his backpack, which lay splayed open on the brown grass behind him. There were tools in there—a wrench set, a pair of pliers, and a coil of copper wire. There was also a revolver, sitting loose in an unbuttoned leather holster.

Be careful, Eva whispered in her mind. *You can do this.*

"Don't you think you'd be better off babysitting the new guy?" the man asked, shoving his arm ever deeper into the device.

Natalie shifted Eva to her left arm. She took a long step toward the open backpack, reached inside, and pulled out the revolver. She peeled off the holster with her teeth, checked the cylinder to see that it was loaded, flipped the safety, and then sighted it square at the stranger's back.

"Be quiet," she whispered.

The man only cocked his head. Then he pulled his arm out of the guts of the device, hoisted himself up, and turned to face her.

"Son of a . . ." He trailed off. He didn't exactly sound shocked—more sort of bemused. And certainly not the least bit frightened, which Natalie found unsettling. The man made a movement as though to run a hand through his hair, but his glove only bounced dumbly against his helmet.

"Well, now," he said. "It's been a little while since I've seen one of you. I mean, out in the open like this. Free-range."

"I told you to be quiet," Natalie said.

"Yup, you sure did," the man answered. His tone had gone soft, almost velvety. "Heard you loud and clear—message transmitted and received. I'm Reggie. It's super to meet you." The man named Reggie offered up his rubber palm for a handshake. "Probably be easier to make friends if you set that gun down," he offered.

Natalie stayed exactly where she was. After a long

moment of silence, Reggie dropped his outstretched hand. Then he tilted his visor up toward the trees and pointed. "Oh—wow! There's a big owl up there. Take a look!"

Natalie just stared at him, baffled.

"It's got a—what's that?" Reggie went on, shifting his weight excitedly from one boot to the other. "It's eating a rabbit! Holy cow, you've got to see this. There's a big owl, right behind you, eating a freaking rabbit or something!"

"No there isn't," Natalie said. "Please. Be. Quiet."

"Oh . . . yeah," Reggie said. His body tilted forward and back. His gloved fingers drummed his thighs. Why the hell was he so relaxed? "You're totally right—that's just a branch, isn't it? Branch." He bopped the palm of his hand against the top of his visor. "Hey," Reggie continued, "you know what would be maybe a lot of fun? How about we start a fire? I've got some butane in my bag, if you just—"

The man took a step toward his open backpack. Natalie's arm tightened. "If you get any closer, I promise I'm going to shoot you."

"Ah. Okay." Reggie eased his foot backward. "But it's just . . . I know a cabin nearby. There are people sleeping inside. We could burn them all up and everything. They might try to get out, but, like, we could shoot them. You could shoot them. I bet they'd scream," he added, as though this might seal the deal.

With that grim offer, the man's behavior finally made sense. He was treating Natalie the same way she would treat her own grandfather.

"I'm not wicked," she said.

For a long while Reggie said nothing. There was a moment of deep, unpleasant silence—no voices, no birds, no singers, no song.

"What do you want?" Reggie asked.

"I want to not shoot you." Natalie intoned the words slowly, deliberately. "I really don't want to do that. But I need you to understand that I will if I have to."

Reggie's arms hung slack at his sides. Natalie could see the shadow of his head tilting this way and that within the dark cavern of his bonnet. Unable to believe what he was seeing and hearing.

"What do you want?" he asked again.

"I want to get away from that cabin," Natalie said, "and all of you."

"What do you—"

"Listen. You can ask me that question all day, and I'm not going to say anything awful. Because I'm not wicked."

"But you're not . . . You're naked out here."

"I'm vexed," she said.

At this Reggie went still. It was freaking Natalie out that she couldn't see his face.

"Take your bonnet off," she said.

"My what?"

"Your bonnet—your helmet," she said. "Take it off and throw it here."

Slowly Reggie lifted his hands up to his collar and unzipped the seal on his bonnet. Then he pulled it off and tossed the rubber thing on the dead grass between them. He was younger than Natalie had expected. He had a soft, pale face and a beard so blond that it was almost invisible. And just like the other stranger back at the cabin, Reggie bore a color tattoo of a singer on his neck.

At first he just blinked at her, as though unsure of what he was seeing. The first thing he noticed was her eyes—he must not have been able to see their purple glow through his tinted visor.

"What's wrong with your—"

"Nothing," she said. "It's a side effect."

"Of the vex . . . ," he said, lingering over the word like it came from some forgotten, holy language. "You're . . . vexed."

His gaze drifted to Natalie's right hand, clutching the revolver. Then across to her left arm, holding Eva. He squinted, apparently unable to puzzle out what it might be.

"You're vexed," he repeated, "and you have a baby."

"She's my sister," Natalie said.

"Your sister . . . ," Reggie said. He looked like he needed to sit down. His hands reached blindly behind him, groping about until they found the edge of the generator-like device. He lowered himself to the dead ground, his knees shaking. "You're vexed," he repeated again. A broad, stupid grin was slowly spreading across his frizzy, pale face. "You have a sister."

Then a small, metallic voice erupted from inside his backpack. "Reggie!" It sounded like the woman—Miranda. "Reggie," she repeated. "Check in."

Reggie just sat there, smiling. Keeping the revolver aimed in his general direction, Natalie hooked one of the backpack straps with the tip of her boot and pulled it close. Squatting down, she rested Eva on the grass and began rooting through the tools with her free hand. She pulled out a strange little radio that was no bigger than an oyster shell—identical to the one Miranda had worn on her belt. It had a brightly lit screen, dotted with colorful little boxes and pictures. This, Natalie knew, was called a phone. But she had never seen one that still worked.

"Reggie!" Miranda called again, her voice slipping smoothly out of the phone. "Get your head out of the disperser and check in. Danny found a kayak down by the jetty. Somebody's been here."

"Don't touch the screen," Reggie said. He'd tipped his head back and was staring up at the bare canopy, still beaming with joy. "As long as you don't touch it, they won't be able to hear you."

Natalie didn't know whether to believe him or not, but before she could make up her mind, he spoke again.

"Help me, Miranda!" Reggie said, his voice not quite loud enough to be called a yell. "There's a girl holding a gun in my face."

"Reggie, I swear," the woman said. "If you've got me on mute again, I'm going to whoop your ass."

"See? She can't hear us." Then Reggie repeated the word: "Freaking *vexed*." He seemed to marvel over the very sound of it.

Natalie slipped the phone into her pocket, careful not to bump the screen as she did so. Then she scooped Eva—amazingly perfect, amazingly quiet—back up, and together they crouched over the open knapsack to see if there was anything else worth taking. Meanwhile, Miranda continued to heckle Reggie from inside Natalie's pocket.

"You know . . . you really don't need to be afraid of her," he said. "Or any of us, for that matter." Reggie looked directly at her. "None of us would hurt you. Not ever."

Natalie had been so frightened for so long that a part of her desperately wanted to believe him. From being locked up in the lighthouse, to helping her mother through the delivery, to escaping the island with the baby, to this. It would be so, so much simpler to take a leap of faith and simply trust this Reggie person. The fact that he looked only a little bit older than her and not the least bit scary made it all the more tempting.

"I can't take your word for it," she finally said. Even to herself, Natalie sounded sad about that. But it was done, and she had to get moving. Now that Reggie's group knew someone had been in the cabin, they'd no doubt start searching the woods. "Where are the singers?"

Reggie seemed like he didn't understand the question.

"I need to find them," she said. "These woods should be full of them."

"Not anymore," Reggie said, tapping the boxy contraption that he'd been trying to fix. Natalie had already guessed that the device was the reason this forest had fallen silent. That blue gunk sticking to the top of the high rotor looked and smelled an awful lot like quiet. The recipe for this insecticide was repeated on every third broadcast of *The First Voice*, and Natalie's father used to brew up a batch for himself whenever they made a scavenging trip to the mainland—he was the only one in their family who needed it, after all. This machine must have been designed to spray quiet out across the treetops. It kept the singers away, but it also killed all the trees and plants.

"Where did they go?"

Reggie shrugged within his bee suit. "There aren't any close by. We have dispersers running every half mile or so. The woods around the highway are pretty safe too. You'd have to go as far as the bog before you hit a swarm."

Natalie nodded. He must have been talking about the swampland outside of Goldsport. "Is it far?" she asked.

"Ten miles, maybe?" he said. "But why would you want to . . . ? Oh. Oh, shit." Reggie pushed himself up off of his butt and stood. "The kid isn't vexed," he said.

"Not yet," Natalie said.

"Congratulations, Reggie!" Miranda snapped through the phone. "You've just given up your next two leave rotations. Danny is coming to get you, and he has my permission to smack you in the head."

"I have to go now," Natalie said.

"You really, really don't," Reggie said, pleading. He leaned forward, as though he wanted to take a step toward her. Then, glancing once more at the pistol in Natalie's hand, he resisted. "We're not going to hurt you."

"I don't know that," Natalie said. "I don't know anything about you." Then she nodded toward the veiled bonnet for Reggie's bee suit, lying crumpled on the dead grass. "Toss that to me," she said.

"Why?" Reggie asked. "You don't need it."

"You will," Natalie said. "You're going to come with us. I can't have you running back to the cabin and telling all of your friends where we went."

"Well, damn." Reggie shook his head. "I should have thought of that." He did as he was told, picking up the bonnet and tossing it to Natalie's feet.

"I promise you that I'm telling the truth . . . ," he said, trying one last time to win her over. "I mean . . . you're vexed, for heaven's sake! Hurting you is the last thing we would ever do."

Again, Natalie almost surrendered to it. She wanted so badly to believe him.

Don't, Eva said.

CHAPTER 24

The Wilted Woods

THEY MOVED SILENTLY THROUGH THE FOREST. NATALIE MADE Reggie lead, and she kept the pistol tight in her grip. A short time later, they could hear hollering in the distance. Several voices, high and desperate.

"Reggie!"

There was a pause as the strangers waited for an answer.

"Reggie!"

"My friends must've found my gear," Reggie said. "They're going to think that somebody snatched me." After a pause, he let out a stifled giggle. "Though I guess . . . they're not wrong about that, are they? There's a word for what you're doing, girl. Kidnapping."

"It's only until we get to the singers," Natalie said, glancing quickly behind them. She saw nothing but bald, wrinkled trees.

"And then what will happen?" Reggie asked. He turned around to face her, walking backward. All of his shock had melted away, and what remained could only be called delight. But Natalie couldn't tell if it was real, or just an act. Just a way to keep her off-balance.

"Will you . . . let me go?" Reggie asked.

"Of course I will," Natalie said.

"Promise?" He cocked his head and gave her a look that was almost cutesy. Was he trying to be friendly? Or was this . . . Was it flirting? Either way, she didn't like it.

"Stop talking," Natalie said.

"Roger that," Reggie said. Then, confidingly: "That means 'understood.'"

Moments later they came upon the small, crumbling highway. Here there was another disperser, looming over a grove of dry pine saplings on the far embankment. This one seemed to be working just fine—the rotor spun atop the aluminum pole, hissing out a faint blue spray of quiet in all directions. Natalie could smell the sharp, soapy tang as they approached. Eva must have smelled it too, because she began to twist about in Natalie's grip. Her closed eyes clenched like little fists, and she whimpered.

"You get used to the smell," Reggie said, forgetting that he'd agreed to shut up only minutes before. "I hardly even notice it anymore. And when I do . . ." He raised his nostrils up into the air, sniffing it the way you might sniff a newly bloomed wild rose. "It just reminds me of home."

He's baiting you, Eva said. *He wants you to ask questions. He wants you distracted.*

"I know," Natalie whispered back.

"Are you . . . ? Are you talking to that baby?" Reggie asked.

Shit. Natalie looked up at him. "I'm not interested in where you come from."

"That is a lie," Reggie said. "But whatever. I for one don't mind admitting that I'm curious about where you and your sister come from. I'm interested in a lot of things about you. Like . . . maybe your names, for starters?"

Natalie stayed silent long enough to make a point. Then she asked: "Why the bee suit?"

"The what?"

"If you've chased all of the singers out of these woods, why do you people still wear bee suits?"

"Oh, you mean my hazmat?" Reggie pinched at the yellow rubber hanging loose about his hips. "Well, it might be quiet here, but we're on the move most of the time. And we can't cover the whole world in quiet. So, you know, better safe than sorry. Speaking of that . . . When we get closer to the bog, I'm gonna need my helmet back."

"When you need it, you'll get it," Natalie said.

Reggie turned south on the little highway, leading them down through the brittle woods. Just as he'd said, the way was lined with dispersers—within an hour they'd passed three. The shining rotors at the top of these strange devices spun rhythmically, hurling blue mist into the treetops. Meanwhile, scattered here and there across the highway embankments, there were older machines. Natalie saw everything from tractors to army jeeps, long since plundered for parts and abandoned to rust. A mobile home lay just off the highway, fronted by a shattered wire fence. White crescents of human bone lay scattered across the brown yard.

Sights like this were a fact of life in the wicked world. Once, when Natalie was just seven years old, a drifting yacht had beached itself on the shores of Puffin Island. It had been a good day for her family—they'd salvaged enough equipment and preserved food from that ship to last a full year. But there were people on the yacht too. Twists of ragged cloth and withered fingers, entombed in the stately cabins. They had all died in their beds, skulls cracked open like crab shells. Natalie's parents' best guess was that one of the crew had fallen wicked and killed them in their sleep.

It wasn't the corpses themselves that had upset Natalie when she was a little girl. It was the sight of those bare, exposed bones. The jagged ridges of cracked skull. The leg sticking out from beneath a blanket, bald as driftwood. It was odd to think that throughout their entire lives, these people had been walking around full of these smooth, hard bones. That same shin had swung and kicked and stepped. Maybe it had danced or been propped up on a table after a long day of work. Stranger still was the thought that Natalie was also filled with these things. One day she would be gone, but her bones would stick around. Maybe in a Natalie-shaped pile, the way they'd been on that drifting yacht. Maybe scattered like they were in this sad, brown garden. Little pieces of herself, lingering in the world. Bits of what she used to be, as foreign as wood or stone.

And Eva? What about her bones, still soft and growing inside her?

Get it together, her sister hissed, impatient.

Natalie shook the thoughts away, and they continued down the road.

For a long time they passed nothing but the mournful shells of trees. Then, after a few hours of walking, Reggie's phone began to speak again. "Hey there, stranger," came the soft, kindly whispers from inside Natalie's pocket. "We bet you must be lonely out there. We bet you must be hungry. Why don't you bring our friend back, so we can cut him up for you? There's plenty of meat on him for everybody."

Clearly, Reggie's group had decided that he'd been taken by the wicked.

"What are we going to do with all of these knives?" they asked.

"We found all these knives, but we can't carry them all!"

"Do you want some of our knives, maybe?"

"Hey, just wondering—did you kill our friend yet? Did you kill our Reggie?"

"Gosh, we hope not."

"We want to help! Maybe with all these knives?"

"We want to give you a back rub, too."

"We want to give you a really awesome haircut."

"Hey, guess what! Did you know that today is Christmas Eve?"

"We bet you didn't know that!"

"Do you remember Christmas? Have you ever had a Christmas?"

"We're going to have a party to celebrate, we think, probably."

"A Christmas party!"

"We've got sandwiches, and we've got orange juice, and we've got candy."

"Want some?"

"They're lying about the sandwiches," Reggie offered. "And the orange juice is powdered. But that candy is for real. It's honest-to-goodness chocolate. Part of the stash we brought with us from home."

Natalie ignored him, but the sound of the word made her stomach turn over. She'd had chocolate only once in her life—a little brown-white brick so ancient and dry that it crumbled to dust in her hands. Still, her mouth watered at the thought. She hadn't had a thing to eat since leaving Puffin Island. She didn't want to stop, but neither she nor Eva could make it much farther without a break. The baby was starting to bawl, and if she got much louder they'd have to find cover and wait it out.

"We'll rest here," she announced, stepping off of the road and down the embankment.

"You are literally the boss," Reggie said.

They sat at the base of a large oak. Natalie set the crying baby down in her lap and then pulled the formula supplies out of her pack. But she found it almost impossible to mix up a bottle with just one hand while still keeping the pistol ready in her other.

"I don't suppose you'd let me help with that," Reggie said.

Natalie didn't answer. She propped the empty bottle in the crook between two roots and began to tip the powder in. But more spilled than made it in through the mouth of the bottle.

"Come on," he said, "what's the worst that can happen? I drink it?" He grinned at her. His teeth were so big and so white. They were beautiful, like his whole face was beautiful. The sight of it was still strange to Natalie. Was everybody left in the world this good-looking?

She scooted aside and let him take the supplies. As he mixed up the bottle, she took the opportunity to eat a little herself, shoving two strips of dried fish into her mouth.

"I'm fine, thanks," Reggie said. "Had a big breakfast."

He passed the bottle back, and Natalie did her best to warm it under her armpit while changing the baby. Then she gave Eva the bottle, and finally her crying stopped. Her little body seemed to vibrate as she ate.

"Are we getting close?"

"Closer," Reggie said. "You know, I could tell you exactly if you let me take a look at my phone. I don't even need to touch it. Just let me see the screen. And if I try anything tricky . . ." He paused, seeming to think over suitable punishments. "You could shoot me in the face. That'd be more than fair."

"Don't joke about it," Natalie said.

"Yeah. I guess I shouldn't. But do you want me to tell you where we are, or not?" He paused, tilting his head like a bird. "I could even help you shut my friends up."

It was an appealing offer. Their grim attempts to lure her back were still crackling out of the phone. Natalie plucked it from her pocket, the screen aflame with cheerful springtime colors. She tilted it in his direction, and Reggie leaned forward so that he could see.

"That's close enough," she said. "If you can't do it from where you're sitting, then we won't do it."

"Lucky for both of us, I can," Reggie said. He directed her to a tab on the side and told her to press it. The moment she did, the voices fell silent.

"That's better," Reggie said. "Now, you see that little picture of a compass? Tap your finger on it."

She did, causing the entire screen to change into a glowing image of the coastline. Natalie could see the town of Lubec on the old Canadian border, and the gutted-trout shape of Grand Manan Island. Puffin Island was there as well—a crumb in the gaping mouth of the bay.

"Do you see a little black arrow?" Reggie asked. "That's us. The bog will look like a purple dot, farther down the road. We mark breeding grounds wherever we find them."

Natalie found the arrow, sitting in the middle of Highway 191. The bog seemed to be just down the road from them, but when she checked the scale she realized that they still had miles to go. They wouldn't make it until dusk, and by then there'd be no way to return before dark.

"You find it?"

"Yeah," she said. "We're not even close yet."

"Don't worry," Reggie said. "I know a safe spot once we get there. We can get your sister bitten, rest up for a few hours, and be back at the cabin in time for breakfast tomorrow."

"I never mentioned anything about going back to the cabin with you," Natalie said, feeling exhausted and discouraged. She tried to switch off the map, but somehow instead she just ended up zooming out. Suddenly there were purple dots everywhere, flashing like storm buoys at sea. They stretched across the entire state of Maine and beyond. But there were also other, different markings. Arrows and flags and *X*s in a rainbow of colors.

"What is all this?" Natalie asked.

"It's all our work," Reggie said, sounding not a little proud. "It's what we've been doing out here for the last three years." Again he leaned toward her. "Those little blue *X*s are our—my—dispersers. And those red flags—those are old radio towers. They're from the world before, but we try to keep as many of them running as possible. Tell me, you ever hear something called—"

Natalie cut him off. "*The First Voice*? That's you?"

"Not exactly," Reggie said. "But without us, nobody would hear it. Whenever we find an old tower, we do what we can to get it running again. That way the old broadcast can still go out. Actually, I'm taking more credit for that than I deserve. It's Danny who does the towers. He's one of my friends—the man on the phone who offered to give you chocolate. I promise you, from the bottom of my heart, that he isn't a bad guy."

To Natalie, this news was almost as shocking as the fact that Reggie and his group existed in the first place. But it also made no sense.

"Why?"

"Oh . . ." Reggie shifted in his bee suit, making the shiny rubber squeak. "Well . . . there's a lot of good information in those old radio shows. The recipe for quiet. The news about the vex. I'm guessing that your folks wouldn't even have known about it if they didn't hear it on *The First Voice*."

Again Reggie smiled, but this time there was a false, sickly quality to it. He could tell that his story didn't sit right with Natalie. She wasn't an idiot. These people traveled open and free in the wicked world. They built things and fixed things. They had working phones, for goodness' sake. Obviously, if they'd wanted to put out a broadcast, they could have made one themselves. So why were they hiding behind a radio show that had been dead for decades now? A radio show that gave only scraps of information about the vex?

But there it was—the answer was in the question.

"You don't want people to know . . . ," Natalie said.

Reggie didn't answer.

"You don't want them to know that it almost never works. You don't want them to know that most of the kids who get it die."

Reggie dropped his gaze to the stretch of dead grass between them. It was a long time before he said anything.

"This is going to sound . . . not good. You're going to need to trust me when I say that it wasn't my decision. I mean, it was made long before I even joined the searchers. But yeah, you're right. If people knew the odds of the vex working, they'd never try it. And if they never tried it, there'd be no you."

With this he forced himself to look back up at her. His expression seemed open, hiding nothing. "You ever meet the wicked?" he asked. "You talk to them or spend some time watching them?"

"Only a little . . . ," Natalie said, pleased with how easy the deception came.

"Well, let me tell you, they can work a radio as well as any of us. So, that's another reason. My people have always been afraid to broadcast something new, because we don't want them to come looking for us."

"You mean there aren't any wicked where you come from?"

"No wicked. No singers. It looks a lot like this, actually." Reggie gestured out at the wilted woods all around them.

For a while neither of them said anything more. The only sounds were Eva's suckling and dead pine needles chiming as they fell. It struck Natalie, in that moment, that her question still hadn't been answered.

"Why?" she asked again. "Why do any of it?"

"Because of you," Reggie said. "All of this—the radio towers, *The First Voice*, my friends and I out here far from home. It's all been in search of someone like you. And now . . ." He trailed off for a moment. It seemed like he might actually be getting choked up, so profound was his happiness.

"And now we've finally found you."

CHAPTER 25

The Bog

NATALIE HAD ABOUT A MILLION QUESTIONS SHE WANTED TO ask. She didn't even know where to start. What the hell kind of place had Reggie come from, this strange land without singers or the wicked—or, for that matter, trees and grass and birds? What had his group of searchers seen in their travels across the country? Had it all fallen wicked? Were there other true sanctuaries, still hanging on behind high walls, or maybe hidden deep beneath the earth? And what were the wicked doing, now that they'd picked the world clean of true people? Had they finally turned their knives and guns and teeth on one another? Had they all slowly starved to death? Or were they still out there, filling the old cities, sleeping in rotting beds, and growing tomatoes on their balconies, like disturbed children playing house? Most of all, what about other vexed people? Natalie could tell from the way that Reggie had reacted to her purple eyes that he'd never seen one in person before. But had he heard rumors? Had some sanctuary out there found success? Or were Natalie and her mother the only two vexed humans on the planet? The urge to ask him these questions was intense, almost physical. But she forced herself to resist it. Reggie hadn't earned her trust yet. Until he did, Natalie couldn't risk revealing what she did and didn't know.

So they walked in silence, heading down the crumbling highway in the direction of Goldsport. Eventually they passed the last of the dispersers, and the woods around them began to come back to life. Natalie heard a distant trill of birdsong, and when the breeze shifted she could even detect the lilting tune of singers up ahead. Then they rounded a bend and came upon a highway sign that made it official—they had arrived.

GOLDSPORT: KEEP OUT.

The words were painted in big white letters across the top of the old sign. When Natalie got closer she could still read the text, faded underneath: PORT EMORY, NEXT LEFT. A few steps later they came upon another sign, this one with more specific warnings. One line read: RESIDENTS OF PORT EMORY WISHING TO CONTEST LEASING TERMS ON THEIR PROPERTY SHOULD REFER TO THE JUDGMENT BY THE SUPERIOR COURT OF MAINE, DATED SEPTEMBER 9. Another said, more directly: REFUGEES NOT WELCOME. TRADERS NOT WELCOME. FEDERAL OR CIVILIAN AGENTS NOT REC-OGNIZED. APPROACH THE GATES AND YOU WILL BE SHOT.

"We've seen warnings like this as far away as Boston," Reggie said.

"What do you mean?" Natalie asked. "About Goldsport?"

"Yup," Reggie said. "All the highways headed in this direction have them." At this he shook his head, almost sadly. "As though the world isn't bad enough already. These rich SOBs are the worst of the worst."

This struck Natalie as an odd thing to say. The people in Goldsport were only wicked, after all. They couldn't be blamed for what they did or said. Not any more than her own grandfather could be. She swapped her gun from one hand to another and then shifted Eva's weight to her free arm.

"It's not like they can help it," she said. "It's just who they are now."

Reggie arched an eyebrow at her. "Um, how's that exactly?"

"Well, it's not like anybody in Goldsport asked to fall wicked."

Reggie kept eyeballing her, saying nothing. "You having me on?" he finally asked.

"I don't know what you mean."

"They're not wicked," Reggie said. It didn't seem to Natalie as though he were lying to her. In fact, when Reggie saw the surprise on her face, he looked genuinely puzzled.

"Of course they are," Natalie stammered. "The whole town is wicked. Everybody knows that."

"Yeah? Everybody, who?"

"My mom. My dad. My grandpa." Little did Reggie know that, in addition to himself and Eva, that list included

literally everybody Natalie had ever spoken to. Not counting the puffins.

"And how would they know?"

"They used to live there. A long time ago." Natalie realized that she was giving away more than she should, but
for the moment she didn't care. Goldsport's wickedness
was one of the founding facts of her life—as fundamental to
Natalie's experience of the world as gravity or the changing
seasons.

"Well, I'm sorry, but I don't know what to say." Reggie
rubbed his gloved thumbs across his eyebrows. "Other than
this: Your parents aren't telling the truth. I mean, you said
that you've met wicked folks, right?"

Natalie had spent more time among the wicked than
Reggie could imagine, but all she did was nod.

"And does this sound like the wicked to you?" Reggie
pointed once more to the sign. He read aloud, enunciating.
"'Terms regarding the duration of all leasing agreements
are final and fully binding. They remain in effect until such
time as . . .' I mean—you ever talk to a wicked person who
sounds like that? The wicked say shit like: 'Could you let
me borrow your face for a minute?'"

Natalie couldn't argue. But it still didn't seem right. "My
mother isn't a liar," she said.

"Okay," Reggie said. "Maybe your mom's not lying.
Maybe she's just wrong. Totally possible. But I'm telling
you, kid, that I've got it on very good authority that the
people in Goldsport are as true as I am. And more than

that, there's supposed to be a vexed girl living there with them."

The words shocked Natalie. Reggie could tell, and he laughed.

"Damn. I'll be real honest. I spent a big chunk of today thinking that vexed girl was you. I figured that you were just a damn good liar. But then I asked myself: Why would she come all the way to the cabin looking for singers when she's got thousands in her own backyard? Also, I thought it was weird that the adults would make you take the baby out all by yourself. But who knows—again, they seem to be the worst. So . . . can we just be a hundred percent clear here . . . ? Are you really not the vexed girl of Goldsport?"

Natalie could only shake her head.

Reggie laughed again, louder this time. He turned in a circle, doing a ridiculous little dance.

"My goodness," he said when he recovered himself. "Imagine that. Two of you. If only one were a boy, we could put you both on Noah's Ark."

"How do you know?" Natalie asked, her mouth dry.

"A man on the inside," Reggie said. "A . . . What would you call it? A real Goldsportian? A Goldsporter?" He grinned, seemingly tickled by everything at this point. "This guy told us all about the sanctuary and the vexed girl who lives in it. That's why we've been hanging around here for so long, filling up these woods with dispersers. My friends and I have been studying the place, trying to figure out how to contact her. According to our source, this girl doesn't like it there, and she'd be more than willing to leave. We don't have the numbers to take on the scumbags inside, and it'll be another few weeks before any help gets here. So, in the meantime, we've just been waiting and watching. Honestly, kid . . ." Reggie shook his head, chewing his lip thoughtfully. "You could have saved us all a lot of trouble if you'd shown up two months ago."

Natalie didn't know what to say, or even think, about any of this.

He doesn't sound like he's lying, Eva offered.

"You're not helping," Natalie whispered.

Reggie gave her a funny look. He must have thought that she was talking to him.

"Really?" he asked. "I'll have to try harder, then."

Just as the highway sign promised, in a few more minutes they arrived. The road here was covered with tire spikes and barricaded by a bus parked end-to-end. The windows were all shot out, the side spray-painted with further warnings. BE ADVISED: WE RESERVE THE RIGHT TO DEFEND OUR INVEST-MENT. A human body sat in the driver's chair, long rotted away to a nest of twigs and leather. One arm hung casually out the window, its stump of a hand missing finger bones. The skull had been arranged so that it would look out at intruders, the scooped-out eyes gazing right at Natalie. She still didn't know what to make of Reggie's story, but he was right about one thing. If these people weren't wicked, they were certainly sick.

"I'm not going any farther without my headpiece," Reggie said.

Fair enough—the singers were getting louder with every step. Natalie tossed the limp bonnet back to Reggie, and he zipped it into place, his pale face once more concealed behind the tinted plastic visor.

Together they stepped over the tire spikes and around the abandoned bus. From there the road sank into a morass of muddy pools and yellow scrub. This was the bog, filled with more singers than Natalie had ever seen in her life. The insects swarmed over the shallow water like smoke over fire, shaking the air with their song. They glimmered on the tips of the scrub grass, perching in rows along the limbs of trees that rimmed the bog. Up ahead the road surfaced again, scaling the slope of a steep hill. And there, at the very top of the hill, stood the high walls and gates of Goldsport.

"There's a watchtower up there," Reggie said, pointing at the distant gates. He had to raise his voice to be heard over the singers. "We've never seen anybody guarding it, but we can't be too careful. If you're really going to do this, you should try to do it quickly."

"All right," Natalie said.

But for a moment she couldn't move.

What the hell are you waiting for? asked Eva.

"Are we really going to do this?"

Now you ask this question? Her baby sister sounded utterly disgusted.

"We don't have to," Natalie whispered under her breath. "We can still turn around. Dad never had the vex, and he was just fine."

So Dad is a role model now? Eva was starting to fall asleep, but Natalie heard her voice all the same.

"That's not the point," she said. "What I mean is that we don't actually have to go through with this if we don't want to. We could just—"

Stop saying "we." There isn't any "we." I'm just a baby. I don't get a vote. Whatever you do, and whatever happens after that, is on you.

"Thanks."

And stop talking to yourself! Walk in there, or don't. But do it fast. Mom must already think that something horrible happened to us.

"My God . . ."

Reggie's voice pulled Natalie out of her own head. She looked up and saw that the singers had already sniffed him out. At least a hundred of the little insects drifted over from the bog to form a bright purple cloud around his body. They bounced against his rubber suit, starving and insistent. But not a single one of them tried to approach Natalie. Even Eva escaped their notice—Natalie's odor must have covered her baby sister.

"I didn't realize . . ." For a moment Reggie struggled to say anything more. "They don't even try to bite you?"

Natalie shook her head. "It's like I'm not even here."

With that she took one step into the muck and then

another. Her shoes sank, and her socks filled with muddy water. Before her, the singers parted like a curtain.

"Hey!"

Reggie rushed to catch up. He splashed from pool to pool, driving the singers into a frenzy of excitement. Before Natalie knew what was happening, he was nearly on top of her. But rather than grabbing for the pistol that was dangling limp in her free hand, Reggie snatched his phone from out of her pocket. Natalie made to elbow him away, but Reggie was already hopping backward and tossing out frantic apologies.

"I'm sorry! I'm sorry!"

Natalie raised the pistol, and Reggie's whole body seemed to shrink. A gloved hand shot up to cover his dark visor. "I'm sorry!" he shrieked once more. "Don't shoot! I promise I'm not going to call anybody. But I can't—I can't not film this."

"That was so stupid," Natalie snapped, shocked not just by what Reggie had done, but by how close she'd come to actually pulling the trigger. "You could have asked for the phone back."

"You wouldn't have given it to me," Reggie said. "Listen, I know you don't trust me yet. But we really are out here looking for vexed people. And now I'm seeing one standing in a swarm of singers like it's no big deal. Not only that, but you're about to expose your own sister. If getting this on tape means you shoot me, then . . . I mean, obviously I don't want you to shoot me."

Natalie took a breath and lowered the gun. Just aiming

the thing made her feel nauseous. "You give the phone back when you're done," she said.

"Absolutely," Reggie said. "The very second."

They continued deeper into the bog. Reggie stayed a few steps ahead of Natalie. He turned the little phone sideways and aimed it at her face, getting close enough to catch the purple in her eyes.

"This Subject Record is being filmed by Reggie Schutt," he announced, speaking up to be heard over the droning insects, "principal engineer, deployed searcher, assigned to the Second Research Expedition. Today is the ninth of July, in the twenty-seventh year of the quiet. The time is 18:24. I am filming this in the wicked territory of the Atlantic Northeast. Specifically, we are in a bog outside of the sanctuary of Goldsport, which I will geo-tag on the completed video. As you can see, I am here with a young woman who is demonstrably vexed. Could you say your name for the camera, please?"

"No."

"Fair enough," Reggie said. "I will refer to her, for the purposes of this recording, as Subject U-39. Subject U-40 will be . . ."

He continued narrating as Natalie approached the center of the bog. All the while, the singers grew ever louder. Their song thrummed through Natalie's bones like a cat's purr, and it pulled Eva out of her nap. She blinked up at the gathering swarms, a galaxy of purple stars.

"No going back now," Natalie whispered down to her.

There never was any going back.

"It's not going to kill you," Natalie said.

Listen. It totally might.

"Don't say that."

I didn't.

Down in her arms, Eva's eyes widened. Natalie had read that a baby this young wasn't much more than a bundle of nerves and potential—a little pre-person. But it really looked like her baby sister was reacting to the sight of the singers. Eva's tiny fingers opened and closed, and her ears seemed to tilt toward the melody. She didn't cry or even fuss when Natalie set her down upon a clump of grass.

The singers descended. Some landed on Eva's arms and on her elbows. Others collected upon her knees and toes. Their little legs, thinner than thread, danced across Eva's skin. Their mouths pressed and tested. But even when they bit her—even as their little bodies swelled with her blood— Eva didn't cry, or make a single sound.

CHAPTER 26

Subject Records

NATALIE BRUSHED THE BLOATED, GROGGY SINGERS OFF OF her sister's little body. She pulled Eva close, and together they waded out of the bog. Reggie suggested that they rest up inside the abandoned bus. Natalie didn't like the idea of lingering this close to Goldsport, but she was so exhausted that she had to agree. Besides, after what Eva had just been through, she was going to need her bottle. The singer bites were already turning red. Her eyes seemed slightly sunken, and her mouth and tongue were dry.

Reggie entered the bus first. He'd been strangely deferential ever since they finished up in the bog, handing back the phone the moment the blood-fattened singers flew off. Now he checked the old seat cushions for exposed nails or shards of glass. Then he produced a tiny little spray bottle of quiet from one of the pockets of his bee suit and doused the shattered window frames. It pushed the singers back away from the bus, giving the three of them as much peace as they were likely to get.

"All set," he called.

Natalie climbed up the stairs and settled into the first row, careful not to let Reggie get between her and the exit. The bus was filthy, but at least the seat was comfortable. Natalie set Eva down on the cushion as she made up a bottle. She wolfed down half of the remaining dried fish and tossed the rest to Reggie in the back.

"I wasn't going to ask . . . ," he said.

"Yeah." Natalie let herself smile at him over the seat back. "I know. Big breakfast."

The baby was dehydrated. Natalie pressed the bottle up to her chapped little mouth. Eva seemed disinterested, barely gumming the rubber nipple. More formula spilled down her cheeks than seemed to go into her mouth.

The sky darkened outside, making the singers glow all the brighter.

"When will we know if it worked?" Reggie asked softly from the back of the bus.

"I don't know," Natalie said. "*The First Voice* says a few weeks, but they're—"

"Wrong," Reggie finished for her. "We guessed that . . ."

"Yes. My mother told me that sometimes babies would die the same day. Other times it might take months. But you knew. You knew that it hadn't worked. From the day they got bitten, the babies would be sick and weak. And you knew they wouldn't ever get better." Natalie paused, remembering once more the look on her father's face when he'd learned that they were expecting another child.

"What about you?"

Again, Natalie looked at him over the seat back. In her arms, Eva squirmed.

"I mean . . . when they gave you the vex," Reggie said. "How long until your mother knew that you were actually going to survive?"

"Soon," Natalie said. "As soon as I got these . . ." She tapped a finger just beneath her eye, indicating the purple shards of light pulsing through her irises. In full dark, on an overcast night, the lights made her eyes shine as brightly as a pair of singers in her skull.

"And your dad?"

"It took him a while longer."

This was an understatement. For the first half of Natalie's life, her father had treated her like she was a dream that he could wake up from at any moment. It seemed like he'd only recently become convinced that she was actually sticking around. What a stupid joke it was that after so many years of worry and doubt, it was he who had disappeared. But the less Reggie knew about her family, the better.

"So . . . you're really sure that the people in Goldsport aren't wicked?" Natalie asked. Through the shattered window she could just make out the high walls cresting a hill on the far side of the bog. The empty watchtower peeked above the wall like a boy's face over a fence.

"I really, really am," Reggie said. "I trust our source."

Natalie still didn't know what to make of Reggie's odd

story, but the notion that Goldsport might be filled with true people—even if they were nasty—was irresistible to her. More than that, the thought that there might be another vexed girl sent a thrill coursing through Natalie. Could it really be possible that she'd spent her entire life just a few miles away from her own reflection? Could it be that there was a girl underneath all of that glass, her eyes gleaming the same color purple as Natalie's?

"Who is it? Your, um, your . . . source?"

"Someone who used to live there," Reggie said. "We found him a little while back, wearing the rattiest old bee suit you've ever seen. He said that he'd escaped from the sanctuary—said that things had gotten real bad there. There's a new man in charge, apparently. Not a good man, to hear him tell it."

"And you believe him?"

From the back of the bus, Reggie snorted. "Come on. You're too young and lucky to be so cynical. He described the whole place in detail, and from what we can tell, it checks out. Anyway, why would he lie about it? I mean, this poor guy is trying to escape from Goldsport. Why the heck would he tell a lie that would make us want to go there?"

For a while they said nothing more. Reggie finished up the last of the dried fish, and Natalie finally gave up trying to feed Eva the bottle. Night stumbled over the treetops, collapsing into the bog. The swarming singers threw shadows across the trees. In the darkness, Natalie could just barely make out the giant white wall.

"He's still with our group, you know," Reggie said. "He's like an honorary searcher now. If you'd like to, tomorrow you can meet him. Ask all your questions face-to-face."

With all that had happened, Natalie hadn't given a thought to how she would return home. Until now everything had been about getting safely away from the cabin and then finding the singers. But with those problems solved, the larger one remained. How would she leave these people behind? Also: Should she leave these people behind? Natalie still knew very little about the searchers. But so far she hadn't learned anything that frightened her.

"It was nice of you," Natalie said. "Taking the man in like that."

"Yeah." He chuckled softly. "We're a nice bunch."

That's not something nice people say, Eva mumbled in her sleep.

Natalie ignored her. For the first time, she was starting to feel comfortable around Reggie, and it caused the floodgates to crack open. There was so much she wanted to know, she could hardly decide where to start.

"So . . . are there other sanctuaries? Other true people out there?"

"Fewer than you'd think," Reggie said. "In all my years out I've come across . . . maybe something like twenty different settlements?"

Natalie gasped. That didn't sound like a few to her. She'd grown up thinking that the number could be as low as zero. Twenty was a whole world. A universe.

"Most of them are tiny, just a handful of families," Reggie continued. "But we've come across a few that are as big as towns. A thousand true souls, maybe more. Goldsport would be on the smaller side."

"And the wicked?"

Reggie sighed. "More than you'd think, unfortunately. The cities are all crawling with them. But that doesn't mean the countryside is safe, either. You're liable to bump into a wanderer almost anywhere. It's worst out on the prairie. For some reason they seem drawn to the old farmland. They're not great at . . . They can't really get organized, the wicked. It's not like they're growing corn and potatoes or raising hogs or anything. I did see one driving a tractor once, but it wasn't a minute before he got distracted and crashed it into a pond. But when it comes to basic stuff like picking fruit off trees or shooting a deer and cooking it up, they do all right. I swear there are a few places out west where you feel like you've gone back to the time of the hunter-gatherers. Except for all the old T-shirts and sneakers and baseball caps." Reggie chortled.

"And what about where you come from?"

"Hey, now," Reggie said, "this is getting a little one-sided, here. How about now I ask you a question?"

"Sure," Natalie said, her eyes still focused on the patch of darkness where the Goldsport gates were.

"Thanks. This has been bugging me for a while, actually. Why the heck did you have to come all the way out here just to give your baby sister the vex?"

"No singers on the island," Natalie said. She realized, the instant the words leapt stupidly from her mouth, that this had been a mistake. She'd let her guard drop, and Reggie had caught her.

"Oh yeah?" he asked, totally casually. "What island is that?"

"It's far away," Natalie said, a breath too quickly.

Not a great recovery.

"That's odd," Reggie said. "You must be a really fast kayaker, then."

"I am," Natalie said, wincing.

Reggie fell asleep soon after. His snores, amplified by the plastic and rubber dome of his bonnet, filled the bus. Eva squirmed atop the shredded seat. Natalie felt her downy little head and found it hot. Whatever was going to happen to Eva, it had already started. There were only two ways it could go.

"You're going to make it," Natalie whispered.

Leave me alone. I'm trying to sleep, Eva raged.

"You're going to be just like your big sister."

Sucks for me, Eva said. Then, in her real voice, she let out a soft whimper. Her fever was inching higher.

Outside, the singers spread into the nighttime forest, looking for deer and moose and birds to feed on, winding through the woods in purple ribbons. Natalie listened to their song, to the wind in the trees, to an owl in the hills above Goldsport, to Reggie snoring away in his bee suit. She checked on Eva every few minutes, to gauge her temperature. It seemed as though time were passing very slowly, but then she checked the clock on Reggie's phone and saw that it was suddenly three in the morning. Had she slept? Natalie couldn't remember nodding off.

She started to fiddle with Reggie's phone to keep herself awake. The device was a marvel—the way light jumped around at the slightest press of Natalie's fingers, reshuffling like sheets of colored ice. She knew that these things used to be everywhere in the world before. They had something like it back on Puffin Island, salvaged on a foraging trip to the mainland. Once, Natalie's dad had managed to bring it back to life by connecting it directly to the solar rig on the roof on their bunkhouse. It didn't last—the splintered screen sizzled, blinked, and died in less than a minute. Still, it was a hell of a thing to see. Even Natalie's wicked grandpa, who'd been watching from the lamp room of the lighthouse, had applauded.

"Text me your number!" he'd hollered.

But Reggie's device seemed different—this wasn't some brittle antique. The sides were worn, and there was a crack in the corner of the screen, but other than that it looked to be in excellent working condition. What kind of place did he come from that could make and sustain a marvel like this?

Natalie opened the map again and traced the yellow line back across the old state border. She thumbed across singer swarms and radio towers. She followed the searchers' path backward as it ducked and swerved, cutting across open country and keeping distance from big cities. It finally terminated somewhere in old California, deep in the heart of the Quiet Lands.

She closed the map and was about to put the phone down when something else on the screen caught her attention—SUBJECT RECORDS. Natalie pressed on the little icon, opening a kind of list with pictures and text. She guessed that these must be videos, just like the one Reggie had filmed of her and Eva some hours ago. The videos were sorted into three categories: SUBJECTS, UNDETERMINED; SUBJECTS, WICKED; and SUBJECTS, TRUE. Natalie selected the most recent one and watched herself carrying her baby sister into the bog. She watched, once more, as the singers descended. The picture got wobbly at that point. Reggie had been so excited that he couldn't hold the phone steady.

Natalie scrolled back through the other records. By far most of the subjects had been categorized as wicked, but there were also a few others within the bunch. She tried clicking one of the videos marked "true," and she was met with the sight of a middle-aged woman sitting on a metal folding chair. The woman held an open tin of peaches in one hand and a mug of coffee in the other. She wore a clean dress, a pair of tape-mended eyeglasses, and a look of profound relief. Her lips moved soundlessly as she answered questions from someone who was off camera.

The phone was still on silent. Natalie stopped the video and glanced back at Reggie. He was slumped sideways in the last row, looking like a deflated yellow raft. This unexpected opportunity to snoop was too good to pass up, but Natalie couldn't risk waking him by turning the volume on.

She lifted herself up off the creaky bus seat as carefully as she could. Waking Eva would have caused a screaming fit, so Natalie left her on the tattered cushion. She padded down the stairs, stepped lightly upon the asphalt, and crept a few short paces down the road. Then she set the volume to low and continued playing the video.

She listened as the strange woman described her life. She'd come from a sanctuary to the south, and the voices off camera asked her every conceivable question about it. How did her community deal with the singers? Did they have any trouble brewing quiet? How often did they have contact with free-roaming wicked? Were they in contact with any other sanctuaries, and if not, did they know of any other communities of true people? Did her neighbors still listen to *The First Voice*? When was the last time someone in her community had tried the vex? Had the vex ever worked, to her knowledge? Had she heard any stories, or even just rumors, of vexed people?

The questions came from many voices—Natalie could pick out both Reggie and his boss, Miranda, in the mix—but none of their faces ever appeared. Just the woman, seated on her metal folding chair, looking through her mended glasses and into the camera. Natalie saw that the video went on for a good two hours more, so she decided to skip ahead and check if there was anything interesting later on.

The scene that greeted her next was entirely different.

The woman was still seated on the chair, but her posture had changed. Her shoulders were slumped forward, and her tight bun of gray curls had come undone. Behind her stood a man, his head out of the frame. Natalie could just make out the tattoo of a large purple singer crawling up the side of his neck. His arms were crossed tightly over his chest—muscles coiled like wet rope.

"Are there any expecting mothers?" a soft voice asked from offscreen. It was, unmistakably, Reggie. The woman didn't answer him. She only sat there, slumped over, her cascading hair puffing back and forth as she breathed.

"Are there any expecting mothers?" Reggie asked again, with the exact same intonation. Still, the woman said nothing.

"Are there any expecting mothers?"

"Are there any expecting mothers?"

Finally, the woman looked up at the camera. Natalie nearly dropped the phone. They had—what had they done to her? The woman's face looked like a boiled lobster, apple-red and cracking, swollen meat bursting out from beneath. Her mouth was moving, but no sound came out. The man behind her uncrossed his arms, and Natalie, tongue between her teeth, stopped the video.

She skipped to the end.

There was the woman again. But now she was lying flat on a wooden table. There was a piece of her head, sitting very close to the rest of her head. Hands in rubber gloves swarmed over her like white spiders. They were using things that looked like knives and spoons to hollow her out.

Somebody—Miranda, maybe?—was complaining that they weren't labeling the samples right. Somebody else said that they were nearly out of sanitary vials. Reggie promised to look for some the next time they passed a pharmacy.

Natalie's stomach spasmed, but there wasn't enough in there for her to puke out. She turned the phone back on silent and closed the video. She tasted blood. In her head, Eva scolded, *Stop biting your tongue.*

"Hey . . . don't be mad, all right?" The voice came from behind her.

Natalie swung around to see Reggie, wide awake, standing in the doorway of the bus. For a second she thought that he'd caught her. That he'd seen her watching the video. But no—it was worse than that.

Reggie was holding Eva in his arms.

"I'm sorry I picked her up," he soothed. "I know you don't want me to touch her. But it's just . . . I think you need to look at this." He stepped down off the bus and onto the road. "I think something is wrong with your sister."

CHAPTER 27

The Man in the Yellow Suit

NATALIE COULDN'T MOVE.

Moments ago she'd been listening to Reggie speak to the doomed woman in the video. She'd watched his gloved hands as they'd reached with ginger precision into the woman's skull. And now those hands were holding her baby sister. Reggie pressed Eva to his chest. His tinted bonnet sparkled with reflected singers in the dark.

"Don't you panic, now," he said.

"I'm not panicking."

Even to Natalie's own ears, her voice sounded remarkably calm. Under the surface she was doing insane, screaming somersaults. Her mind spun with the image of the woman's face—before and after. Sipping coffee one moment, dripping with blood and tears and snot the next. But none of that showed in Natalie's expression or in her voice. It was like some other, better, stronger version of Natalie had suddenly arrived and taken control.

"That's good," Reggie said. "I'm going to hand her over now."

"Do it, then," Natalie said.

All in one movement Reggie closed the distance between them and pressed Eva into Natalie's arms. She could tell right away that Eva's fever had worsened. The baby shivered against her, eyes clenched tightly closed. Her little chin was slick with mucus, and her blanket was soaked through.

"She was vomiting," Reggie said. "It must have woken me up. At first I didn't know where you were, or if you'd . . . I thought you might have run off."

"I wouldn't leave her with you," Natalie said curtly. She peeled off Eva's blanket, found a dry corner, and used that to clean her up.

"Yeah, I didn't think so," Reggie said. "But, I mean . . . I also don't know you that well. Not even, like, your name."

After what Natalie had just seen, Reggie's little "aw, shucks" act was both disgusting and impressive. She resolved to do as good a job hiding what she knew about him as Reggie was doing hiding what he truly was.

"Do you have any spare water?" Natalie asked.

"Absolutely," Reggie said. He began to pat down the many compartments of his bee suit, as though searching for his canteen. Then, from one of the pockets he fished out a pistol. His pistol. Reggie held it just high enough for Natalie to see that he'd gotten it back, then returned it to his pocket.

You left the gun on the bus? Eva asked through her fever and her chills.

Natalie glanced down at her sister and nodded.

Eva writhed weakly. *Don't beat yourself up about it*, she said.

"Here it is!" Reggie announced, grinning wide as he produced a dented tin canteen from a cargo compartment on his upper thigh.

Natalie took the canteen from him, moistened her fingers, and rubbed them across Eva's gums. Then Natalie poured more water into her hand and patted down Eva's head. Steam rose up off of her baby sister's scalp.

"I guess it doesn't look so good," Reggie said. He sounded like he was already preparing to offer his condolences.

"It looks how it looks." Natalie waved him off. Then she gently placed her fingertips on Eva's face and pried open one of her eyelids. The eye beneath was cloudy and sunken. And glowing. Natalie let the eye shut and opened it again, just to be sure. Still glowing. The light was faint, but it was there. Tiny purple embers sparked in Eva's iris, throbbing and fading in the darkness. Natalie couldn't believe it. She hadn't expected it to happen so quickly.

"Holy shit," Reggie said, genuine awe in his voice.

"Yeah," Natalie said. Despite everything she'd just seen, she felt a surge of relief. Carefully, she released Eva's eyelid. It snapped closed like a shade drawn over a tiny lamp.

"Does that mean what I think it means?" Reggie asked, his voice wobbly. "Does that mean it worked?"

"It only means that it's started to," Natalie said. "She still has to make it through this fever."

"But if she does?"

"When she does," Natalie said. "Yes. She'll be vexed."

"Holy shit," Reggie said for the second time. "I can't . . ." For a moment his words became lost in a swell of light-headed laughter. "Man. I can't believe I didn't get that on tape."

"You'll just have to remember it," Natalie said. She poured water into the cap of the canteen and tried tipping some into Eva's mouth. But the fluid came right back out, chased up by a film of cloudy mucus. Eva's fists beat the air, and she began to bawl.

"I have a friend who can help," Reggie said. "Miranda— she's not a doctor, exactly. But she knows some stuff. If you'd like, we could go back to the cabin together. . . ." He trailed off, allowing his words to hang among the singers. Again, Natalie saw the wooden table in her mind. She saw the woman, cut to chunks and hollowed out.

"You mean I have a choice?" she asked.

"Absolutely," Reggie said. "Nothing's changed about that."

"Something has." Natalie nodded toward the pocket in which Reggie had stashed his pistol.

From inside the dome of his helmet, Reggie sighed. "I just didn't like having it aimed at me is all." He sounded wounded by her implication. "Honestly, after everything I've told you, can you really think I'd hurt you? As far as I'm concerned, you are the most valuable person on the planet. You and your sister."

Natalie believed him that they were valuable. But, if anything, that made her feel even less safe with him.

"Miranda can probably help us get that fever down." Reggie raced on, almost tripping over his own words. "She can help with the dehydration and anything else that comes up. We've got a place where your sister can rest, and . . ."

As Reggie rambled on, Natalie considered bolting into the woods. Even with the baby in her arms, she'd be faster than he would be in that bulky suit. And she was pretty sure he wouldn't dare shoot her. But how far could they go with no supplies? How would she and Eva ever return to Puffin Island without their kayak? And even if they did . . . what if Eva wasn't going to be all right? She was burning up, gagging out little threads of clear bile. Natalie had apparently gotten better all on her own, but what if Eva couldn't? What if she really did need medical help?

Meanwhile, Reggie was selling as hard as he could. "We have plenty to eat as well—picked up a resupply a while back. I think there's even some powdered milk in there. It isn't baby formula, but it's better than—"

"Sure. Sure." Natalie had to say it a few times to get him to stop talking.

Reggie paused, uncertain. "Yeah?"

"Yes. Just promise me something." Natalie opened her eyes as wide as they would go and looked right into the blank darkness of his bonnet. "Promise that when I'm ready, your people will let us leave."

"Of course we will!" Reggie said, so eager to reassure

her that he nearly leapt out of his bee suit. "Absolutely! Yes. And, I mean, not only that, but we can help you get wherever you're going. It's a wicked world out here." He gestured out at the sparkling woods on either side of the road. "We can all use more friends."

"I think that's true," she agreed.

That, right there, was another reason not to run. Because running would sacrifice that last advantage that Natalie still had—the fact that Reggie didn't yet know that he'd been unveiled as a monster. The fact that Natalie had seen him. So she stood there and forced herself to smile.

"My name's Natalie, by the way."

Reggie was positively giddy. He babbled nonstop as they headed back up the road, returning once more to the dead, silent forest. He told her about his life in the Quiet Lands, where he'd grown up. About joining the searchers and taking his first expedition into wicked country. What it was like to see his first tree and first singer. What it was like to meet his first wicked person. Natalie pretended not to believe any of it—a place without the wickedness? But that was just to keep Reggie rambling. And ramble he did.

"They don't mention this in any of those old radio shows, but it used to be called Agent Blue. The quiet, that is. It was invented by a woman who came from my hometown—a first-class pesticide, herbicide, and defoliant. California still had something like a government back then, and they were the ones who decided how to use it.

I mean . . . you think this is bad?" Reggie gestured out at the rotting trees flanking the road. "You should see where we come from. They literally dropped the stuff out of airplanes. They poured it directly into the lakes and rivers. They even seeded the clouds with it, so that the rain came down blue. And sure, it did get rid of the singers. But this is one of those cure-is-worse-than-the-disease situations. Because it got rid of everything. Basically, if it's green or it moves, then we don't have it in the Quiet Lands. That's one of the reasons we send searchers into wicked country," he said. "I mean, other than looking for you, of course. We're also here to study the singers. And to study the wicked. We even study the true people who have managed to hang on in this environment. We're all just out here, looking for a better way to survive."

Of course, Reggie didn't mention the pictures and films on his phone. Not a peep about the interviews that started with snacks and ended with scalpels, metal scoops, and sanitary vials. Was that simply what they were doing— studying? Slicing up the brain of some true woman, just on the off chance that she might be vexed? Or in search of some clue as to how she had survived out here, in wicked country, for so long?

"But the vex . . . Good Lord, the vex!" Reggie's satisfaction was uncontainable. "That's always been the prize. We've been searching for it for years. Then suddenly . . . boom! Here you are. Two vexed ladies."

"Here we are," Natalie agreed gamely.

Her attention was divided—listening to Reggie as carefully as she could while examining the woods beyond the road for a way out. Dawn had broken, scattering sunbeams among the dry trees. In the gathering light, Natalie could see slivers of the seashore beyond. If she could just make it down to the beach, she could follow it back to her kayak, bypassing the cabin. She could hear the roar of the waves. They sounded close. It was Eva's voice that pulled Natalie out of her own head.

Those aren't waves.

She looked up the road. A pickup truck was approaching rapidly, shiny metal plating bolted to the hood and doors. A long antenna, floppy as a fishing rod, sprouted up from a mount on the roof. The headlamps blazed with white light.

"Don't freak out, now," Reggie said. "Everything is going to be all right."

Somehow, Natalie found it within herself to answer. "If you say so."

As the pickup truck got closer, she could make out yellow and black bonnets bobbing in the rear bed. Four—five of them. Another pair of heads was visible behind the windshield. The driver gunned the engine, and the pickup leapt the final distance toward them before screeching to a stop. Five bee-suited figures vaulted out of the back. They carried rifles. One had a coil of rope slung over his shoulder.

"It's all right!" Reggie hollered, rushing to put himself between Natalie and the others. "She isn't wicked," he shouted. "Stand down!"

Still the searchers approached, forming a crescent around them. They raised their rifles, and Natalie saw to her surprise that they weren't just aiming at her, but also at Reggie himself. The next person to speak had a voice that Natalie recognized. She must have been their leader—Miranda.

"What do you want?" she asked.

"That's the wrong question," Reggie answered.

"Good boy," Miranda said, nodding. "How far away is the lake?"

"The lake is not far," Reggie said, not missing a beat. "This is the lake. We are in the lake right now." It must have been some kind of passphrase, because the very second Reggie finished, his friends relaxed. They lowered their weapons, and there was a general commotion of relieved grunts and gurgles.

"What the hell, Reggie?" Miranda said. "You couldn't have called?"

"The kid had my phone," Reggie said, stepping aside so that his group could get a better look at Natalie and her baby sister. "No need to be shy, now," he said to Natalie soothingly, as though to a baby deer. "Come forward and introduce yourself."

Reggie brought the searchers up to speed during the ride back to the cabin. Their reaction, much as his had been, was one of utter glee. One of the men, in the privacy of his domed bonnet, actually wept. But it was too early to celebrate. Eva's fever still hadn't gone down, and she seemed to be growing weaker from one minute to the next. Miranda ordered the truck off-road so that they could get back to the cabin as soon as possible, sending them crashing down the embankment and through the wilted woods. Once there Miranda took control, gently but firmly removing Eva from Natalie's grip.

"Do you know how much the baby weighs?" she asked.

It seemed, to Natalie, an entirely baffling question. All she could do was shake her head.

"All right," Miranda said. "When was the last time she fed?"

"I tried a few hours ago," Natalie said. It was all she could do to keep from reaching out and grabbing her sister back. "She didn't get much down. . . . The last time she really ate was yesterday evening."

Miranda had heard all she needed to. She rushed Eva to the cabin, barking orders at the various searchers. "I want that scale, Danny. Also, get some water going. Reggie, go check the kit to see if we have any Tylenol left and cut me a few half doses. Nathan, the IV, and don't forget swabs. Quickly, people! As far as we know there are exactly two vexed people on the planet, and we aren't about to lose one of them!"

As sickened as Natalie was by these people, she couldn't dismiss a feeling of relief at this very moment. They were going to help her sister. At least that—she had to stay focused on that. And stay alert for whatever might happen next. Miranda continued giving orders as she and Reggie peeled off their bee suits and pulled on pairs of horrifyingly familiar surgical gloves. Eva battled and brawled as they set upon her. She hollered so loudly when Reggie pressed the IV needle into her arm that her jaw looked like it might unhinge. But as the fluid began to flow into her, Eva calmed. Not five minutes later, with her hot head snug under a damp cloth, she fell asleep.

Natalie was determined to act her part, making herself every bit as sincere and as thankful as the doomed woman in the video. But all the while, she kept half an eye on the bee-suited figures rushing in and out under Miranda's command. She took stock of the room, looking for anything that she might be able to use to defend herself—and her sister—with. She tried her best to picture the short path that led back down to the jetty. Would she be able to find it in the dark after everyone had fallen asleep?

"You know, I may have some more formula back in my kayak," Natalie lied. "Would it be all right if I went to get it?"

"That's a silly question," Miranda said.

"What she means," Reggie said, "is of course you can. You're not a prisoner here, Natalie." Reggie paused to look up and give her a wide grin, which made it look like his singer tattoo was trying to climb into his mouth. "Do what you need to do."

"Thanks," Natalie said, smiling right back.

Not wanting to leave Eva alone with these people any longer than she had to, Natalie bounded down the cabin steps and through the yard of brown ferns. She traced her way back to the jetty, committing each turn and twist in the path to memory. Once she got there, she saw that her kayak had been hoisted out of the water and pulled onshore. She wasn't surprised that they'd found it, but the sight gave her a sinking feeling. The day hatch lay open—clearly they'd searched it. Natalie took a few steps closer to see if anything was missing, and that's when she noticed the hole. It was about the size of a littleneck clam, smooth around the edges, drilled right through the kayak bottom. As fatal as a hole in the heart. Unless she patched it up, the kayak would sink like a stone.

"They aren't good people," a familiar voice said very softly.

Natalie froze. One of the bee-suited searchers had followed her to the jetty. He was the tall one—the man who had wept at the news of two vexed girls. Until that very moment, Natalie hadn't heard him speak. So . . . why was his voice familiar?

"I don't understand what you mean," she said, struggling to keep up her part of the act. "They're helping my sister."

In answer to this, the man only shook his head.

"They . . . They're giving her medicine," she stammered, "to get her fever down." Natalie peered past him to see if somebody else was out there as well. Was this some kind of test? Some kind of trap?

"Please try to stay calm," the man whispered, bringing one of his gloved fingers up in front of his tinted visor to make a shushing motion. "They're watching you. Very carefully. They're listening. If you get loud, they're going to hear."

Even at a whisper, even muffled through the tinted visor, Natalie knew that voice. But before she had a chance to say anything, the man began to unzip his bonnet. Then he pulled it off, revealing a face still wet with tears.

It was her father.

So at least there was this—Natalie didn't get loud. She just stood there, frozen, staring. Her father. He looked different from how she remembered. In just a few months his skin had grown pale, and his hair had thinned. There was a broad, peach-colored scar on his temple, and his opposite ear was blistered and burned. His nose had also changed shape and fattened. It looked like it had been broken and reset. Maybe more than once.

"Please, please stay quiet," her dad whispered. "Don't shout."

Natalie couldn't have shouted even if she wanted to. She fought an urge to run to her father and wrap him in a hug. She fought an even stronger urge to shove him off the damn jetty. Instead, she just sat down upon the slatted wood. Her knees felt wobbly, and the jetty swam beneath her.

"Natalie, I—"

"No." She cut him off. She wasn't sure what he'd been about to say, but "no" was the correct answer for any and all of it. She suddenly remembered what Reggie had told her, about a stranger joining their group. An honorary searcher.

"It's you? You're the new guy?"

"What?"

"The one helping them study Goldsport. That's you?"

At first her dad could only nod. Then he started again. "Honey—"

"No," Natalie said.

"Sweetheart—"

"No."

She had as many "no"s for her dad as he had stupid bullshit garbage words for her.

"Natalie, please. It happened on the first day. Otherwise, I never would have . . ." Her dad trailed off. He glanced over his shoulder. Through the dead bramble, they could see flashes of yellow as searchers came and went in the yard.

"I can't stay here long," he said, lowering his voice back to a whisper. He squatted down and began gathering fallen branches for firewood. "I'm pretty sure they believe my story, but Miranda will start asking questions if she sees me hanging around near you."

Natalie glared.

Her father kept his attention locked on the ground at the base of the dock, searching for sticks. Searching for words. "Look, we don't have time right now to go through it all, but I was being an idiot, Natalie. I think I must have . . . I must have just been blowing off steam. It was always in the back of my head that I might need to take a few days to cool down. I was always going to come back. But then I met these—"

"You never told me you were going to come back," Natalie said. "You looked right at me as you packed up that kayak. And then you left." Her voice was getting dangerously loud, but she couldn't help herself. Her dad shifted uncomfortably and once more glanced back toward the cabin. He tried to reach out to touch her on the shoulder, but Natalie slapped his hand away. Hard.

"Leaving is leaving."

"I know," her dad said.

"You left Mom all alone, and me all alone."

"I did," he said.

With those two words, his whole body collapsed within his bee suit. Natalie found it impossible to look at him—both because of her rage and also because of the unbearable shame that was pouring out of the man. She loved him and hated him and was embarrassed for him all at once. So instead, she kept her eyes on the water just beneath their feet. It was crystal clear. A green anemone waved gently up at them.

"The searchers were already here when I arrived," her dad said, his voice nearly inaudible. "They seemed . . . They pretended to be good people. They asked where I'd come from. I told them Goldsport, only because I didn't want them finding out about Puffin Island. And then, when I realized how . . ." Her dad tried wiping his tears with the back of his rubber glove, but that only smeared them.

"They did that to you?" Natalie asked. She meant the marks all over his face—the broken nose and burnt ear.

Her father's eyes darkened. "They did. But it's nothing. They're capable of so much worse."

"I know," Natalie said. "I saw a video on Reggie's phone."

Hearing this, her father's back straightened. "Does Reggie know?"

Natalie shook her head.

"Thank God," her father said, glancing around at the woods. "They were getting ready to cross the bay and head into Canada when I met them. The plan was to search the islands on their way. That's why I've been trying to keep them busy here. Keep their attention on Goldsport. It's also the only reason they decided not to . . ."

Her father didn't finish. He didn't have to—Natalie got it. By diverting the searchers and keeping them occupied on the mainland, he'd not only been protecting her, her mother, and the baby, but he'd also been protecting himself. Otherwise, Reggie's group would have had no more use for him than they'd had for the true woman in the video.

"So you held them off going to Puffin Island by telling them that there was a vexed girl in Goldsport," Natalie said. It was the closest thing to a peace offering she could manage.

"Yes," her father said.

"So that's not . . . It's not true, is it?"

For the first time since he'd sat down beside her on the jetty, her dad looked Natalie directly in the face.

"It used to be," he said.

PART V

COMMEMORATION

CHAPTER 28

Pay It Back

THERE ARE SOME WORDS THAT, WHEN SPOKEN, BECOME wrecking balls. Astrid's mother might as well have knocked down the town of Goldsport with her story. The sanctuary would never be the same again—at least not for Astrid, it wouldn't be. What she'd learned about her town, about her own family, shook her to her core. How could her grandfather—that wide-grinning, hand-shaking, deal-making, wall-building savior of their history—have done something so evil? The more Astrid thought about it, the more disgusted she became.

Here was the simple, awful truth of it: Ronnie Gold had built this life, her life, on the blood and suffering of other people. It was cruel, and it was unnecessary. There wasn't an investor in Goldsport who didn't have at least one bedroom to spare. Hell, they'd converted three of the houses into storage space for antiques and family heirlooms! So, if they'd wanted to, they could easily have kept their promise to the people of Port Emory and shared the sanctuary. To exile them in order to survive was bad enough. But what Astrid's family had done—what all of the investors had done—was so much worse. They had harmed others, left them out beyond the walls to die or fall wicked simply to preserve their own comfort. To protect their stores of freeze-dried treats, their supply of milk and cheese, their stupid damn billiard rooms. And whether Astrid liked it or not, she was a part of that. Every good thing in her life had been stolen from someone else. In the end, what did it matter that it wasn't her who'd done the stealing?

Now nothing was going to stop her from going to Puffin Island. It went beyond Astrid's old childhood curiosity—it had become a matter of duty. There might not be anyone left alive on that little rock in the bay, but if there was, Astrid had to find them and do whatever she could to help. Hank was in complete agreement.

They decided that the best time to sneak away would be during commemoration, when the whole town would be distracted—not to mention drunk and happy. That gave them a few days to get ready. First they went out to the docks to fuel up the lobster boat and pump out the bilge. They gathered food from the dairy garden and underground grocery, taking enough to make a serious peace offering to whomever they might find out there. Eliza may have hated the ice cream, but Astrid was willing to bet that hungry people on the island would be happy to have it. At Hank's insistence, they also stashed a hunting rifle in the boat, just to be safe.

The preparations reminded Astrid of that time she and Hank once played at running away to the island, when they were children. Despite all of their planning back then, she was pretty sure they'd never have gone through with it. But things were different now. Astrid meant to get to Puffin Island even if she had to swim. Of course, her dad's thoughts on the issue hadn't changed a bit since she was a little girl. It was only fair to tell him, and Amblin threw a fit when he heard.

"You are not going anywhere," he yelled, hammering on the bolted door of the quarantine house. "Neither of you."

"I'm sorry, Dad," Astrid said, standing on the other side of the door. "But you can't stop us."

"The hell I can't." Her father stormed over to one of the barred windows and called out through the heavy-duty screen. "Tommy! Are you there?"

He meant Mr. Collins, who was supposed to be posted on guard duty.

"He isn't," Astrid said.

"Chipper! Hey, Chip!"

"Mr. Gregory isn't there either," Astrid said. In fact, neither of them had shown up for their last few shifts. She could only guess that the two old men were busy decorating the plaza with streamers and balloons. Still . . . it was a little odd that Henry hadn't thought to send a replacement.

There was a hard bang from inside the quarantine house—the sound of her father kicking something. "And what about your mother?" he asked, his voice sinking down into an angry rumble. "I suppose she's just fine with this?"

"Not exactly," Astrid said. "But she isn't trying to stop us."

"She might as well be helping you, then," Amblin fumed. "It's stupid, Astrid. This is a stupid way for you to get back at me. It's unsafe, and immature, and—"

"I'm not getting back at you," Astrid cut him off.

"Aren't you?"

"Of course not. How do you . . . ? How do you not get that?" Astrid asked.

There was a long silence from inside the quarantine house. She heard a slide, followed by a soft *thump*. Her father must have sat himself down upon the floor. When he spoke again, his anger had drained away.

"I shouldn't have waited so long to tell you," he said. "But I was going to."

"I know that you were," Astrid said.

"I thought if . . . I thought that there might be a way to tell it so that you wouldn't think I was . . ."

"Think you were what?"

"I don't know, honey," he said. "I guess I didn't want you to hate me."

"I don't hate you, Dad." Astrid took a step closer to the door, sat down in the sand, and tried again. "You were a kid. You couldn't have stopped it. But I'm still . . ." Words failed her momentarily. "I'm angry. And I'm ashamed."

"There isn't any reason for you to be ashamed," her dad said.

"Of course there is."

"Neither of us can change what happened."

"We can't," Astrid said. "But if anyone is still left out there, then we need to pay it back. We need to pay something back." She reached out and touched the door. The wood stank, sticky with dried quiet. "Please don't worry, Dad. It's been a long time. There probably isn't anybody on the island anyway."

"And if there is?"

Astrid didn't hesitate. "Then I'm going to talk to them."

CHAPTER 29

One Crack

COMMEMORATION WAS THE FOLLOWING DAY. THE CEREMONY would begin at dusk, with the hours before a frenzy of last-minute preparations. There were speeches to practice, pits to dig for the clambake, banquet tables to set, champagne to ice, tuxedos to press, and evening gowns to steam. Astrid and Hank, on the other hand, just had one thing left on their to-do list: retrieve the boat key from the Bushkirk house. If they could do so without bumping into Hank's dad, so much the better.

They made their move in the morning, avoiding the plaza by taking the long way around the greenway and entering through the western hatch. Happy voices echoed down the halls, and they could see fuzzy shapes racing through the layered glass. But they managed to make it all the way to the Bushkirk house without bumping into a soul. They knocked just to be sure that no one was home and then stepped inside.

It was filthy. Half-eaten cans of soup crowded the coffee

table in the living room, and the carpet was littered with crumpled tissues. Somebody must have caught a cold. "The key is in my father's study," Hank said, casting his eyes over the mess. He hadn't been home since the day Eliza was shot, and it didn't look like he'd missed the place. "You can wait here."

Hank disappeared into the back of the house while Astrid stepped deeper into the living room. She noticed an empty bottle of cough medicine among the many soup cans, along with a packet of heavy-duty painkillers. There was also a thermometer, sticking out from between the couch cushions. Whoever was sick, they had it bad. Astrid hoped that it was Mr. Bushkirk.

"I didn't hear you come in."

Astrid started at the voice from above. She looked up to see Klara standing on the second-floor landing. She was dressed in a bathrobe. Her hair was a tangle, and there were shadowed bags under her eyes.

"I'm sorry," Astrid said. "We knocked. Did we wake you up?"

"I didn't hear any knocking" was Klara's only answer.

There was a very long and awkward moment when neither of them spoke. Astrid shifted her weight on the dirty carpet. It felt odd to be staring up like this at Hank's stepmom, who was wearing nothing but a bathrobe. She'd rarely seen Klara in anything other than her Sunday best. The robe revealed the woman's sharp collarbones. Her skin looked like expensive paper.

"Hank's just getting something," Astrid offered. "We won't be long."

"Oh . . . I thought he was in his room?"

For a moment Astrid just stared up at her. Had Klara really not noticed that her stepson had been gone for more than a week? Had she gotten worse since the last time Astrid spoke to her, or was this the other kind of unknowing—the willful kind? Klara had been here when Henry had whipped Hank with leather gloves, plastic coat hangers, and his own fat hands. Over the years she must have become an expert at not noticing things.

"Well, he's not," Astrid said. "We'll be out of your hair in a minute."

"You aren't in my hair," Klara said, running her fingers across her scalp as though to double-check. Then she leaned forward and gripped the railing of the stairwell with both hands.

"Can I ask you something? Show you something, I mean? Can I show you something upstairs?"

"Oh. Sure."

Klara smiled. "Come up with me," she said, releasing the railing and turning down the second-story landing. Baffled, Astrid followed her. They headed to Hank's room. The door was open, and Klara walked right in. The room looked very much as Astrid remembered it—bare and boring. There were no posters on the walls, no books on the shelf. It looked like a room in a stranger's house that Hank had been renting, rather than one he'd grown up in. Clothes hanging in the closet and the unmade bed were the only clues that anybody had ever spent a night here.

"Look what I did," Klara said.

"What?"

"I didn't think I could do it, but I did," Klara said. She sounded proud, grinning sheepishly as she pointed at the bed.

Astrid wasn't following. She looked at Hank's bed; it seemed perfectly normal. The big comforter was twisted and overturned, as though from a night of restless sleep. But then she noticed bits of fluff—they looked like cotton balls—strewn here and there. It was . . . stuffing? Astrid stepped closer and saw that there were little gashes punched here and there through the comforter. She pulled back the bedding. The mattress below had holes as well—jagged stab wounds, bleeding stuffing and springs. It was as though the bed had been butchered. A kitchen knife lay in the middle of the mattress, discarded among the fluff.

"He didn't hear me coming," Klara said. "He was under the covers, so he couldn't hear me. He doesn't even know that I killed him yet!"

Astrid looked from the bed to Klara. Hands shaking, she put the torn-up comforter back into place, covering the knife.

"Astrid! Where'd you go?" Hank's voice rang out from below.

"She's up here with me," Klara called. Then, to Astrid: "He's going to be so surprised when he sees what I did!"

Hank's footfalls hammered up the stairs. A moment later he appeared in the doorframe. As soon as he saw the expression on her face, Astrid could tell that he understood. Something had gone horribly wrong.

"Don't touch her," Astrid said.

"I killed you," Klara said, spinning around to beam at her stepson. Then, once she actually saw him standing there, her expression soured. "Why didn't you die when I killed you, Hank? That doesn't seem fair to me."

Astrid reached out and grabbed at the sleeve of Klara's bathrobe. She gently pulled the woman backward, lowering her down into a chair that sat against the wall. Then, careful to use her other hand, she took Hank by the elbow and led him through the doorframe and out of the room. Klara made no move to chase after them. She just sat there on the chair, patting down the sides of her robe.

"Did either of you see where I put my knife?" Klara asked.

Astrid didn't respond. She closed the door behind them, keeping her fist tight on the knob. Hank just stood there, his whole face drained of blood. "She's . . . Is she . . . ?" He couldn't bring himself to say the word.

Just as Astrid nodded, Klara called from inside the bedroom, "Oh, forget I asked—I found it!"

The doorknob began to jostle in Astrid's grip.

"How could she have caught it?" Hank asked.

"It has to be your dad," Astrid said, holding tighter to the knob. "He must have gotten it when he moved Eliza's body."

This sent a jolt right through Hank. He recoiled from

her, his back pressed up against the railing. "God, if my dad . . . Then I—then I could . . ."

For a moment Astrid was afraid that he might throw himself over the railing to get away from her. To keep her safe from himself in case he, too, was infected. But in his panic, Hank wasn't thinking.

"I can't catch it, remember?" Astrid said, as soothingly as she was able while still keeping a firm grip on the doorknob. "And it's been a week. If you'd been exposed, you'd be sick by now."

Hank nodded at her frantically. "I'd be sick by now," he agreed. "If I had it, I'd be sick by now." Slowly he released his grip on the railing. "And my dad . . . He hit me before he moved Eliza's body. I didn't ever . . . I never touched her," Hank said haltingly, talking himself off the ledge.

"That's right," Astrid said. "And you've been staying with my mom ever since."

For another moment Hank just stood there, nodding. The horrible irony of what had happened wasn't lost on either of them. In his attempt to make Amblin Gold look like he'd risked their safety, Henry Bushkirk had completely shattered it. He'd cast himself, and Klara, down among the wicked. And if the two of them were sick, there was no telling how many other people he might have exposed. Mr. Bushkirk may as well have opened all the hatches and let a whole swarm of singers into the greenway. Meanwhile, on the other side of the bedroom door, Klara continued to fiddle with the doorknob.

"A little help?" Astrid said.

"Shit—sorry!" Hank leapt back into action, rushing into the master bedroom at the far end of the landing. He emerged with a length of rope, and for a second Astrid was worried that he meant to try to tie Klara up. But instead Hank knotted one end of the rope around the doorknob and the other around the landing railing. It was such an odd, such a specific thing to do. Astrid understood without asking that Hank's father had done this to him when he was small. To lock him inside. To punish him for . . . who knew what. God, Henry Bushkirk had been wicked long before he'd ever caught this disease.

Carefully, she released the doorknob. The door pulled back about an inch, just enough to see the gleam in Klara's delighted eyes, before snapping closed again.

"Hey, I think there's something wrong with this," she called to them. "Could one of you help me out, please?"

They both took a step away from the door. For a moment they could only stare at it, dumbfounded about what to do next.

"Did you find the boat key?" Astrid asked.

Hank nodded.

"I don't need a boat key." His stepmom groaned from inside the bedroom. "I need a door key."

"Can she even understand us?" Hank asked.

"I don't know," Astrid said. "I think so."

"Klara," he called out. "Are you . . . ? Are you in there?"

"Of course I am, honey!"

"I'm sorry about this," Hank said.

For a moment his stepmom quit tugging at the door-knob. "No, I am," she said. "I'm the one who's sorry. I tried so hard, Hank. But I didn't do it right the first time. I'd like a second chance, please."

Of course, she only meant a second chance at stabbing him.

They left Hank's house in a daze. Astrid's legs carried her numbly down the stairs, out the front door, and through the greenway shunt. The enormity of what had happened seemed too much to fit into her head all at once. She and Hank agreed, without saying a word, to go to the plaza. They crept through the dairy gardens, peeking through the opening and into the big airy space.

The scene that greeted them appeared normal at first. A large banner hung above the stage, reading: THANK YOU, RONNIE GOLD! THANK YOU, INVESTORS! Below that, smaller text read: FORTY YEARS THRIVING IN A WICKED WORLD. The banquet tables had already been set up, each draped in white lace. Name cards, empty glasses, and bouquets of greenhouse flowers sat atop each table. Ribbons and streamers cascaded from the glass walls, and Mrs. Lee's party-planning committee had hung the old photographs up around the edges of the plaza. Some of the members—Mrs. Wrigley and Mr. Pratt—were still there, fussing with the decorations. Trying to make every-thing perfect.

But something was wrong. Astrid's eyes were drawn to the Abbitt twins at the center of the plaza, in the midst of a gathering crowd. The twins were huddled over what looked like a ruined sandcastle. They seemed not to care one bit that they were getting sand and grit all over their evening gowns. When Astrid looked more closely at the castle, she could see a pair of bare feet sticking out, near the base. She searched the other side of the sandcastle, but she couldn't find a head to go with those feet.

"There's my dad," Hank hissed, pointing down at the far end of the plaza. There, a group of investors were digging pits for the clambake. The work had a frantic quality to it, with shovelfuls of sand flying out of one pit and into another. But nobody seemed to mind—the diggers cackled like children at play. They chucked unearthed shells and stones at one another. Henry Bushkirk himself stood atop a mound of sand, surveying the work with his hands on his hips. Beside him was Mr. Gregory, wearing nothing but a pair of boxer shorts, a smashed-in party hat, and an expression of placid delight. He was seated in a wheelbarrow.

"How did it spread so quickly?" Hank asked.

"I don't know . . . ," Astrid said. Instinctively, they reached for each other. Astrid squeezed Hank's hand, and he squeezed back.

It was clear to her that while they'd been pawing through the archives and sneaking food from the grocery, the wickedness had marched steadily through the sanctuary. But could it have touched everyone in just a few days? Astrid scanned the crowd, catching sight of Abigail Lee seated upon the stage, gazing out at the other investors with glazed horror. Missy Van Allen was beside her. They both looked awful, with red noses and dark circles under their eyes. Mrs. Lee blew wetly into a handkerchief.

"We have to go," Hank said.

Astrid nodded at the two ladies on the stage. "They still look true."

"They're already sick," Hank said, desperation rising in his voice. His hand tightened on Astrid's, and he began to pull her away from the opening. "If they haven't fallen wicked yet, they will soon."

"But there have to be others," Astrid said. "Others who haven't caught it. This isn't even half the town."

It was almost as though Mrs. Lee sensed that somebody was talking about her, because at that moment her bloodshot eyes settled upon Hank and Astrid lurking by the plaza entrance. Mrs. Lee stood and made a very clear shooing motion. She mouthed: *Don't run.*

"We can't stay here," Hank whispered, pulling harder now. "You know that."

He was right. Together they backed out of the plaza. It was all they could do to keep from breaking into a sprint. They returned to the western hatch, where Hank began to pull his bee suit on with shaking fingers. While he did this, Astrid dunked her left hand—the one she'd touched Klara with—into the big bucket of quiet to disinfect it. She might not have been able to catch the wickedness, but she didn't want those germs hitching a ride on her. The frothing blue liquid burned her skin.

Outside, the singers rejoiced.

"I thought I heard you two!"

Astrid and Hank turned and saw Mr. Collins standing about twenty paces down the glass hallway. He was ready for the ceremony—all done up in a three-piece suit, complete with a pocket square. He'd even combed and trimmed his beard.

"Hurry up, please," Astrid whispered to Hank.

"That is you two little lovebirds I hear, isn't it?" Mr. Collins asked. He wasn't wearing his glasses. Astrid could see the pair of golden bifocals sticking out of the breast pocket of his suit jacket. "Just say something so I know it's you. Someone turned off my eyes, I think."

Neither of them answered. Hank stepped into his rubber boots. Astrid helped him tighten the elastic on his pant legs while he pulled the coarse fabric of the bee suit up over his waist. Mr. Collins stood there, tapping his finger against his bearded chin.

"Oh, I just remembered!" the old gentleman yelped. "There's something that I want to show you." With that he began patting down the pockets of his vest and trousers. His fingers settled lightly on the golden frames of his eyeglasses, and he pulled them out of the pocket. "No . . . ," Mr. Collins said, "that's not what I want." He flicked the eyeglasses away, both lenses popping out as they smashed against the greenway wall.

"Did either of you kids happen to see where I put it?"

"Yes," Astrid said, breathless. "I think you left it at home."

The top half of Hank's suit was all twisted up. His arms couldn't find the sleeves. Astrid tried her best to help, but it seemed like they were succeeding only in tying themselves into knots.

Mr. Collins mustn't have liked Astrid's answer, because he continued patting himself down. He finally reached into his belt and fished out a pistol. He held the gun up to his own face for a moment, giving it a look of loving surprise. Then he aimed it roughly at Hank and pulled the trigger. All that came out of the pistol was a *click*, like snapping teeth.

"Fuck." Hank was in a full-on panic. Astrid wasn't far behind, her hands shaking as she tried desperately to help him into the bee suit.

Mr. Collins seemed utterly tickled. "I know! Stupid me. But don't you worry, I'll get this sorted out." He dug his fist into his pants and pulled out a handful of glittering bullets. Flipping the cylinder open, he tried to load the pistol. A single bullet slid home before he spilled the rest. They clattered down onto the tiled floor of the greenway. Mr. Collins began to giggle as if this were simply the most hilarious thing he had ever seen in his life.

"What a klutz I am!"

With great effort he squatted down and began to recover the bullets. One by one he slid them into the cylinder of his pistol.

Astrid yanked one of Hank's arms through the suit, yelling at him to hurry up. But he froze—stuck between fight and flight. Without warning he lurched toward Mr. Collins, hands clenched into fists. But Astrid held him back.

"If you touch him, you'll get it!" she shouted. "Just get your other arm in!"

It was too late to charge him anyway. Mr. Collins had finished loading his pistol.

"There I go," he said, winching himself back up into a standing position. He aimed the pistol once more and squeezed off a shot. The sound in the enclosed space was deafening as the bullet struck right between their heads. The reinforced greenway wall made a sucking sound as it absorbed the shot, and a thousand milky cracks blossomed across the ballistic glass.

"It sounds like I missed," Mr. Collins announced, undaunted. He very deliberately moved the pistol a few inches to the right and fired again. This time the shot cut through the quiet-laden woolen curtains. Again, he adjusted his aim.

Astrid tugged, Hank shoved, and in went his other arm. His bonnet remained unfastened, but they were out of time. Astrid reached through the curtains, grabbed the bucket that sat in the quiet room, and hurled the contents at Hank. The blue liquid splashed across his chest, spattering up over his face. Some of it got into his mouth and eyes. It would have to be enough.

"Run!" Astrid cried as Hank pawed at his eyes. "Run!"

And they ran, dashing through the curtains, across the quiet room, out the western hatch, and into the open air. The singers cried hallelujah, and Mr. Collins kept on shooting.

CHAPTER 30

Mom

THE SINGERS CHASED HANK ALL THE WAY ACROSS THE BARREN north shore. They swarmed a few paces behind him, diving for his bare head, pulling away only at the last minute. The quiet must have been just enough to keep them at bay. Mr. Collins chased them as well, though much more slowly. The sand jumped up around Astrid's and Hank's feet as he shot at them. "I sure wish I could see you better!" the old man called, full of good humor, as he stopped to reload.

By the time they got to Ria's house, she'd heard them coming. Ria stood guard just inside her makeshift quiet room. She opened the front door the moment their boots hit her deck, slamming it shut again as soon as they were through. But as fast as Ria had been, a single singer still managed to make it inside.

Ria took cover behind the treated curtains. Hank, terrified, just kept running through the house. He knocked over chairs and splashed blue poison everywhere, yelping with fright, wild as a mad horse, the singer always only inches behind him. Astrid tried to keep herself together. She chased after Hank, catching the singer in her bare hands. It took all her strength to crush the nasty little thing between her palms.

"That wasn't . . . Was that Mr. Collins chasing after you?" Ria asked, coming out from behind the curtains. She went into the den to peek through the screened-in window.

Before they could answer her, another shot rang out, splintering the banister of the veranda outside. They all dove to the floor.

"Yes!" Hank spit quiet out of his mouth as he spoke. "They're wicked," he sputtered, his eyes enormous.

"What? Who is?"

"Everybody!" Hank cried out. He rolled onto his back, cradling his head in his hands. "My father—my father—he gave it to everybody." Hank made a choking sound.

Ria looked at Astrid. Her face said that she didn't want to believe it.

"We don't know if it's everybody," Astrid said. "But it's most of them. They're all in the plaza, getting ready for the party."

Hank began to pull at his hair. "How could I not have said anything?" he moaned. "It's my fault. I didn't say anything about how he—how he touched the wicked lady's body. I didn't say!" It still sounded like he was choking, like he couldn't get his breathing right. Hank began to roll from side to side on the floor, deep in a full-blown meltdown.

Astrid had never seen him like this. Then he rolled over one of the unfastened buckles of his bee suit and nearly jumped out of his own skin.

"What is that?" he screamed. "Is that a singer?"

"Hank." Ria crawled toward him. "Hank, look at me now."

"Get it off me," Hank shrieked, flopping around like the floor was a hot skillet.

"Hank." Ria put both hands flat on his chest and pressed down hard, pinning him. "That wasn't a singer. You need to calm down."

Hank looked up at Ria and took a long, quavering breath. "Okay," he said. "Okay. I'm sorry."

From outside there was another gunshot. A window shattered on the second floor, the glass chiming as it fell. Mr. Collins whooped with delight. Then he shot out another window, this time on the ground floor. The wire screen puckered inward, and shards of glass went flying. They landed at Astrid's feet.

"Nothing to be sorry about," Ria said, ignoring everything that was happening outside. She rubbed her hands in a slow circle on Hank's chest. "Let's get that suit the rest of the way on you." Ria glanced at Astrid, nodding toward her own bee suit hanging on a peg by the quiet room. With Mr. Collins shooting out windows, it was only a matter of time before more singers found their way inside.

Astrid scooted over to the wall and slipped the suit from the peg. Then she helped Hank and her mother dress. Just as she fastened her mother's bonnet, they heard footsteps on the front stoop.

"Hi there, Tommy," Ria called out, keeping her voice nice and steady.

"I can hear you, but I can't see you," Mr. Collins answered. "Somebody made my eyes go all fuzzy."

"You should probably get that fixed," Ria said. Then, without missing a beat, she continued. "Tell me, Tommy, do you have any bullets left?"

"I don't," Mr. Collins said, crestfallen.

"That's a shame," Ria said.

"I know. There might be some back at my house. I'm pretty sure there are, actually. But I'm tired. I don't want to go all the way back home." Mr. Collins went quiet for a moment, perhaps weighing his conundrum. Then an idea struck him. "Actually," he continued, "do you have any bullets that you could give me? My gun needs a special kind. . . . Thirty-eights, I think?"

"Thirty-eight caliber, you say?" Now that Ria knew Mr. Collins couldn't shoot at them anymore, she allowed herself to stand and look at him through the window. "Definitely," she said. "Just give me a few minutes while I find them."

"I'm going to put those bullets into my gun," Mr. Collins explained. "And I'm going to use my gun to shoot you in the heart and stomach."

"I bet you are."

Ria headed upstairs, motioning for Astrid and Hank to follow. Hank was still shaking, his legs wobbly, but he seemed better now that he was properly fastened into his suit. They passed through the second floor, which already had a few singers floating down the hallway, and up into the turret room. There, Ria kept an old telescope by the window.

"We have to get back to the greenway," Astrid said, looking at her mother.

Ria didn't answer. She turned the telescope toward the plaza and put her eye up to the viewfinder.

"There must be people in town who haven't caught it yet," Astrid pleaded, gulping down a breath. "It's only been a week!"

"A week is a long time," Ria said, adjusting the focus. "And if the wickedness really has spread, it won't be safe to just walk around the greenway asking everybody the question. Even if they don't have any symptoms yet, they could still . . ." Whatever her mother had been about to say turned into a long, deep sigh.

"Hank. Did you manage to find that boat key?"

"I did."

"And the boat?" Ria asked, not taking her eye off of the telescope. "Is it ready to go?"

"It has some food and water," Hank said. "And it's all gassed up."

"Mom, what are you talking about?" Astrid said. "We can't just go. There are people back there. And we can't leave Dad in quarantine."

"We're not leaving your father anywhere," Ria said. "But

whatever was going to happen on the greenway has already happened. I'm sorry, Astrid. It's too late to go back."

With that she pulled away from the telescope, allowing Astrid to look for herself. The scene that greeted her through the viewfinder was like something out of a nightmare. Henry Bushkirk stood astride the stage—it looked like he was delivering the annual commemoration speech. But instead of holding a microphone in his hand, he was talking directly into the severed head of one of the milk goats from the dairy garden. Henry's arms were pure red from his elbows to his fingertips, marinated in blood. Meanwhile, the Abbitt twins had begun setting off the fireworks early. They were lighting them right inside the plaza, sending the rockets bouncing off of the glass dome and tumbling back down again, exploding here and there upon the sand. One of these rockets set the hem of Mrs. Wrigley's lace party dress on fire, and she ran in circles, trailing smoke. It looked like she was laughing. Astrid's head snapped back from the telescope as if the metal eyepiece had burned her.

"Guys?" Hank had drifted over to the opposite side of the turret room. "I think it's too late to get to the boat, too."

Ria spun around. "What do you mean?"

"Just look." He pointed. "The harbor."

Astrid and her mother raced to the far window. Down beyond the plaza, the docks were swarming. The newly wicked had surrounded the lobster boats, playing catch with wooden buoys. Some grabbed at the singers like kids chasing fireflies, while others leapt into the shallow water, splashing with a kind of frenzied joy. Still more wicked were pouring out of the eastern hatch of the greenway, headed directly for the north shore.

Down on the veranda, Mr. Collins must have seen the fuzzy shape of the approaching crowd.

"I think those are my friends!" he announced. "They're going to help me blow your house down."

The investors arrived at Ria's house one by one, gathering in a crowd outside. They greeted Mr. Collins with laughter and embraces, rocking back and forth as they hugged. Chipper Gregory was there, still wearing his crushed party hat. So was Mrs. Wrigley, her dress in ashen tatters. Even the Abbitt twins came, their slender hands blackened and blistered by the fireworks. But the wicked didn't claw or scramble, like a horde of monsters at the door. They all just stood around the house, as if waiting expectantly for their friends to come out and play.

Astrid, Ria, and Hank ducked down and kept clear of the windows. They snuck downstairs and took cover behind the couch.

"Let's give it some time," Ria whispered. "Sooner or later they'll forget why they came out here."

"How do you know?" Astrid asked.

"I don't," Ria said, scowling.

The wicked began knocking on the door. The sound continued for a time and then stopped. The doorknob jostled and then went still. This happened again and again. It seemed that none of them could truly understand that the door was locked until they'd all tried it for themselves. There was a soft murmur of conversation as the wicked puzzled over the problem of how to get inside. When nothing worked, they tried the exact same thing all over again—jostling the knob, knocking, asking with hopeful voices if somebody could please open up. They didn't sound the least bit discouraged.

Then one voice rose above the rest.

"Is my son in there?"

Hank went rigid.

"I saw him!" Mr. Collins said, bursting with pride. "At least . . . I think it was him." Less sure now. "I would have shot him. But I was out of bullets."

"I agree that we should shoot him," Henry Bushkirk said. He sounded officious—the very formal chairperson he'd always wanted to be. "I agree with you on that."

Astrid reached out to take Hank by the hand, but he snatched it away from her. Slowly he began to inch out from behind the couch. He was heading for one of the windows. Astrid crawled after him.

"Be careful!" Ria whispered.

"Do any of us have bullets?" Henry Bushkirk called out. "If anyone has bullets, please pass them forward to me now!"

There was a general commotion as the investors searched their pockets and purses. "I have scissors," Mrs. Wrigley offered. "Are my scissors enough?"

"My scissors," Henry said.

There was the sound of a brief scuffle, followed by an agonized cry. Hank and Astrid scrambled the rest of the way to the window. They cracked the curtains open and peeked out to see if Mrs. Wrigley was all right. She was sitting down on the front stoop with her head in her hands, sulking. Standing before her was Mr. Bushkirk, his arms still dripping with goat blood. He held the scissors in his fist, gripping them like he would a tiny ceremonial dagger.

"I don't think he'll hurt her," Astrid whispered to Hank.

Hank looked at her. The panic had left him, but something else had taken its place. "He already has," Hank said. "He made her like this. He made Klara and Mr. Collins and everyone else like this."

Hank's eyes were glassy with shame and rage. A strange expression passed over his face, and an instant later his hand darted into the compartment of his bee suit. Astrid remembered, a second too late, that he kept a sanctuary-issued pistol in there—the same one he'd aimed at poor Eliza when they'd first met her. Hank must have forgotten about the pistol too, because he seemed almost surprised when he pulled it out. He pressed it through the curtains, the barrel making a clinking sound as it touched the window glass.

"Hank." Astrid grasped his wrist. "Stop."

"It's an easy shot from here."

"Don't do it," she whispered.

Outside, Henry Bushkirk climbed up onto the stoop and faced the crowd. He couldn't have been more than a few feet from them. "What about our mother?" Mr. Bushkirk called out. "Does anybody remember how our mother works?"

"He deserves it," Hank said, pulling against Astrid to steady his aim. "He deserved it even before he fell wicked."

He finally wrenched his wrist out of Astrid's grip, but before he could pull the trigger, Ria landed on top of him. She was not messing around. She got an arm up under his chin, squeezing so hard that she knocked the wind right out of his throat. With her free hand Ria pressed on the back of his head, completely cutting off Hank's air. She yanked him away from the window, and together they fell backward onto the floor. They wrestled without speaking. After a few short moments Hank began to go limp. The pistol dropped from his hand, and Astrid snatched it up from the floor. It was only then that Ria released Hank.

"I'm sorry, honey," she whispered. "Not about to let you put us in danger."

Hank was gasping too hard to answer back. He put a gloved hand to his throat and rolled over so that neither of them could see his face.

Meanwhile, the baffling conversation outside continued. Mr. Collins said that he remembered everything there was to remember about their mother. Mrs. Wrigley offered up that she was also on good terms with their mom. Then the two of them trotted off together across the north shore, heading in the direction of the greenway.

"What the hell are they talking about?" Astrid whispered.

Ria didn't answer. Her face had drained of blood.

. . .

It began soon after.

A great whooshing noise split the air above Ria's house, as though the sky were being pulled inside out. No more than a second later, there was an explosion that sounded like two thunderclaps butting heads. It was so loud it made the windows shake. Even the singers fell silent. The gathered wicked oohed and aahed, like this was just another one of the fireworks. There was a round of enthusiastic applause.

"That's our mom!" Mr. Gregory shrieked.

"Hooray for our mom!" the Abbitt twins cheered in unison. They clutched hands and jumped up and down.

"I'm not ready to celebrate," Mr. Bushkirk said curtly. "I'd rather they don't miss!"

Astrid couldn't believe what was happening. She parted the curtains again and looked up at the hills beyond the greenway in horror. At this distance she could barely make out the puss-yellow smudge of Mother, the tank, sitting before the Goldsport gates. Mr. Collins and Mrs. Wrigley must have climbed inside and gotten it working. All the times she and Hank had spent in and around Mother, they'd had no idea they were sitting inside of a loaded gun.

At that moment a thick puff of smoke burst from the tank, and Mother rocked back and forth. The sound of the cannon reached them a few seconds later—a deep double boom. This time the shot struck the peak of the plaza dome, shattering it. Giant chunks of greenway glass went cartwheeling into the sky. One landed on the Pratt house, smashing through the roof. Another crashed into the archives, shearing off the old wooden steeple. Moments later the plaza dome itself collapsed. Sharp claws of glass slashed down onto the stage and the banquet tables. A great plume of sand and dust rose up, obscuring Astrid's view.

There was more cheering from the wicked crowd, but Mr. Bushkirk was still dissatisfied. He cupped his hands around his mouth and called out, "I think you're aiming too high!" as though Mr. Collins and Mrs. Wrigley could possibly hear him all the way up in the hills.

Astrid turned to her mom. But for once in her life, Ria seemed paralyzed. Astrid ran to the back door to check if they could get out that way. But there was a host of wicked behind the house as well. Mr. Gregory saw Astrid's face at the window and gave her a thumbs-up. He tipped his party hat to her. He pointed at Astrid, pointed at his own mouth, then rubbed his belly and grinned.

"That means I'm going to eat you," he said, concerned that Astrid had somehow missed this.

There was another boom from Mother.

The shot ripped across the sand, passing directly through the crowd. The shock wave knocked some of them back onto their butts. Others, who'd been standing in the path of the shell, simply vanished. Right before Astrid's eyes, Missy Van Allen and Joshua Lee turned to mist. Their shoes alone remained at the edge of a smoking crater. Mr. Gregory gawked. He looked like a happy child, wowed by the most amazing magic trick—disappearing people.

"Could you show me that again, please?" he asked.

Over in the front yard, Mr. Bushkirk was still hollering in vain to his friends in the tank. "You guys, are you even listening to me? We want to hit the house!"

Astrid stood at the window in shock. Something was floating in the air out there, above the crater. Missy Van Allen's favorite silk scarf, patterned with purple and golden lotus flowers. She wore it to every Sunday picnic, and of course to every commemoration. Missy had once told Astrid that she'd bought it on a vacation in Vietnam, back in the world before. Back when Vietnam was a place. Back when America was a place. Back when you could go from one of those places to the other. The scarf rippled through the air, still riding the wind of the tank shell.

It looked to Astrid like it would never land.

Again Mother exploded, shredding the air.

The shot flew wide, crashing somewhere on the far end of the north shore. Mr. Bushkirk had had just about enough. "How the hell does that help us?" he screamed. "I meant this house, not that one!"

The words pulled Astrid's attention back into the moment. What did Mr. Bushkirk mean when he said that house? She looked farther down the shore and saw what looked like a crashed ship, broken to pieces on the rocks. It was the quarantine house. It lay in shambles under a faint cloud of smoke and dust.

Her father was in there.

"Mom!" Astrid screamed. "They hit Dad!" She ran back

into the living room, but just as she got there, Ria's house flew to pieces.

For some reason, Astrid saw the scarf again.

Missy Van Allen's silk scarf, whipping and twirling on the breeze. Astrid closed her eyes and opened them again, but the scarf was still there. She could see it in perfect detail. The individual petals of the lotus flowers glowed as the sunlight passed through them. All of a sudden Astrid decided that she needed to have that scarf. It would be something to remember Missy Van Allen by. Something to remember everyone by.

Astrid reached out and snatched at it. But her hand came up empty. The scarf floated out of her grasp.

Astrid tried to take a step forward, but her foot found nothing to land on—no sand or rock or hardwood floor. She looked down to see why this might be and couldn't make sense of what she saw. There was a doorway beneath her, and piled wood. It was almost like Astrid was floating too. Soaring over a pile of wreckage, right along with Missy Van Allen's Vietnamese silk scarf.

"Astrid! Astrid! Are you hurt?"

Two big, bee-suited heads swam over to her. Hank and Ria. It was only when they grabbed her and pulled her up into a seated position that Astrid realized she'd been lying down on the living room floor. The roof of her mother's house had been torn away, as if by a hurricane, and she had been looking up into the sky.

"Are you hurt?" Hank asked again.

Astrid had no damn idea. She examined herself and found that she was covered in a blanket of dust and splinters. There seemed to be some blood here and there. But did anything hurt? Not yet, it didn't.

"I'm all right," she decided.

"Thank God." Ria squeezed the words out through clenched teeth, one hand pressed against her ribs. She was bleeding too. A thick, red flow that oozed between her gloved fingers.

"It's nothing," Ria said quickly.

It didn't look like nothing.

"We're almost there!" Mr. Bushkirk announced from outside, pulling all of their attention to the front door. It stood askew upon sagging hinges. The top of the doorframe was splinters, and the curtains of the quiet room had been blown off their rails. Henry's naked hand was reaching through a gap in the wood, tugging and prying. Ria leveled Hank's pistol at the door—their last defense against what was coming. But it wouldn't be enough. It would, at best, delay the inevitable. Astrid was beyond fear now. All that remained was a certainty that she, and everyone she loved, was about to die.

"I'm not as young as I used to be!" Mr. Bushkirk said, laughing to himself. Finally, he managed to yank the door off of its frame. He stepped into the ruined house, tossing the door aside. For a moment he stood there, beaming at the three of them.

"Tell me honestly," he said. "Do you think I'm strong for someone my age?" He took another step inside, cracking his knuckles expectantly. Then, in a flash, a second man flew into the house. He leapt upon Mr. Bushkirk's back, knocking him forward and pinning him to the floor.

"Why did you do that to me?" Mr. Bushkirk gasped, winded and shocked.

The man's only answer was to strike him once on the back of the head. He did it with such tremendous force that Astrid could feel the impact through the floor. It knocked Henry Bushkirk out cold, breaking his nose against the hardwood. Then the man looked up at them.

It was Amblin Gold.

He was a mess, bleeding from a gash over his eye, but alive! He must have escaped from the quarantine house when Mother blew it to pieces. And now here he was, crouching like a leopard over Henry's unconscious body. Alive. They were all still alive. And they were going to stay that way.

"Everyone on your feet," Amblin barked. "We need to get to the boat."

"There are wicked there," Hank said.

"There are wicked everywhere." With that Amblin stood and turned to block the doorway; Mr. Gregory was trying to get inside. Amblin punched him in the throat so hard that he fell like a sack of cement.

"Can you all run?" Amblin asked.

They all could.

They all did.

Out the back door of Ria's broken house and through the crowd of giggling wicked they raced. Amblin led the way, clearing a path through their once-beloved neighbors, down to the harbor. Whenever someone got too close, he laid them flat upon the sand. He wore no bee suit, but it was too late to do anything about that. The singers were already on him, thick across his arms, and back, and neck. They glowed upon his body, making Amblin Gold look like a bolt of purple flame, burning a path for his family to follow.

CHAPTER 31

The Boat from Home

NATALIE WAS LEANING OVER EVA'S MAKESHIFT COT, CHECKING her temperature, when she heard an engine in the distance. It had been two days since she'd returned to the cabin with the searchers. Two days of watching and waiting as Eva recovered from her ordeal in the bog. Two days of smiles, of gratitude, of pretending not to know that she was in the grasp of beasts. So far nothing bad had happened. Miranda seemed obsessed with getting the baby healthy again, and Reggie was still committed to his nice-guy routine. But Natalie knew that it was only a matter of time until the searchers showed their true faces. She had to get her family out of here before that happened.

Outside, the engine sounds grew louder. Natalie scooped Eva up from the cot and walked softly down to the jetty to investigate. It was an overcast morning, and that quilt of summer fog was back. But Natalie didn't have to see to know what was out there—she would have recognized that familiar wheeze and gurgle anywhere. The outboard motor gagged as it dipped beneath a swell, hacking for breath as it came up again. It was her family's lobster boat. The only question was who would be aboard.

"Maybe Mom came looking for us," Natalie whispered into Eva's tiny ear.

Sure, her sister said. *Or maybe Grandpa found the keys.*

Of course, they weren't the only ones to hear the motor. Soon the searchers began to gather on the jetty as well. Miranda in the lead, her yellow bee suit pulled up only halfway, the sleeves tied about her waist like a belt. Reggie and the others followed. Natalie's father was there too, keeping a low profile in the back of the pack.

"There you two are," Miranda said. Plucking Eva out of Natalie's grasp, she held her up for inspection. Purple light poured out of Eva's eyes, illuminating Miranda's face. The baby writhed in her grip, whimpering. Natalie had to fight the urge to snatch her sister back. She only smiled, grateful for the woman's kind attention.

"Her fever is almost gone," Miranda said, passing the baby back. "But still, you should have let her sleep."

"Sorry," Natalie said, docile as a fawn. "I heard the boat and got excited."

"You, um . . . You expecting somebody?" Reggie asked. Behind him the men in yellow shifted nervously. They'd all brought their rifles with them.

Natalie made brief eye contact with her dad. They'd managed not to give themselves away over the last two days, but they also hadn't come up with anything like an escape plan.

"Natalie, do you know who that might be?" Miranda asked. She put on a smile the way you might slip on a hat. "If it's a friend of yours, I'd hate for there to be any confusion."

If you lie, and it's Mom, then we're screwed, Eva said.

Helpful as always.

"I think it might be my mother," Natalie said. "It sounds like her boat, at least."

"Your mom." Reggie nodded slowly. "From the island?"

"Puffin Island," she said—no use keeping it secret, as the searchers had long since guessed. "Yes. I think so."

The engine grew louder. Soon Natalie could make out the rough outlines of an approaching lobster boat—the peaked stem and exhaust pipe, the level platform and transom. A sheltering roof stood above the wheelhouse, capped with a defunct radar antenna. As the boat drew closer, Natalie immediately recognized the figure at the wheel. Her glowing irises gave her away—it was her mother. Her eyes pierced the fog like a pair of purple flames. Everybody else noticed them at the same time. On the jetty, there was a collective intake of breath.

"Oh my God," Miranda said, taking a step backward.

Reggie gawked at Natalie. "Your mom is vexed too?"

She nodded.

"You might have mentioned that."

Natalie gave a half shrug. "I wasn't sure if I could trust you. I didn't know you."

"Well, you do now," Reggie said. He actually sounded hurt. "You should have told us."

"I do now," Natalie agreed. Again she saw the woman in the video. Her bruised, split cheeks. The insides of her skull scooped hollow as a lobster shell. "I know you."

The boat was close enough now that Natalie's mom must have been able to see that there were strangers on the jetty. She cut the engine, allowing the lobster boat to coast forward on its own momentum. She hobbled out of the wheelhouse, using an oar as a crutch. Natalie's mom may have been strong enough to escape the island, but she was still in rough shape.

"That must be how both girls survived it," Miranda said. She sounded a million miles away. Natalie couldn't tell if she was talking to herself, or to everybody. Maybe both. "Resistance passed from the mother. Otherwise the chances for both siblings to survive the vex would be . . ."

"Damn near impossible," Reggie finished for her.

"We need to get a look at this island," Miranda went on.

"Among other things," Reggie added. Then, to Natalie: "You know, it really would've been helpful if you'd told us about this sooner."

"I know," she said, sheepish and obedient. "I'm sorry."

Her mother had made her way out onto the platform, grabbing at the railing and leaning over the side. She stared at them all through the thick fog. She closed her eyes, rubbed them, and looked again. Natalie couldn't guess what was shocking her most—the sight of her two vexed daughters, the half dozen strangers in yellow suits, or her missing husband. It was a good thing that her mom had a poker face like a brick wall.

Hey, Eva snapped at her. *Wake up. Dad's trying to say something.*

Natalie glanced at her father. His mouth was moving, but no sound was coming out. He shaped a pair of words over and over.

Signal flag.

Damn, Eva said. *You should have thought of that.*

"I need something white," Natalie announced.

Miranda and Reggie raised their eyebrows, glancing at each other.

"What do you need it for?" her father asked. It was as much help as he could offer without giving himself away.

"It's how we communicate on the island," Natalie said. "A white flag means all clear. If my mom doesn't see it, she won't dock."

Naturally, this was the precise opposite of the truth—a white flag was a signal that something was wrong. The signal for good news was no signal at all.

"Hurry, please," Natalie said. "She must be worried about me—about us."

"Give her your shirt, Reggie," Miranda said.

Reggie only cocked his head, looking skeptical. Miranda glared at him.

He gave in. "Fine. You can have it. But don't look. I'm bashful." He pulled his bee suit down and then yanked his

T-shirt up and over his head. His skin beneath was pale, his chest lean and freckled. Reggie tossed the shirt to Natalie. The white cotton was warm and moist in her hands.

"Just kidding," Reggie said. "You can look all you want."

Natalie's father shifted his weight almost imperceptibly.

"Don't be gross," Miranda snapped. "And don't forget to pull your suit back up before we leave this quiet zone. I can't have you bitten." She looked to Natalie: "You go ahead, honey. Let your mom know that we're nothing to be afraid of."

Natalie lifted Reggie's shirt into the air and swung it in a wide arc back and forth. Out on the boat, her mother went still. Then she hobbled back into the wheelhouse and began to bring the lobster boat in toward the jetty.

As the boat approached, Miranda called out to her, "Don't you worry, ma'am! Your daughters have been safe with us!" Then, to Natalie: "What's her name, anyway?"

"It's Astrid," she said.

It felt slightly odd to say out loud—on the island they barely used names. There'd always been just one of each of them. Mom and Dad and Grandpa. But of course, her mother had a name. It was Astrid.

"Can you hear me, Astrid?" Miranda called, waving both her hands in the air. "We're true. We're friends. We're here to help!"

CHAPTER 32

Eliza's Family

ASTRID WOULD ALWAYS REMEMBER THE DAY SHE AND HER family escaped Goldsport. The same day that their life on Puffin Island began.

They landed on the western shore, beaching the lobster boat on a narrow strip of gravel and sending thousands of terrified birds screaming into the sky. Off in the distance, they could still hear Mother booming. White columns of water flew up as the shells crashed into the bay. But the island was out of range.

The wicked couldn't touch them here.

Hank helped Ria out of the boat and settled her down on the stones. Her breathing was shallow, and her face had turned pale beneath the mesh of her bonnet. Blood had been oozing steadily from her side, leaving a stain that ran down to her boots. It would turn out that a small length of copper piping had blown out of the wall when her house exploded, plunging itself through Ria's ribs and into her liver. She would be dead by the following morning. Though Astrid didn't know that yet. None of them did—least of all Ria herself. That night, as she began to fade, Ria would fight. She'd claw back at the life slipping out of her. And when it finally ended, she would seem, more than anything, surprised.

But that was still hours away.

And ages ago.

In Astrid's memory, the time stretched. It was as though her mother had sat on that stone beach for years, facing the ocean and breathing hard. The puffins came and went. They laid eggs and warmed them. They fed chicks and fledged them. They flew off to sea and returned and flew off to sea again. Winters froze the rocks, and Ria with them. Summer storms brought the waves up to her chest. Amblin, long wicked, grew old in his locked tower. Astrid and Hank grew older too. They had Natalie. They learned to hunt and to fish and to make do with their feelings for each other. Sometimes it seemed as though there might be something more than friendship between them. Other times it felt like there was nothing at all. Like they were simply an accident—two beans forgotten in the bottom of a can. And all this while, Ria was there. Now she sat on the western shore, looking across the bay at the shattered speck of Goldsport. Now she lay atop a moldy cot in the bunkhouse, cursing at the ceiling as she lost her fistfight with eternity. Now she was buried beneath a pile of stones, in a graveyard at the shadowed foot of the lighthouse.

That was where Astrid had found Eliza's family back

on that very first day. Three graves scratched into the soil. Wooden crosses, blasted smooth by the ocean winds. Astrid could just make out the name carved into the largest cross—Solomon Jones. Eliza's father. The man who'd traded away everything when Ronnie Gold came to town, told Solomon to be afraid, and offered him a good deal on a wall and some glass.

Beyond the graveyard the bunkhouse door stood open and rusted upon its hinges. A stink of ammonia stung Astrid's nostrils as she approached. The house was a warren for lean, angry-looking rats—it would take her and Hank months to clear them all out. It was here where Astrid found Eliza's mother. The woman sat at the table in the common room, slumped to one side in a big chair. It looked like she'd been dead for a very long time. The rats had picked her clean and had carried off all but a few strips of her dress to line their nests. Her bones were the mottled color of coffee, with milk only half stirred in.

After that Astrid went to investigate the lighthouse. She stepped into the engine room and found the generator clicking like a broken clock. A red light was still flashing on the instrument panel. After all that had happened, her father had been right. Puffin Island was deserted, and the only thing keeping the lighthouse alive was a ghost of electricity haunting the old engine. It would actually be her dad's idea to lock himself up in here. Amblin even took charge of bricking over the windows to ensure that he couldn't get out once he'd fallen wicked.

Actually, locking himself up in the lighthouse had been her father's second choice. When Astrid had returned to where they'd beached the lobster boat, she'd found Amblin and Hank wrestling in the shallows. Her dad was trying to get into deeper water, while Hank, still in his bee suit, struggled to pull him out. Ria simply watched, helplessly, as she bled out upon the rock. Eventually Hank managed to drag Amblin back onto the gravel shore and pinned him down. Amblin wept, begging to be let go.

"I don't want to hurt anybody," he said between sobs.

"I know," Hank cooed, pressing his knee into Amblin's back. "We won't let you."

This was the Hank Astrid remembered. A man who was weak and strong all at once. A man who was always afraid and still not a coward. This was the Hank she saw twenty years later, standing on the jetty. He wore a strange yellow bee suit and a look of dull panic. Their eldest daughter stood beside him. In one hand she was waving the warning flag. In the other she held Eva, her little purple eyes ablaze. All around them were strangers bearing open arms and wolf smiles. One of these people, a woman, was calling out to her.

"Hello there, Astrid! I promise that we're not going to hurt you."

"I know," Astrid answered softly into the fog. "Because we won't let you."

CHAPTER 33

Home Again

AN HOUR LATER THEY WERE ALL CRAMMED ONTO THE LOBSTER boat, motoring slowly away from the cabin. Natalie passed Eva to their mother, who clutched the little baby tight against her chest. Then Natalie took over the helm, steering them out into the open water. Soon they were lost in the fog.

Back at the cabin, Astrid had played it exactly right. She'd docked the boat and pretended to be overjoyed to meet the searchers. She'd thanked them for keeping her children safe. When Miranda asked if her group could take a little visit to Puffin Island, Astrid acted as though she were only too happy to agree. She must have realized that if she said no, things would get ugly.

The searchers peppered her with questions as they went. How long had Astrid been vexed? Was she experiencing any side effects other than her purple eyes? Did she know of any others who had survived the process? How long had her family lived on the island? Did she have any other children?

What about Natalie and Eva's father—was he immune as well?

"Oh no," Astrid answered, speaking up over the drone of the engine. "He wasn't vexed. Anyway, he's dead now."

"I'm sorry to hear that," Miranda said.

To Natalie, she didn't sound sorry at all.

All the while the fog outside grew thicker. Astrid had Natalie slow the engine to a crawl. Then she asked Reggie to go out on the bow and keep an eye out for rocks. But they were in deep water—there was nothing out here that they could crash into. Her mother must have had an idea in mind.

Reggie glanced at Miranda, getting a nod of permission before leaving the wheelhouse. "I didn't know there was a shoal out here," Miranda said, only the faintest trace of suspicion in her voice.

"Oh, it's bad for miles along this stretch of coast," Astrid said casually. "That's why they built our lighthouse, all those years ago." With this she let one of her hands drift down to the wheel, pulling it slightly to the right. Natalie didn't know why, but her mother was steering them away from Puffin Island.

"You know," she went on, "I think everyone should keep an eye out. I got banged up a little bit on the way out this morning. And the boat is riding a lot lower and heavier now."

For several long seconds Miranda only stared at her.

"Normally I wouldn't think of taking her out in this fog," Astrid continued. "But, you know . . ." She nodded down at Eva, snug in her arms. "I couldn't wait any longer."

"Of course," Miranda said. "You must have been worried sick. About both of them."

"I can't even describe . . ." Astrid paused, seeming to blink away tears. "I knew that my Natalie could do it. But the baby—Miranda, I am so very grateful to you." With this she reached out a hand and placed it on Miranda's cheek. She looked right into her eyes. "I can never thank you enough for keeping my girls safe," she said, soft as new grass.

That sealed the deal. Miranda smiled back at her and turned to the others. "Let's keep our eyes peeled, everyone!" she said, stepping out onto the rear platform. She posted lookouts along the port and starboard sides and pulled the rest into a loose huddle, whispering secrets into the white morning. Plans unfolding. But Natalie's mother had plans of her own. It was just the four of them in the wheelhouse now. Natalie, Eva, Astrid, and Hank, who was pretending to stand guard.

For a moment it seemed as if the weight of what wasn't being said would be enough to sink the boat.

"I didn't mean to—"

"Of course you didn't." Astrid spoke quietly and quickly. They could barely hear her over the drone of the engine. She glanced at her husband, lingering over his face. His broken nose and fresh scars. "Let's not get into it now," she said.

"I was being an idiot," Hank said.

"That's true too." Astrid clutched Eva tighter, and the

baby squirmed a little in her sleep. At this point she'd spent as much of her short life away from her mother as with her. "Have you had a chance to hold her yet?" she asked.

"Once," Natalie's dad whispered. "When everybody was sleeping."

"So they definitely don't know that you and Natalie are . . . ?"

"No," Natalie said. She glanced behind them and saw that the searchers were still talking to one another. Miranda stood in the center of the group, her ponytail lank with fog, her tattooed singer flexing as she breathed.

"They think I escaped from Goldsport," Hank said.

"Well . . ." Astrid sucked in a long breath through her nose. "They're not wrong." Again she put a hand on the wheel, dragging them even further off course.

From up on the bow, Reggie called back to them, "How much longer?"

"It isn't far," Astrid said. "Can't be too careful in this fog." Then she dropped her voice again. She looked from Natalie to Hank. "How bad is it, with them?"

"Bad," Hank said.

Astrid squinted through the rain shield. She reached out and folded a strand of Natalie's hair behind her ear. Rather than reassure her, it made Natalie light-headed. She was so very frightened.

"They're going to want to take us?" Astrid asked.

"Just the baby," Hank said. "They were discussing it last night."

"Makes sense," Astrid said, nodding to herself.

"Easier to bring Eva back alive. And they know Natalie would give them trouble."

"They're damn right she would," Astrid said, turning the wheel ever further. In the fog, it was impossible to tell that they'd changed direction. For all anyone knew, they might as well have been traveling backward.

"For Natalie, they're going to take samples," Hank said. "Blood and . . . well. Samples. I assume they'll want to do the same with you."

Again Natalie saw the woman's hollow head placed neatly upon the wooden table. How long would this image haunt her? Someone would have to scoop out her own skull just to get rid of it.

"Ah" was all Astrid said. Then she leaned in to nuzzle her baby, kissing her on the cheeks and scalp. Eva writhed, pulled halfway out of her sleep. "You did so good," Astrid said. She was talking to both Natalie and Eva. "You did so, so good."

"Don't cry," Hank whispered to her. "Don't give it away."

"I'm not about to," Astrid said, rubbing her cheeks with the back of her free hand. The water collecting in her eyes sparkled with purple light. "How long do you think it'll be?" she asked. "Before they turn sour?"

"Not long," Hank said. "But it won't happen just yet. These people are . . . They're thorough. They're going to want to inspect the island. See what you've been eating.

Maybe ask permission to run some blood tests. They'll want you to feel relaxed, and cooperative, for as long as possible."

"Well, then." Astrid adjusted the wheel again. "We'd better keep our smiles on."

"What are you thinking?" Hank asked. "The grocery?"

"No. We could get trapped in there. There's no way out if they follow us. I was thinking the quiet room. Plaza side."

These words—"grocery," "plaza," "quiet room"—were all familiar to Natalie. Her mother's plan dawned on her in an instant.

"Do you think it's still standing?" her father asked.

"I'm not sure," Astrid said. "I don't think it got hit in the attack. But who knows what's happened since then."

"Can you run?" Hank asked.

"I can barely walk."

"Okay."

Natalie watched her father's face as he took this information in. His expression hardened. She could almost see her dad willing his own fear away. But before he had a chance to say anything further, Miranda hollered into their little shelter, "Hank! Would it be too much trouble for you to join us?"

"Of course," he yelped, ducking his head out of the wheelhouse and joining the other searchers in the back. Miranda shot them both a commiserating look.

"Sorry if he was bothering you," she called out over the engine. "He's a bit of an odd one, our Hank."

Astrid only laughed and waved her off. The searchers returned to their conversation, and Astrid stepped up next to her daughter, so close that their hips were touching.

"We're going to Goldsport," Natalie said.

"Yes," her mother said. "Going back home."

"What about the wicked? Won't they try to . . . ?"

"We'd better hope so," Astrid said. "We can't get through this without them."

In the distance, they heard bells. Soon the rocking shapes of buoys became visible in the fog.

"Not long now!" Astrid announced.

Miranda stepped back into the wheelhouse, her ponytail and shirt saturated with the wet sea air. "Is it safe to land in all this fog?"

"Don't worry," Astrid said. "I've done it a thousand times."

She passed Eva back to Natalie and took over the wheel. Meanwhile, Hank began to fumble around by the bulkhead. Pretending to lose his balance, he yanked on the pull cord to the air horn. The horn blasted, booming out into the still morning. Natalie heard it echo back off of the approaching shore. Ringing the dinner bell for the wicked. Miranda looked like she could kill him.

"Whoops," he said, all sheepish. "I am so sorry."

"Maybe you'd better go up front with Reggie and help look for rocks," she snapped at him.

"Yes, ma'am," Hank said, climbing out onto the bow. "Sorry!" He got down on his belly and inched toward the stem, joining Reggie there.

"Idiot," Miranda grumbled.

"Not a problem," Astrid said, revving the engine. "The worst he could have done is scare the puffins."

"You know, I've never actually seen a puffin," Miranda said.

"No? They're cute, but they stink."

"And um . . . your daughter tells us that you don't have singers out here, either?"

Astrid winced, almost imperceptibly. Natalie did too—she wished she'd never let that detail slip. "That's right," her mother said brightly. "Too windy and too small. They've got no place to breed."

"Cute birds, no singers, and the whole family is vexed . . . ," Miranda mused, a half smile on her face. "Some people have all the luck."

Astrid didn't argue the point.

A few moments later a large dock exploded out of the fog, looming right over them. The pilings were as big around as full-grown trees. To one side of the dock sat a ramshackle boathouse with rotting walls and a caved-in roof. Natalie gawked up at it.

"Wow!" Reggie called from up on the bow. "You guys don't mess around. Who the hell built this?"

"No idea," Astrid said. "It was here when we arrived."

She reversed throttle as they closed the final distance, causing the engine to groan and hiss. Then, as the lobster boat kissed the edge of the dock, Hank and Reggie jumped ashore. They guided the boat into its moorings, tying it off as Astrid cut the engine.

"Here we are," she said, limping out of the wheelhouse. Natalie could detect the faintest quaver in her voice.

Still using the oar as a crutch, Astrid climbed out of the boat and headed down the warped wooden planks into the fog. Miranda and the rest of the searchers followed. Natalie knew that somewhere ahead of them lay the ruins of the greenway. The moment they arrived at that shattered heap of glass, or came upon a swarm of singers, the searchers would surely realize they'd been tricked. When that happened, Natalie's family would be done for.

We should probably get ready to run, Eva said. *Or, I mean you guys should.*

"I'm not sure exactly what you'd like to see first." Astrid spoke up, allowing her voice to carry over the silent shore. "But why don't we begin with our—"

Suddenly Natalie's mom stopped in her tracks. The rest of the group did too. Natalie peered around their backs, examining the white wall of fog ahead. There was a dark shape out there. Two dark shapes.

"I thought I heard you coming," one of the shapes said.

The sound of his voice made Hank go rigid. The searchers were also uneasy, tensing up and exchanging glances.

"Who is that?" Miranda asked.

"It's—oh. It's our neighbors," Astrid said. She must not have expected to come upon the wicked so soon. "It's not just my family who lives on the island. Did I not mention that?"

"No," Reggie said crisply. "You didn't."

"Oh? I'm sorry," Astrid said. "Let me introduce you."

She limped forward another few paces, gasping in pain with each step. The dark shapes resolved into two tremendously old men, seated in a pair of wooden dining room chairs that they'd dragged outside and jammed into the wet sand. The men were dressed in open shirts, tattered pants, and shiny black shoes. One of them was on the fat side, with folds of his body spilling out over the chair. The other was tiny and withered. Between the men was a chessboard set upon a rotten ottoman. Most of the pieces were gone, replaced with buttons and seashells. The men were in the middle of a game.

"Everybody, this is Henry Bushkirk and . . ." Natalie's mother trailed off. She seemed to be having some trouble recognizing the man on the left.

"I'm Mr. Gregory." The smaller man came to her rescue. "But everybody calls me Chipper. You can call me that too, if you want."

"Henry, Chipper—it's a pleasure to meet you both." Miranda stepped forward and made to shake their hands. The two old men only looked at her offered palm. Then they looked at each other. They seemed not to know what to do.

"You'll have to forgive them," Astrid said. "They're both a little, um . . . They have good days, and they have bad ones."

Miranda nodded. "Well. You certainly have your hands full, Astrid!" she said admiringly. When she addressed the old men again, she spoke loudly and slowly. "My friends and I are here to help you all."

"Help us with what?" Mr. Gregory asked.

"Don't be stupid—help us with them obviously." Mr. Bushkirk reached over and pinched his friend.

"Don't pinch me," Mr. Gregory said.

"Stop me," Mr. Bushkirk said, pinching him again.

The two old men giggled.

It lasted a while.

"So . . ." Miranda turned back to face Astrid, eyebrows arched. "How many people live out here with you?"

"Not so many of us, these days," Mr. Bushkirk answered for her. "We're all pretty old. Well, I guess not all of us. I see you in there, Junior. Don't think I don't see you."

At this there was an uneasy commotion among the people in yellow suits. Miranda and Reggie exchanged wary looks. Almost casually, Reggie dipped his hand into the compartment of his suit—the one that contained his pistol.

"Sorry, what?" Miranda asked.

Henry Bushkirk ignored her. "I always knew this would happen," he said, hoisting his round self up off of the dining room chair with a labored grunt. "I always knew you'd come back home, Junior."

"Come on now, Henry . . . ," Astrid said. "You know Junior has been dead for a long time." She gave Miranda a shrug, stretching the lie as far as it would go. "Like I said—good days and bad days."

Mr. Bushkirk smiled at them both. "I don't have bad days. For me every day is a good day. And today, I think, is a best day." Then, without any warning whatsoever, he cupped his hands around his mouth and called out into the fog. "Everybody, listen to me! Junior has finally come home to us! Come down to the docks so we can say hello!"

Reggie had finally had enough. He took a quick step forward and yanked Mr. Bushkirk's hands away from his face. "Take it easy, old man," he said.

"You don't need to remind me that I'm old!" Mr. Bushkirk laughed. "I feel it in these knees every day."

"Who is Junior?" Miranda asked, turning on Astrid.

"He's my son!" Mr. Bushkirk said.

"I told you to take it easy." Reggie took him by the shirt collar and pushed him back down onto the fancy dining chair. He landed with an *oomph*.

"I'm taking it super easy," Mr. Bushkirk said, winded.

"Astrid, you need to tell us exactly what is going on," Miranda said.

"I can explain," Mr. Bushkirk offered, still regaining his breath. "Let me!"

"Buddy." Reggie grabbed Mr. Bushkirk by the chin with his bare hand and leaned in close. He had no idea yet, but he might as well have just walked naked into a swarm of singers. The wickedness was already on him, worming desperately through his skin and down into his blood. "What are you not understanding about this? Be quiet, or I'm going to hurt you."

"I'm actually understanding all of that," Mr. Bushkirk said, beaming up at him. "I'm old, but I've still got my marbles."

"You think I'm kidding?"

With that Reggie finally pulled the pistol out of his suit. The two old men gazed down at it like they were in love. Their eyes widened. Natalie could guess what was going through their minds at that moment. *Guns. Guns are lovely, lovely things.*

"I've got one of those," Mr. Bushkirk said wistfully.

It was at this point that they began to hear sounds in the fog. Approaching footsteps and the tittering of soft voices. Natalie caught flashes of color in the cloudy air—turquoise and orange, deep black and daisy yellow. The colors drew closer. They grew legs and arms and weathered faces with inviting smiles. Natalie had heard about these people in her parents' stories. The Pratt family, the Whites, Abigail Lee. And, of course, Mr. Gregory and Henry Bushkirk—her other wicked grandfather. At the sight of the approaching strangers, Miranda became truly upset.

"Astrid, if you don't tell us right now what is—"

Hank sprang into action before she could finish. Natalie had never seen her dad move so fast. In one movement he lurched toward Astrid, grabbed the oar that she'd been using as a crutch, spun around on Reggie, and brought the oar down hard on his outstretched arm. Natalie could hear the bone snap. Reggie's pistol spun away across the gravelly beach as he howled. The gathered crowd of wicked men and women showed their appreciation with a smattering of applause. Mr. Bushkirk actually cheered.

"I always knew you had it in you, son!"

For a moment the searchers seemed too stunned to react. Hank launched the oar at Miranda and scooped Astrid up into his arms. "Follow us," he said, sprinting off into the fog. Natalie was right on his heels, Eva bouncing and bawling in her arms.

Behind them there was pandemonium. Natalie didn't look back, but she could hear Reggie still shrieking in agony. One of the searchers fired a shot, and it ripped through the fog above their heads. But then Miranda screamed, "No! We can't risk hitting the girls." Moments later they could hear more footfalls behind them, heavy and hard. The searchers, giving chase.

The greenway emerged ahead of them—great slabs of glass slick as melting ice. Natalie's father headed right for the quiet room. The curtains had long since rotted away, leaving nothing but a little transparent box that sat adjacent to the shattered plaza. He opened the hatch, and the four of them dove inside. No sooner had he closed the hatch behind them than one of the men in yellow suits crashed into it.

Miranda and her searchers stood beyond the glass, panting and puzzled and furious beyond words. Reggie was still doubled over in pain. He tipped his head up to give Hank a deadly look.

"I'm going to kill you," Reggie said. "I should have. Months ago."

"I'm glad you didn't!" Mr. Bushkirk's voice rang out from behind them. "I'm glad I got to see him again."

They weren't as fast as the searchers, but within a few moments the wicked people of Goldsport had caught up. They approached, pinning the searchers against the outside of the greenway. Miranda and the rest of her searchers all drew their pistols. The wicked looked at the guns with hungry, blazing joy.

"I see," Mr. Gregory said, excitedly searching his own pockets. "So that's what we're doing."

"Everybody just needs to relax," Miranda said. Her group was surrounded by now. Everywhere Natalie looked, she saw grinning wicked people in evening dresses, pinstriped blazers, and swimming costumes. "If you all just stay calm, then I promise nothing is going to happen."

"Oh, I don't think I can agree with that," Mr. Bushkirk said, shaking his head. "I think everything is going to happen."

And then the wicked fell upon them.

CHAPTER 34

Under the Wall

BEFORE SAILING AWAY FROM PUFFIN ISLAND, ASTRID HAD done what she could for her dad. She'd limped out of the lighthouse while he slept, leaving the iron door wide open so that he could return to the tower if he wanted to. She tightened the taps on all of the rain barrels, righted the overturned plants in their greenhouse, and even took the fishing gear out of the toolshed for him. It wasn't a lot, but if the wicked folks in Goldsport had managed all these years on their own, then surely Amblin could fend for himself on the island for as long as he needed to. Natalie and Eva had already been gone for three days, and Astrid had no idea how long it would take to find them. If anything had happened to her girls, then she might not return at all.

But she couldn't leave without saying good-bye. After loading up the lobster boat with some water and food, and topping it off with fuel from the storage tank, Astrid slipped into the bunkhouse. She found Amblin Gold asleep in his granddaughter's bed, the blanket pulled snug up to his chin. He stirred as she entered the room, blinking as though he'd just emerged from a pleasant dream.

"I see you," he said.

"Hi, Dad."

"That's me." Amblin writhed beneath his blanket, stretching. He rubbed his eyes and dug a finger into his ear. "I don't know about that foot," he said.

"It's getting better."

"I bet it hurts."

"Less than it did yesterday," Astrid said. She kept one hand on the doorframe to steady herself. "I'm going to go for a little while. I don't know when I'll be back."

"I'll come with you," Amblin said.

"Sure." There was a sudden rising in her chest, and the word came out broken into chunks. Astrid felt almost dizzy with sadness. But her father took in none of this. The emotions on her face were written in a language forever lost to him. He might not even have realized that she was real.

"Maybe in another hour, though," Astrid said.

"Sounds good to me." Her dad grinned and stretched again. "As long as we go in time for *The First Voice*. I'd hate to miss that."

"I love you, Dad."

"Thanks for telling me," he said, already slipping back into sleep.

. . .

Astrid's plan in Goldsport was ludicrous—a whim, born of desperation. She knew that. But it was the best she could come up with, and in the end it worked. After all, no one had spent more time among the wicked than her, Hank, and Natalie. They'd all sensed that the turn was about to come—like sailors able to read a current that was invisible from the surface. That was why Hank made his move when he did. That was why Natalie knew what to do without anyone telling her. The searchers in their rubber bee suits didn't realize what was happening until they were surrounded, their backs pressed against the greenway glass. And then it was too late—they hardly had a chance to raise their weapons before the wicked fell upon them.

It didn't happen quickly. Hank stared at the floor of the quiet room, while Natalie covered her eyes and ears. Astrid could only bring herself to look at their feet through the glass—shuffling, scrambling, running. And falling. There were a few gunshots and some surprised squawking. A single bullet hit the wall of the quiet room, throwing out a halo of cracks. It looked like a snowball, thrown up against the glass.

Astrid opened the inner hatch, and the four of them stepped into the plaza. From outside, they could hear Henry Bushkirk laughing. The sound rang with impossible, joyous purity. It was hard not to feel happy for him.

"I hope none of them get hurt," Natalie said. She meant, of course, the wicked people.

"Me too."

Astrid, still barely able to walk, leaned on Natalie for support. Hank took Eva, holding her for only the second time in their lives. Together the four of them felt their way through the fog and across the shattered plaza. Grasses and young saplings had taken root in the sandy soil, curling around the fallen chunks of glass. Singers floated in the mist, casting bright rings of purple light around them. They sniffed out Hank as he passed, and descended to land upon his bee suit. They glowed there, like a string of lights wound about a Christmas tree.

Then the family put the plaza, and the rest of the ruined greenway, behind them. They passed into the woods and up the crescent hills. At the top they paused so that Astrid could rest in the shadow of Mother. The tank cannon was still aimed out at the north shore, as it had been for the past twenty years. It still looked, and smelled, exactly as Astrid remembered.

Eva cooed in Hank's arms. She seemed taken by the singers perched on his suit, her arms flailing happily. The purple lights of her eyes reflected on the shining black veil of Hank's bonnet. He looked from her, to Natalie, to Astrid. The three vexed women in his life.

"I'm going to try to deserve this," he said.

"You'd better," Astrid said. Then: "We'll help you."

In the far distance they heard one final gunshot. The wicked, having finished with the searchers, would soon come for them.

"We should probably get moving," Astrid said.

"Where?"

"The searchers had a truck," Natalie said.

"And food," Hank added. "And medicine."

"Is that right?"

"Yeah. I have a map."

"Well. It's an idea," Astrid said. "Do either of you know how to drive?"

She'd meant it only lightheartedly, but Natalie answered her with total seriousness. "We can learn, Mom."

"That we can," Astrid agreed.

Hank pressed the baby into her arms and headed over to work on getting the gate open. They didn't have the keys, but the big padlock was so rusted that it looked like it was made of old chocolate. Hank picked up a sturdy branch from the side of the road and began working it like a crowbar, trying to wedge the padlock open. Meanwhile, Natalie stepped a few paces back down the road, keeping a watch on the greenway below. In the distance they heard more sounds—the wicked, singing carols as they trickled through the greenway and slowly ascended the hill.

All this time Astrid rested at the base of the tank, holding Eva. She gazed up at the wall towering over them all. Concrete and steel, built with her grandfather's money, if not his own two hands. This was Ronnie Gold's legacy. Amblin's legacy. Her legacy. A strange thought struck Astrid then—for as much time as she'd spent at the base of this wall, she'd never actually seen the other side of it. She didn't even know what color the outside of the wall was painted. She'd left the sanctuary, of course, but never this way. And never completely. The wall, with its metal gate and razor wire, had always been there. Astrid was born beneath it. She'd grown tall under its shadow. When she and her family escaped Goldsport, the wall had followed them. It ringed Puffin Island just as surely as it did the greenway. Astrid had never, truly, gotten out from under it.

But she could. Hank could get out. Natalie could get out. Even her baby, her Eva, could get out. All it takes is one crack.

The singing was growing ever closer. Hank strained at the lock, but it wouldn't give. Natalie went to help him, and together they pushed as hard as they could. And then, in an instant, the rusted metal snapped to pieces, and the gates swung open.

Epilogue

From the Diary of Amblin Gold

Dear book,

Hi, book. It's me. It's me, Amblin.

I lost you for a little while, book. I tried looking in the lighthouse, but you weren't anywhere. It made me pretty angry. But then I remembered that Natalie threw you out of a window. I found you down on the rocks by the graveyard. I'm glad I found you again. I've been carrying you around for a little while now, but I haven't had much time to talk.

So much has happened to me, book! Here's a list that I made, starting at the beginning.

1. I went to live on Puffin Island for a little while.
2. I ate a lot of lobster and sometimes some crab and eggs.

3. Sometimes I ate other stuff, too, but mostly lobster and crab and eggs.
4. Also, I got to live in a big lighthouse!
5. And my daughter had a daughter.
6. I think she maybe even had a second one?
7. Then everybody left, and I was all alone.
8. Then I went home to Goldsport, and I wasn't alone anymore.

Now that I think about it, eight things aren't that many things. But still it feels like a lot to me.

I was really lonely on the island after everybody was gone. First Hank left me, and then Natalie left me, and finally Astrid left me. And Puffin Island sucks when you're the only person on it. Natalie told me once that the puffins talk, but I think she was lying. Or else they only talk to her and not to me for some reason.

But I have good news!

A few days ago, some people came to visit me in a boat! They had beautiful yellow clothes that they wouldn't let me touch. They told me that they were looking for their friends. They asked me if I had seen a woman named Miranda. I told them that I didn't know anything about any Mirandas, but hi, I'm Amblin.

I used the knife on one of them. The other, I got with a rock.

Now I have a boat!

Having a boat is nice because now I'm in Goldsport.

Everything here is different than I remember. Henry got SO OLD I CAN'T BELIEVE IT! And a lot of other people I used to know aren't even alive anymore. But the good news, book, is that they said they saw my family. They saw my Astrid and her babies! Henry told me that they came by a few months ago, and that they left town through the big gate, up in the hills. Henry told me that he and some of the others tried to follow them, but that they got tired.

Book, I need you to believe me when I tell you this. I am NOT going to get tired. My family is out there somewhere. And I'm going to find them. I don't care if I have to walk for a million years. I'm going to find them.

It'll be so great when I do! Do you know why I think it'll be great, book?

It's because I love them.

Acknowledgments

Thank you Ellen Levine. Your support over the last decade means the world to me. Thank you Caitlyn Dlouhy. Your belief in me and my work makes a sometimes-frightening business less so. I continue to learn from your wise edits, and my writing is so much stronger for the attention that you give it. Thank you Brett Finlayson and Calvin Hennick for being great readers, advisors, and friends.

Thank you Emily Rupp. Life was on the brink of turning upside-down as I finished this book, and you stepped in and righted it. Terhi and I will be forever grateful. Thanks also to so many close friends in Vietnam who gave support when we needed it. Thank you Nguyễn Thanh Huyền, Vũ Thị Thảo, Trương Thanh Miền, Trần Ngọc Hà, Pakawan O'Leary, and Michael O'Leary for taking such good care of our dear Onyx and Isabelle. Thank you Hoàng Vũ Huyền Trang for your advice, and friendship. Thank you Jack Cooper, Sundi Bonfiglio, and Nathan Bonfiglio for never allowing Terhi and I to feel alone out there. And thank you to all of my friends in the Office of Infrastructure in Kabul, Afghanistan, for welcoming me and for inspiring me.

And Terhi. Always Terhi. Thank you for being brave. Thank you for making me brave too.